BRIEFCASE WARRIORS

American Indian Literature and Critical Studies Series
Gerald Vizenor, General Editor

BRIEFCASE WARRIORS

Stories for the Stage

E. DONALD TWO-RIVERS

UNIVERSITY OF OKLAHOMA PRESS : NORMAN

Also by E. Donald Two-Rivers

Survivor's Medicine: Short Stories (Norman, 1998)

Published with the assistance of the National Endowment for the Humanities, a federal agency which supports the study of such fields as history, philosophy, literature, and language.

Library of Congress Cataloging-in-Publication Data

Two-Rivers, E. Donald, 1945–
    Briefcase warriors : stories for the stage / E. Donald Two-Rivers.
        p. cm.—(American Indian literature and critical studies series; v. 38)
    Contents: Winter summit or, The bang-bang incident : a play in one act
— Forked tongues : a play in two acts — Chili corn: a play in two acts —
Coyote sits in judgment : a play in one act — Shattered dream : a play in
two acts — Old Indian trick, or, An old urban Indian story as told by an
old urban Indian : a play in two acts.
    ISBN 0-8061-3301-5 (alk. paper)
    1. Indians of North America—Drama.   I. Title.   II. Series.

PS3570.W6 B75   2001
812'.54—dc21
                                                                00-059978

Text design by Gail Carter

Briefcase Warriors: Stories for the Stage is Volume 38 in the American Indian Literature and Critical Studies Series.

The paper in this book meets the guidelines for permanence and durability of the Committee on Production Guidelines for Book Longevity of the Council on Library Resources, Inc. ∞

1 2 3 4 5 6 7 8 9 10

CONTENTS

PREFACE

It is spring 1994 and I'm sitting in my favorite restaurant on North and Clark in Chicago, eating and reading the newspaper to see what the theater critic has to say about a play I'm acting in up at the Center Theater. It's a Friday night and I'm with the beautiful and talented Beverly Moeser. We're out on the town . . . well, at least hoping to be. Our relationship is brand new; we're finding out things about each other, and that, as most of you know, is a very exciting time for any couple. She being a film maker and I a poet, and a romantic one, y'all know what life is about. That's right—good wine, poetry, and those romantic moments just like in the movies.

I read the critic's words and throw the paper aside with an angry feeling boiling in my stomach.

"You should read what she said! Called my character a "quiet presence." It's always like that. It seems that any time there is an Indian character in a play, he always has to be this quiet presence or else a violence freak. You know, I'm getting tired of this crap. Whatever happened to the regular Indian guy? You know, the guy who is into betting on the horses, or watching the birds in a tree, or pissed off at the dog shit in the park, or putting the make on some pretty lady?"

Beverly gives me a look that says, cool it. One of her "watch the mouth" looks.

"I mean, think about it," I continued in a lower voice.

One thing about this woman is that she knows how to get me talking. She's a good listener, so I continue.

"I was reading somewhere that Russell Means said we need to be writing our own roles. Telling our own stories. I think he's right on about that."

"You mean the Indian activist turned actor?"

"Yeah, that's who I mean. You know I'm an old AIM man myself. Hell, woman—I led a demonstration right over there across the street. At the Hysterical Society. What do you think?"

"That playwrighting stuff you can learn."

"Like I got time to go to college?"

"College isn't the only place. You ever hear of the Chicago Dramatists?" she asks as she leans forward. I sit back, because I'm beginning to know this woman. I correctly figure that she has a plan of some kind. I'm beginning to wonder if I've stuck my foot in my mouth—and all I want to do is impress her.

"Chicago Dramatists? What's that?" I ask.

As we ate she talked to me about the works of Sam Shepherd and David Mamet. I got excited, seeing that she had given some thought to it. I had never met a woman more in tune with what was going on in the Indian community. We discussed how the stage would be a good way to tell Indian stories. In my lifetime I had seen only two plays. One was *Of Mice and Men*, directed by Robert Falls at the old Wisdom Bridge Theater many years before. I had been stimulated by it. A few years later, when I saw *Antigone*, the political intrigue excited me. I had always had a feeling that plays would be a good way to bring people to a better understanding of the Indian Community. Beverly urged me to make learning how to write plays a goal—one that she said was very attainable. Thank God, she made a believer out of me.

And so, seven years and three children later, we're sitting in the same restaurant eating. Of course I'm not eating steak anymore. Eating habits have changed and so has the nature of our conversations—tonight we're discussing finances, kids, and our art. I tell her that I've signed and sent back the contract for *Briefcase Warrior*. She smiles. It's her special smile that tells me what she's thinking about. A sentimental look comes into her eye, and we begin reflecting back on the past seven years.

First, I think I wrote the plays for the political reasons, as weapons to use to tell the other side—our version of the story. Then, later, I began to catch myself writing for specific people in my community, and that is where the humor comes in. I *know* Indians have a sense of humor. The six plays that I have chosen are all very loosely based on different aspects of my life. Maybe all writing is like that. *Winter Summit* is a retelling of a story my grandmother, Minnie Johnson, used to tell. For *Forked Tongues* I drew on my own experiences of roughing it in the South. Of course I changed details in *Chili Corn*, a story right out of my community here in Chicago. As I wrote the play, a young woman in my life was actually undergoing the same sort of mistreatment from her boyfriend that my character Chili was. I loosely wrapped the story around a true incident involving the Chicago Historical Society. The Society used to have a large statue of an Indian man scalping a white woman. In the summer of 1973 two friends and I wandered into the Historical building. There were children running everywhere. At the sight of us they got scared and stopped to stare at us, because of the statue. We organized to have it removed.

Coyote Sits in Judgment is one of those stories that you pick up somewhere. It may have been a gift from my grandmother. She gave me so many stories that I expect I could write for the rest of my life about the things she told me. Inspired by the Hydro Quebec issue in Canada, I wrote *Shattered Dream* while studying playwrighting at the Chicago Dramatists under the direction of Kathleen Thompson and Michael Novak. Then, while taking a playwrighting course taught by Claude Allen, I began writing *Old Indian Trick*, which was triggered by a guy I knew who was always getting into dilemmas. I have been very lucky to have had the opportunity to study under some of the country's best teacher/playwrights.

I want to dedicate this book to the memory of three people: my grandmother Minnie Johnson; my mother, Nancy Johnson/ Broeffle, or Keewaygoonabeak; and Sam Angel, who had more natural comedy in his little thumb than I could ever hope to develop. This book is also dedicated to my community in Seine River, Ontario, and in Chicago. But most of all it is dedicated to the very lovely woman who has blessed my life with her love— Beverly Moeser, the mother of my children.

PERFORMANCE HISTORY
Red Path Production Company

Plays are listed in order of first performance.

OLD INDIAN TRICK
1994 Beacon Street Theater, Chicago
1995 American Indian School, Milwaukee
1996 Around the Coyote Arts Festival, Chicago
1999 St. Mary's College, South Bend, Indiana
1999 Truman College, Chicago
1999 University of Illinois, Chicago Campus

FORKED TONGUES
1995 Truman College, Chicago
1996 Joliet Junior College, Joliet, Illinois

SHATTERED DREAM
1996 Truman College, Chicago

CHILI CORN
1997 Great Lakes Naval Station, Waukegon, Illinois
1997 Truman College, Chicago

COYOTE SITS IN JUDGMENT
1998 WINTER, Time of Telling, Newberry Library, Chicago
1998 Menominee Club Celebration, American Indian Center, Chicago
1998 Pegasus Global Theater project, Chicago

WINTER SUMMIT
1999 WINTER, Time of Telling, Newberry Library, Chicago

BRIEFCASE WARRIORS

Winter Summit, or the Bang-Bang Incident

A PLAY IN ONE ACT

CHARACTERS

NARRATOR

LYNX: Very fussy and temperamental.

WOLF: Likes to joke but is constantly aware of himself.

BEAVER: Gruff and impatient.

CHICKADEE: Very nervous.

CANADIAN JAY: An impatient and argumentative kinda guy.

SQUIRREL: Grouchy and always fighting with the Canadian Jay.

OWL: Grumpy and wise.

NARRATOR

This is not a traditional Indian story. At most, it is a story about strange memories—perhaps even ancestral memories. It comes from a nervous night in the bush. It was the year of the snow. The story takes place on the edge of Sapawe Lake—a real place, a magical place, isolated and rich with Indian history. A beautiful kingdom of pine, cedar, and granite.

A blizzard blew in from the west. It lasted four, maybe five days. It was middle to late March, which was unseasonably late for a storm of that caliber. Snow started falling. At first it was a warm snow—you know, the kind that kids like to play in. Then it seemed like these strange sensations rode on each flake. Shortly after that the wind picked up. That wind was something else. Vibrations rode it. Some outcome could be expected, but what would it be?

That storm raised total havoc with the wildlife. It upset the natural rhythm of Mother Earth. Moose and deer floundered about in the deep snow, helpless against the wolves and other predators. Rabbits stayed still, hunched under tree boughs.

A close-knit family of Beaver listened as the storm raged above their home. The Whiskey Jack which some people call Canadian Jay, usually squawked and fussed with the squirrels but now lay still, sheltered from the wind. Everything, even the playful otter, waited quietly. During the night a lynx could be heard yowling nearby.

Snow continued to fall. Belts of dense clouds rolled over granite cliffs. The wind blowing across the lake was ever so pleased with itself. Sometimes it pranced through the bays, then it rushed headlong up steep, pine-laden hillsides and rolled over the hilltops like an athlete jumping the high bar. Like an early morning mist over an open pond, swirls of snow moved like fancy dancers paying homage to the spirit of an unexplainable event. Time surrendered to the sounds of that wind and wrapped itself around eternity. An atmosphere of stalemate prevailed over the affairs of the bush, and that, my friends, is where this story begins.

SETTING: The stage is laid out with a log or two and some pine boughs.

As the curtain rises, the cast lines up center stage.

ENTIRE CAST
> Tonight, tonight while the west winds howl,
> We gather, we gather,
> All from this place
> To discuss if we may
> The affairs of the bush.
> We gather, we gather, humbled
> To discuss the affairs of the bush
> While the west winds howl.

Cast exits. The Lynx stays onstage. He dances around preening himself and spreading cedar boughs around. He also backs up to certain items and sprays.

LYNX
> Hi! I'm Elvis the Lynx. I have the moves and the grooves and that's why I'm such a cool cat. (*Sprays and sniffs.*) Ah—the wondrous scent of me. The essence that makes the kitties go wild, and—I must add (*grins diabolically*)—on occasion others, like some of those macho-looking Toms. This is an age when sexual preference is a personal choice—an enlightened age! Many of the Toms are attracted. (*Sniffs again.*) And who can blame them? I am, after all, such a—Lynx—three and a half feet of sexuality. I got eyes that can see—that can spot an ant three and a half miles away. I'm bad and you know it—oh, I just love me. Don't ya just love it? (More seriously.) So this year I was selected as the host with the most, and to see to it that everyone who's attending the meeting is made comfortable. An easy task, because I do like to entertain—for me it's sort of like being on the upside of a bipolar experience. Easy for the likes of me. (*Offstage, the sound of someone approaching can be heard.*) Ah—the first of my guests. Who, I wonder, can it be?

Enter Myeengun, the Wolf.

LYNX
> Oh—it's you! Well anyway, welcome to my humble abode.

WOLF
> And humble it is. (*Sniffs the air.*) What's that stank?

LYNX
> I would be very careful if I was you. I am not in the mood.

WOLF

It smells like cat wee-wee. Is that what it is? (*Holds paws over nose.*) That, my friend, is the most disgusting odor in the entire bush. Can't you do something about it?

LYNX

And what would you have me do?

WOLF

Change your diet or something.

LYNX

When I was asked to host this year's Winter Summit, I didn't hear anybody say I had to take any abuse. You know we're supposed to be as one at these summits.

WOLF

Yeah, right! You and I?

LYNX

We both have similar issues to present. (*Pause.*) I will accept your apology.

WOLF

Yeah—I guess you're right. Okay, okay, Elvis, I apologize (*short pause and turns to audience*), but hot damn—this place stanks.

LYNX

You are such a . . .

WOLF

A fine wolf. That's what you were gonna say, right? (*Grins.*) Oh—by the way, what is this year's theme?

LYNX

Habitat! (*Pause.*) Here comes someone else. I wonder who?

WOLF

(*Listens closely.*) Beaver—and it's dragging something.

LYNX

I hope its Wally! He is so nice.

WOLF

Wally is the brother. He doesn't have any rank, really—you know—in the beaver gang. An upstart. You just leave it to beaver to send his brother to represent their species.

LYNX

Well, he is, after all, as busy as a beaver—which he is, I might add!

WOLF

(*Mocking the Lynx's words.*) Which he is, I might add! You make me wanna vomit.

LYNX

Must you be so graphic? (*Pause.*) He has a big responsibility, taking care of the water.

Enter the Beaver.

LYNX

> Welcome, Mr. Beaver. (*Smiles.*) Just to clarify my thinking, which one are you?

Beaver looks somewhat confused.

WOLF

> Yeah, like what he's asking—are you Wally or the other one? I can see why he's confused—you sure did get big in a year's time. We gonna be calling you Sir Tree-Top pretty soon.

BEAVER

> (*Shakes Wolf's hand.*) Neither. I am Amick . . .

WOLF

> AMICK? The Mack daddy of all beavers? I'm very honored. (*He holds the Beaver's hand. Beaver pulls it away.*) Hey—it ain't every day a wolf gets to meet the main guy from the Beaver House.

LYNX

> (*A tone of admiration in his voice.*) Amick! Sounds very ethnic.

BEAVER

> I take care of all water that flows through here.

WOLF

> And he ain't lying, either. He doesn't talk no jive! You tell him, Mr. Amick.

BEAVER

> Why are there so few of us here? Is everybody late?

LYNX

> Its called being fashionably late. A buzz word for the ultimately hip group. The one (*glances at the Wolf and grins proudly*) which, incidentally, I am a charter member of.

WOLF

> Its called Indian time, and it irritates the crap out of everyone—especially the Indians.

BEAVER

> I hear someone approaching. Listen! Listen!

WOLF

> The cat's pissin'.

LYNX

> Would you mind?

The sound of someone coming can be heard, but very softly.

LYNX

> It has to be Chickadee. (*Turns to the other two.*) Like she would have something to say.

Hesitantly, enter Chickadee. Goes to Lynx.

CHICKADEE
Is it safe here?

LYNX
Greetings, and welcome to my home.

CHICKADEE
Thank you, Elvis.

LYNX
Are you the one they call Polly, perchance?

CHICKADEE
Polly? What's this Polly? Who told you such a thing? (*Glances at the Wolf.*) Who? Who?

WOLF
Cool it, Chicken Wing. You ain't an owl.

CHICKADEE
What's with the Polly thing? Did you start that? You did start that, didn't you? I know it was you.

WOLF
Man, you are one uptight little bundle of feathers. (*Laughs.*) Why you be like that?

CHICKADEE
(*In a shrill voice.*) Why do you talk like that? Come on, tell us why? Why?

LYNX
Like Myeengun said, cool it. You got a complaint, bring it up at the meeting—but I can't imagine what you'd have to complain about.

CHICKADEE
You can't be serious. But never mind. I never complain. I'm not one to bellyache and moan around, but—now that you've brought it up (*pause and throws hands in air*)—ah, what good would it do anyway? (*Goes to background, depressed.*)

BEAVER
We all have issues that need to be resolved. Elvis, are you sure you invited everyone?

LYNX
But of course. I was given the list, and like the big guy in the red suit, I been checking it twice. Like, I am the ultimate at parties. That's why I was asked to be the host.

WOLF
You were asked because no one else agreed. Don't flatter yourself.

Beaver laughs and starts conversation with Chickadee.

LYNX

(*Irritated.*) You know, I really don't like you very much. So please don't try my nerves. I do have a claw with your name on it.

WOLF

Like, I'm shaking in my paws.

CHICKADEE

Someone is at the door.

A knock at the door.

LYNX

Come in, come in, and come in.

WOLF

I think he means come in.

LYNX

Would you please! There's going to be problems if you don't stop. (*Short stare-down with wolf. Enter Squirrel and Canadian Jay, pushing and shoving each other.*) Come in please and take off your fur and feathers and give me some skin. (*No one laughs.*) Ya'll don't get it, then? Oh well—welcome to my home!

CANADIAN JAY (CJ)

Next year I'm joining the migration. I could be sunning myself instead of dealing with this mouthy little fluffy tailed . . .

LYNX

With the summer birds?

SQUIRREL

I really do hope so. Oh, that would be such a delight. You seed-cracking, fluttering piece of . . .

BEAVER

Now, now!

CANADIAN JAY

They always come back so nicely tanned.

WOLF

You get any darker and you'll look like a . . . blue jay!

CANADIAN JAY

So be it! At least I'd be away from that bushy-tailed, nut-burying pile of fur.

SQUIRREL

Up yours, you walking hangover.

BEAVER

Moving right along here.

CHICKADEE

I hear it's an unbearable flight. All kinds of dangers—not to mention time, especially the future.

LYNX

(*Truly alarmed.*) Now you've done it. That is never to be mentioned—alluded to, yes, but never mentioned. Come— we must do the dance.

BEAVER

Oh, I can't bear this—my sacroiliac's on the blitz from dragging a poplar tree around.

WOLF

Gotta make it tough to shake a tailfeather, huh, Chickadee? Is your sacroiliac okay? (*He reaches down like he's gonna touch the bird's butt.*)

CHICKADEE

Don't you dare.

They all gather in a circle and begin to dance around, shaking their butts. Chickadee refuses.

LYNX

Come on, Chickadee—get in here and shake a tail feather.

CHICKADEE

What's going to happen if I don't, huh? Will the sky fall or something? (*Looks up and laughs.*) To the future! To the future! (*The others begin dancing and shaking their butts in sincerity.*) It's all superstition and nothing more. Look— nothing's happening to me.

WOLF

(*Stops dancing.*) Boy, Chicken Wing, you are asking for it— big time!

CHICKADEE

I'll thank you not to call me Chicken Wing. I do have a name, you know.

CANADIAN JAY

It's Wandellie. I'm CJ for short and she's Wandellie. (*Points at Chickadee, laughing and dancing and shaking his butt.*) Wandellie, Wandellie, Wandellie!

SQUIRREL

Why don't you stick it?

LYNX

Actually, Wandellie is a good name. (*Laughs.*) Oh come now, do tell—what is your name?

CHICKADEE

See what you started? You . . . you . . . nothing but a walking hangover! (*Pause.*) For your information—for all of your information—it is Parus.

Her announcement causes a stir.

WOLF

Parus? What kind of handle is that for a pint sized bird like you? (*To Lynx.*) Now that's ethnic if anything is.

CHICKADEE

It is Latin—or maybe Greek, but it predates anything you might be called.

BEAVER

I am Amick!

CHICKADEE

Yeah, yeah, we all know that. King of the Waters isn't it?

LYNX

(*Brushing Beaver's fur.*) Pay no mind to her. She should be medicated or something. Cheekadee the PROSAC QUEEN! (*Pause.*) Oh, and that fur you got—no finer is there in the land—such rich texture. (*Turns to Wolf.*) Not like yours, Myeengun, which—incidentally—smells like last year's carrion.

WOLF

Ah, yeah! Prime road-kill! A good smell, if I remember correctly. I had to chase you away from it three or four times.

BEAVER

Let's get this meeting going. Felix, why don't you call us to order?

LYNX

It's Elvis, not Felix. You been watching too much TV. Felix is in the futu . . . oh no, now you made me do it.

They all start dancing again.

WOLF

What about the owl? I demand that we wait a while longer, at least until Owl gets here.

LYNX

I hear someone coming. Can we stop dancing now? Yes— it's the flapping of wings.

Cast freezes and the Narrator steps forward. Casually and matter-of-factly explains things.

NARRATOR

As the group gathered, those strong
west winds began to lessen
in intensity.
The group became aware of that,
but like a bunch of cool cats,
never did they mention it—
that's why I'm doing it now.
As an objective observer,
of course.

Anyway, back to the summit—
the summit in the night!

Enter Owl, rumpled and unorganized in appearance.

LYNX

You're just in time to eat. Shall we share a few morsels, then
get right down to business?

OWL

Would you be offended if we forgo the snacks? I don't want
to . . .

WOLF

Yeah—let's get this show on the road, for Pete's sake.

CHICKADEE

Who is Pete?

WOLF

Not now, Chicken Wing—oh, I'm sorry, Parus! Well, at any
rate can we hurry the thing up? I like, got places to be, those
to see, and things to do. What about you, CJ for short?
That's what you said, right? CJ for short.

CANADIAN JAY

It's CJ, not CJ for short as you just said. Never mind the for
short.

WOLF

But you *are* short!

SQUIRREL

And short of brains too.

CANADIAN JAY

Why don't you stay out of this, you fluffy-tailed bush-
whacker.

SQUIRREL

(*Sing-song voice.*) Sticks and stones may break my bones, but
names and faces will never hurt me.

BEAVER

(*Sternly.*) Would you two stop? Every year it's the same thing. Always bickering or playing grab-ass.

WOLF

Grab-ass? Hardly what I'd call grab-ass.

BEAVER

We have serious work to do.

LYNX

All work and no play makes Jack a dull boy.

OWL

So be it, but let us begin. Are we in agreement?

Everyone but Lynx says "Yea!"

LYNX

Oh well. I shall still endeavor to be the perfect host in spite of this outrageous rudeness. Okay, everyone, shall we begin? (*No one answers.*) Okay all together then. On three.

He counts and the group, who have formed a semicircle, all shake their booties three times, then begin reciting.

THE GROUP

We are the species,
We live in harmony.
To care for our Mother Earth.
We are the species—
We are the species—
We stay in the winter's winds.
Ours is the paradise.
We are the species.

LYNX

Yes, we are the species—
The one thousand and twentieth summit begins.

OWL

Point of order! Point of order! It's one thousand and twenty-first, not one thousand and twenty.

LYNX

Oh great, now I'm a year older than I thought. Oh joy! Thank you ever so much, Mr. Owl, for that information.

BEAVER

My name is Amick. I am the oldest and meanest of all beavers. None has lived longer. It is our duty to care for the waters—the blood of Mother Earth, if you will.

OWL

And you are encountering problems.

BEAVER

Not right now, but our visionary sees a time . . .

WOLF

Hey—hold on a minute. You're talking about the unmentionable time. Oh—now we must pay tribute again . . .

They all begin to shake their booties and reach up to the sky. Chickadee and Beaver refuse to do it.

LYNX

You are aware of them rules.

SQUIRREL

They must be obeyed.

BEAVER

Of course I'm aware, and I disagree with that rule.

OWL

But nonetheless, a rule is a rule. Ignore them and what have you? A condition known as havoc. We don't want that. It isn't wise.

WOLF

(*Begins singing.*) Oh, vippity-voppity-vou!

CHICKADEE

Would you get serious?

WOLF

About what? Can't nobody have no fun?

OWL

Point of order! Point of order!

LYNX

What now?

OWL

Who, who, who, I ask, is running this meeting? We need a chairperson.

WOLF

Lynx is the host with the most, or so he did boast. Lynx is chair, that's who, who, who!

OWL

(*To Lynx.*) Robert's Rules, then. Please Mr. Felix, bring this meeting to order.

LYNX

It's Elvis! E-L-V-I-S! You dig it?

SQUIRREL

My, but are we getting formal. No wonder the deer and moose passed this year. You know they gave me their proxie?

CANADIAN JAY

No, no! That's not allowed.

SQUIRREL

Are you questioning me?

CANADIAN JAY

I am. I have a major problem with your integrity.

Squirrel and Canadian Jay have a stare down. Cast freezes.

NARRATOR

And so, those characteristics that divided the species had to be dealt with speedily and with much understanding.

LYNX

(*To Wolf.*) Yo, Hound's Tooth. What's the old who, who, who talking about now? You know where the old irritating bastard can put that, right?

CHICKADEE

He's definitely a "go by the books" kinda guy.

WOLF

(*To CJ.*) You smell anything foul in here?

CANADIAN JAY

I have a beak, sir. Not a set of nostrils. (*Looks closely at Wolf's nose.*) My, but you have some long nose hairs. What are they for?

LYNX

(*Laughing.*) For smelling butts (*Pause.*) and turds . . .

WOLF

Like the one in your ass! Hey, feline, you have a dingleberry the size of a potato dangling from your butt.

Lynx is embarrassed and tries to see his butt. Wolf laughs hysterically.

LYNX

(*Hisses at the Wolf.*) Oh—I hate you. Don't you start with me, leg-lifting cousin to a jackal, cause I'll get on your case so bad you'll wish you had no relatives.

OWL

Please—this bickering is not wise.

LYNX

(*Laughs.*) We're not wise guys.

BEAVER

We need to get busy. (*To Owl.*) Every year! You'd think by now they'd know what to do. I am becoming disenchanted with this whole deal.

OWL

I understand, but we must give guidance.

Chickadee stares at Wolf with a mean glare.

WOLF

What are you looking at? You're acting like you some kind of hawk's eye!

CHICKADEE

You have such a smart-aleck attitude.

WOLF

You think it's easy, huh? Everyone hates me. The big bad wolf, the noble savage of the north. I've been stereotyped. I don't know why you're complaining—everyone likes you.

CANADIAN JAY

That's not entirely true. Listen, Myeengun, I like you. I do not like that "nut-cracker" over there in the corner.

LYNX

Yeah—what's up with that? Why are you off by yourself? Do we stink or something?

WOLF

I done told you.

LYNX

Don't even go there.

SQUIRREL

I just don't want to be nowhere near . . . you know who.

BEAVER

(*To Owl.*) Perhaps you and I might caucus together and fashion a resolution. I really do feel compelled to get some work done. They want only to filly-fally.

OWL

Perhaps it would be a wise thing to do. Yes—let's go off and get same work done. We should invite Rocky the Squirrel. In many ways he's actually worthy of our company. Filly-fally? Is there such a word?

Beckons to Squirrel, who stands up to follow. Beaver, Owl, and Squirrel exit.

LYNX

An unholy alliance if I ever saw one. I wonder what scheme they'll hatch up.

WOLF

Whatever it is, I'm voting against it.

CANADIAN JAY

What if it's something good?

LYNX

Anything those two old stodgies and that Squirrel come up with won't be in our favor. Maybe for you, but not for me and that Wolf.

CHICKADEE

(*To audience.*) Talk about your unholy alliances. It's scary, actually. (*Turns back to others.*) I suppose we should get some of our concerns down so we have an agenda. I don't want it said that we wasted our time.

CANADIAN JAY

Well, what have we to discuss other than a general lack of nesting areas?

CHICKADEE

Hello! You don't think that's important?

CANADIAN JAY

Wait a minute here. What did you just ask me?

WOLF

All right—let's not get personal. We should discuss hunting grounds. You, swivel hips (*dances like a Spaniard*), are always trespassing into my territory. Not only that, then you have the audacity to spray the sickening stench around. I am getting sick and tired of it.

CHICKADEE

I thought you said not to get personal. Sounds personal to me.

LYNX

It's you that is the problem. You and your pack keep claiming more and more territory. A bunch of thugs. Paw-and-fur Mafia is what you are.

WOLF

Don't go getting ripped to the tits about it. There's a reason for it.

LYNX

Yeah? Well I'd really like to hear it.

WOLF

We keep getting pushed farther and farther back.

LYNX

By whom?

CHICKADEE

Yeah! By whom?

CANADIAN JAY

In case none of you have noticed, we're all, like, getting the shaft here. The whole bush is in disarray. You'd have to be blind not to see it.

LYNX

Well, I always say, clean up your own backyard first. That's what I say.

WOLF

Yeah—sure you do.

CHICKADEE

But who is doing it? Can we defend ourselves?

CANADIAN JAY

Take off the blinders, Chicken Wing. See the world! Smell the coffee!

CHICKADEE

And what, may I inquire, is that supposed to mean?

CANADIAN JAY

You don't get the point? Oh well, whatever! (*Pause.*) A distant cousin returned to his home breeding grounds this spring. He was thinking he was gonna have him a rockin' good time with the robinettes.

CHICKADEE

(*Reacting strongly.*) I should have known it'd be something about the birds and bees. Making eggs is all you have on your mind.

CANADIAN JAY

Like you don't make eggs?

CHICKADEE

Discretion! You ever heard of it?

CANADIAN JAY

Well anyway, wham, bam, thank you ma'am, a highway had been built right smack dab through the middle of his traditional breeding ground.

LYNX

And what, may I ask, is a highway?

CANADIAN JAY

I'm not exactly sure, but it was sometimes referred to as the Dawson Trail.

WOLF

It must be a hunting trail.

CANADIAN JAY

I can't say. The Indians aren't too happy about it. I can tell you this much, however—the robin's feathers been ruffled since. He's afraid he's gonna become impotent.

CHICKADEE

That's more information than I need.

LYNX

You know, that reminds me of something. It may even be related.

WOLF

Does anybody smell anything foul in here?

LYNX

(*Gives the wolf a dirty look.*) I was talking with that new otter the other day, and he said the same thing. Only his was a real horror story. (*Pause.*) I don't know for sure, but do you think it could be connected?

CANADIAN JAY

Connected? You aren't making a whole lot of sense here. Connected to what?

LYNX

Some kind of mining operation. That's what he called it.

WOLF

What is that?

LYNX

They dig up Mother Earth and smash her bones.

CANADIAN JAY

How savage! Strange! A Windigo maybe? Did the sky turn red or anything?

LYNX

He didn't say, but it does stand to reason. He said all the fishes in his stream were floating belly up.

WOLF

Not too good—not good at all. This should be reported to Amick.

CHICKADEE

Yeah—he'll know what to do. Between him and that Owl they should be able to come up with something.

LYNX

At first the brother thought he'd hit it big. He figured it was a blessing from the BIG OTTER IN THE SKY. When he ate the fish, he started getting these real bad cramps.

CHICKADEE

What kind of cramps?

LYNX

Like Mrs. Otter gets when she's on her moon.

CANADIAN JAY

Would you mind? We're in mixed company.

CHICKADEE

(*Lots of attitude.*) Don't be such a prude. We're all adults here. (*Steps closer.*) Hello!

LYNX

To make a long story short—she was pregnant and died. All her fur came off. I tell you, it's some bad vibrations going down.

CANADIAN JAY

Could be a Windigo.

WOLF

Sure do sound like it. (*Pause.*) There's a bounty on my butt.

CANADIAN JAY

What, may I ask, is a bounty?

LYNX

Payment for killing. This is most depressing.

WOLF

You ain't kidding. It's like being on a bad trip. Can't trust anybody behind your back.

LYNX

This is really awful. Totally wrong and against all our ideas of fairness. A concept that our elders adopted in earlier summits.

CHICKADEE

I'm sorry, Brother Myeengun. (*Pause.*) This is really awful. What about compliance? Our mandates must be adhered to.

WOLF

It's bad, my friends. I've lost three sisters over the last year. We'll be wiped out soon if we don't do something about it. This is why I brought it up to you guys. I need the council to help out.

CANADIAN JAY

This is extremely disturbing news. Have the perpetrators been identified?

WOLF

(*Very concerned, shakes his head.*) Only as Bang-Bang!

CHICKADEE

Bang! Bang! What is that? What species?

WOLF

I don't know, but I'm told they smell terrible and are real noisy.

LYNX

Smells terrible . . . hmmmmm. Are you sure it isn't one of your own kind?

Everyone hollers at the Lynx.

LYNX

Okay, okay. You're right! What, then, would you have us do, Brother Myeengun?

CANADIAN JAY

We must have information.

CHICKADEE

A spying mission perhaps.

Everyone bursts out laughing, but then gets serious.

CANADIAN JAY
That might be a good idea.

WOLF
But Chicken Wing, who can do it? Could you? (*Everyone bursts out laughing.*) It would take a special breed.

LYNX
One who is courageous, that's for sure!

CANADIAN JAY
And swift and fleet and very, very quiet.

WOLF
And stealthy and wise.

LYNX
The Owl? No, no—I doubt that.

CHICKADEE
Or the Beaver either. He'd reveal himself with his compulsive building.

LYNX
That's true. As chair of this summit I move we send a spy to the Bang-Bangs. Can I have a second?

CANADIAN JAY
Take a day, heck, take all the time in the world.

LYNX
Oh no—you did it again. Why do you insist on doing that?

Beaver, Owl, and Squirrel come back onstage. Everyone gets into a semicircle and begins the dance routine again. They reach for the sky as they shake their butts.

NARRATOR
They worked hard at the task of crafting a resolution that summer. One that would achieve what they knew must be done. Meanwhile, the Owl, Beaver, and Squirrel had also reached a concensus regarding their discussion, which centered on their loss of habitat and the deteriorating condition of life in the bush. They expressed concern about POPs— the unseen enemy. Persistent Organic Pollutants. And so the group came together. Like thirty-five different kinds of Indians, they spent thirty-five days discussing, and finally . . .

OWL
And so we are in agreement that our homes are being encroached upon by—let me see here, what is that we called them? (*Searches paper.*) Where was that?

CHICKADEE
By the Bang-Bangs. We referred to them as the Bang-Bangs. It's right there.

OWL

Oh yes—here it is. Thank you, Chicken Wing.

CHICKADEE

Oh no—not you too. (*Looks at Wolf.*) See what you've started?

SQUIRREL

We've decided that a spy must travel to the Bang-Bangs and gather information.

WOLF

Which will be reported to this committee. What, may I ask, are we to do about the POPs?

BEAVER

I will personally deal with that due to the fact that fish are being contaminated first. My responsibility is the waters. Oh—this is such bad business. Well at any rate we must discuss the spy.

WOLF

The spy of our choice must possess character traits that will allow him or her to go unnoticed.

CANADIAN JAY

Traits like bravery.

LYNX

And stealth. (*Turns to audience.*) We need a sneaky spy. (*Makes the sound of 007 music.*)

BEAVER

One who can stay focused and works hard. (*To Lynx.*) Did you take note of that, Felix?

LYNX

ELVIS! It's Elvis, and yes, I did take note.

SQUIRREL

We need a spy who can be busy and observant.

CHICKADEE

(*In alarm.*) Oh my! Who have we got like that? (*Walks around thinking.*) We can't send the Wolf, although he is brave. The Bang-Bangs would bang him on sight.

WOLF

(*Very macho-like.*) Good point. I tell you, were it not for that, I would be the first to volunteer. I am indeed a brave one.

LYNX

And obnoxious to boot. Too much so to make a good spy.

WOLF

Hey—I resent that remark, so I'll ignore it. The Beaver is ruled out, because on land he's so clumsy and the Bang-Bangs must be observed at close quarters.

CHICKADEE

What are we to do? Oh my—this is a quandary.

WOLF

Don't get yourself a case of the twitters. We'll think of something. Elvis certainly has an abundance of stealth. Nobody is sneakier, but that odor would give him away. The Lynx cannot go.

LYNX

(*Smiling sweetly.*) Thank you. I think.

OWL

The spy must be wise. (*Pause.*) Perhaps I should go.

SQUIRREL

No, no—you're too old and slow. We need somebody who is not so crutchedy.

OWL

Hey! I resent that!

SQUIRREL

Don't pop a nut.

WOLF

And besides, we need you here. To advise on everyday affairs.

BEAVER

There won't be any everyday affairs if we don't deal with this quickly. Besides, you'd probably taste like chicken to them.

CHICKADEE

Hey—that's close to home. Like Chickadee . . . chicken. You hear it.

BEAVER

Semantics. Don't sweat it. You're nothing alike, you and the Owl. Don't make me laugh.

CHICKADEE

I'm just concerned.

OWL

I can take care of myself.

CHICKADEE

I'm sure you can. It's just that . . .

OWL

Never mind. Point of order! Point of order!

LYNX

What now?

OWL

Let's stay focused here, please.

CANADIAN JAY

Okay! Okay! This is it. (*Walks center stage.*) I volunteer. I wouldn't make much of a meal, and if I must say so myself, I am brave.

SQUIRREL

Rejected! Rejected! You argue too much.

WOLF

The same could be said about you.

CHICKADEE

Those Bang-Bangs sure are a problem. I would like to see them firsthand. Could I volunteer?

Everyone laughs.

WOLF

Wait a minute here. Chicken Wing might just be the ticket. Would you all take a minute to think about it?

CHICKADEE

I'm willing.

They all start pairing off and discussing the possibility. Chickadee watches them, waiting.

WOLF

I've always admired her bravery for staying here all winter instead of flying the coop and heading south. Why, heck— she's no bigger than a snowflake, and yet she's got a heart as big as an eagle.

BEAVER

And I've noticed she is industrious.

SQUIRREL

And she does seem to be considerate of others. (*Pause.*) I can't believe I just said that. It must be the moment.

CANADIAN JAY

And she is deceptively innocent appearing. Especially with that singing of hers. CHICKADEE . . . DEE . . . DEEE. How sweet.

LYNX

No one is stealthier. She's almost like a shadow or some- thing. I've spent hours watching her.

CHICKADEE

And don't you think I haven't noticed you. No wonder my nerves are shot.

BEAVER

And she is resourceful and quick witted. I accidentally felled a tree that she was perched in. Before it hit the ground she was already on her way to another.

CHICKADEE

I remember that. I was taking a nap. A rude awakening if you ask me. Of course no one is.

WOLF

I got Chicken Wing by a tail feather one time, but she got away on me. She was too quick for me, and I was one hungry dude too.

CHICKADEE

It took me a month to fly straight again. (*Pause.*) Now that's what I came to this summit for. To complain about each and every one of you. You've all transgressed against me. However, in light of this development, it seems pointless. Especially the POP thing. I hope we can figure out what needs to be done.

BEAVER

Worry not your little head. And I do suppose that apologies are in order. I mean, after all . . .

LYNX

I want to be the first to apologize.

WOLF

And I.

CANADIAN JAY

I'll never call you Wandellie again.

LYNX

I'll never call you Prosac Queen again, either. Hey—wait a minute here. Well, once in a while, okay?

CHICKADEE

I guess that's better than nothing.

BEAVER

And I will always look before I chew down a tree. I'll make sure you aren't in the middle of your nap.

CHICKADEE

I'll sleep on that.

OWL

The entire realm is indebted to you. You have the heart of an eagle. The wisdom of a crane. The loons will sing praises to you this summer. Bears shall wake up, lean and mean, and they shall hear of your brave deed. Indeed—all shall hear about you. It shall be a public proclamation.

CHICKADEE

I am speechless. Chickadee . . . dee . . . dee . . . dee. Chickadee . . . dee . . . dee . . . dee.

The Cast begins to exit, but stops.

EPILOGUE

OWL

And so it was that the Chickadee became the tiny hero of the north woods.

SQUIRREL

And the Bang-Bangs? Oh well . . .

LYNX

It doesn't take a rocket scientist to figure out who they were.

BEAVER

So when you're in the north woods camping or tramping about,

CANADIAN JAY

especially in wintertime, and you hear her singing,

WOLF

look closely and remember

CAST AS ONE

Winter Summit of One Thousand and Twenty-one.

Forked Tongues

A PLAY IN TWO ACTS

CHARACTERS

MACK IRON-HORSE: Laid-back old cowboy-type Indian.

KEN HOPS-GROUND: A boxer in good shape. Has short hair. Nervous and on edge.

CLAUDE DELORME: A poet. Quiet, dark skinned, and artistic looking.

NORA HEART-GRAVE: A down-home type woman.

REV. CLYDE TURNER: Mr. Clean. A sneaky kind of guy in fancy clothes.

ROSE HALL: A quiet and beautiful half-Indian, half-Black woman.

DARREL RICHMOND: Wild-eyed businessman. Superpatriot.

AMANDA JONES: Southern belle.

SHERIFF SWAIN: Black hillbilly, dressed roughly.

ACT ONE

Scene One

SETTING: An automobile in the predawn morning.

As the curtain rises, three Native American men ride in a car. Country music plays on the radio. Mack is driving. He wears cowboy clothes. Ken is in the passenger's seat. He appears energetic. An ex-boxer, he bobs and weaves and throws make-believe punches. He wears a jogging suit and has a towel around his neck. His gym shoes are old and scruffed. Claude sleeps in the backseat.

MACK

This is the way Indians should be living. We got it made, pal. Don't get much better than this. I mean to tell you.

KEN

Yeah, right! Here we are, maybe six hundred miles from home, and we're running low on gas.

MACK

The Great Spirit will provide.

KEN

I'm getting worried, Mack, and you know when I get worried I get hungry.

MACK

So don't worry and you won't get hungry.

KEN

I don't like it here in Georgia.

MACK

What's wrong with it? This is beautiful countryside.

KEN

I think we should have stayed on the main highway. There are so many southerners here.

MACK

Well, what did you expect? We're in the South. (*Pause.*) Look, did I ever let you down?

KEN

Not really, but I'm getting real hungry.

MACK

Because you're worrying? (*Pause.*) Man, you eat too much anyway.

KEN

Don't you think that I don't know that. Boy—you know how to hurt a guy's feelings. (*Pause.*) How we gonna get back to Chicago, Mack?

MACK

> Have some faith, would you? (*Thinks for a moment.*) Wake up the poet.

KEN

> (*Looks off into the distance.*) What's that over there? Is that a carnival or something? Can you see it?

MACK

> Yeah—I can see it. (*Short pause.*) Ain't no Ferris wheel, so it ain't no carnival.

KEN

> What is it, then?

MACK

> I can't tell. What's that on those banners? Can you read them?

KEN

> Let me see. J-E-S-U-S. It says "Jesus Saves." That other banner says, "Pastor M. Simmons."

MACK

> (*Laughing.*) Boy—you know what that means?

KEN

> You got a plan, Mack?

MACK

> (*Overjoyed.*) Does a Lakota like buffalo meat? Does a Shinob choke rabbits? Do Ho-Chunks like casinos? You damn right I have a plan. I mean to tell you. (*Short pause.*) Wake up that poet! He'll like this.

Ken reaches back and shakes Claude. Claude tries to roll over and sleep some more. Ken keeps shaking him.

KEN

> Wake up, Shakespeare! Wake up! Look and see what we done found. A sure-enough revival tent. Wake up, Poe. They'll be Christians.

MACK

> Come on, Whitman! Wake up! We done found us a ticket home. I mean to tell you. Wake up, you riddle-saying poet.

CLAUDE

> (*Sits up.*) My name ain't Poe or Whitman, and sure it as hell ain't Shakespeare. It's Claude! C-L-A-U-D-E! Claude! You get it?

KEN

> Yeah—we got it.

CLAUDE

> What do you mean, Christians?

MACK
You'll see! I mean to tell you.

Blackout

Scene Two

SETTING: The inside of the revival tent. "Amazing Grace" is playing softly.

As the curtain rises, a man and woman are in a heated argument offstage. Reverend Rev. Turner wears a white suit with matching shoes. Nora wears a dress, and a kerchief to cover her hair. She appears almost motherly.

REV. TURNER
(*From offstage.*) Woman, I fail to understand your logic.

NORA
(*Also offstage.*) Of course you do. All you want is their money. You could care less about their souls.

Nora and Rev. Turner enter the stage and continue to argue.

REV. TURNER
I am a man of the Lord. You are not to address me like a common criminal.

NORA
And why not? That's what you are.

REV. TURNER
I DEMAND that you give me proper respect.

NORA
You demand? I've given you more respect than you deserve. You're a leech on society, a backstabbing leech. You hear me, Clyde TURNER?—a leech.

REV. TURNER
(*Steps threateningly toward her.*) Why, if I wasn't a gentleman, I'd slap your face.

NORA
You're by no means a gentleman. You're a coward, and if you dare to put your hands on me, I'll have you arrested. After I beat the piss out of you.

REV. TURNER
Is that language absolutely necessary? I swear, between your foul mouth . . .

NORA

Don't even go there. Do you understand me, Clyde TURNER?

REV. TURNER

Why is this burden on me? What have I done to deserve you? An ex-whore and a nut case to boot.

NORA

You know what, Clyde TURNER? You're just a cheap hustler.

REV. TURNER

That's your opinion! I'll thank you to keep it to yourself. It would help if we'd work together here.

NORA

You might start by getting off your high horse, you piss ant.

REV. TURNER

Piss ant? Such nice language. (*Short pause.*) It would be most helpful if you'd attempt to pull yourself up from the gutter. You need to use a little more restraint in your language. In other words, clean up your act.

NORA

Why? I'm talking to a snake.

REV. TURNER

Nora, you are the child of the devil.

NORA

Go piss up a rope.

REV. TURNER

You are trying my nerves. The Lord's curses are upon you.

NORA

You know what you can do with your curses. When that committee of town folks gets here to inspect, I'm gonna tell them all about you.

REV. TURNER

You wouldn't dare. They wouldn't believe you anyway. You seem to forget that you're a whore.

NORA

That's ex-whore.

REV. TURNER

Do you honestly think for a moment that they'd believe you over me? Nora, I am, after all, an ordained minister. That certainly carries some . . .

NORA

Ordained, my ass. That piece of paper you got comes out of a Cracker Jack box.

REV. TURNER

I'm going to the staging area. I've had enough of your foul mouth. I'll make sure everything is as it should be outside.

Rev. Turner exits. Nora makes an obscene gesture. A second later he returns.

REV. TURNER

There are three men outside. I don't think they're committee people. They look like gypsies, or maybe they're (*hesitates*) Indians. My God—what would they want. Indians make me nervous.

Nora goes over to peek out of the tent door.

NORA

(*Peeking out.*) It's because your ancestors stole their land. You feel guilty.

REV. TURNER

You are trying to be funny, of course.

NORA

(*Straightens her hair.*) Well, I can tell you this much—they sure are some handsome fellows. I know from experience when I see a good man.

REV. TURNER

Once a whore, always a whore. Must you be so sluttish?

NORA

You have some nerve. What about that young girl over in Jackson County? She wasn't more than fifteen. You ought to be locked up.

REV. TURNER

Aren't you the kettle calling the pot black? At any rate she had the demeanor of a twenty-one-year-old. She was as ripe as a Georgia peach. Just ready to be plucked.

NORA

Plucked? You are sickening. But she was still fifteen years old. That makes you a child molester. You aren't even man enough to deal with a mature woman. You need to pick on little girls because you don't have enough brains to hold a conversation with a real woman. (*Pause.*) Or is there some other way that you don't measure up? Huh, Clyde TURNER?

REV. TURNER

I'm warning you, Nora. Do not overstep your bounds. You are really beginning to try my nerves.

Nora gives him the finger. Rev. Turner grabs her by the throat and pushes her against the wall.

REV. TURNER

(*Continues.*) I'm warning you, if you don't go along with this whole deal, I'll go to the police. DO YOU UNDERSTAND ME? You'll rot in jail. Now get out there and see what they want.

He pushes her roughly toward the door.

NORA

You slime ball! I'll go along now, but Clyde TURNER, there'll come a time . . .

Rev. Turner shoves her again.

REV. TURNER

I said get out there, woman! NOW!

Blackout.

Scene Three

SETTING: The outside of the revival tent.

As the curtain rises, Mack, Ken, and Claude stand around the front of the car trying to straighten up their clothing to look presentable.

CLAUDE

Does this choker look all right?

KEN

Yeah, you look nice.

CLAUDE

Does it really look okay? Do I look Indian?

Ken goes into a peekaboo stance and throws fake jabs at Claude, who ignores him.

KEN

Shit—you look like you just jumped off a nickel.

CLAUDE

Are you sure you ain't just pulling on my pud?

KEN

I done told you, you look just fine. You going to a beauty contest or something?

Claude slicks back his hair and polishes his shoes on the back of his pant leg. He throws a fake jab at Ken, who skillfully pushes it aside and counters to Claude's head. They both laugh and slap five.

KEN

> Got ya! You'd be out like a light. (*Short pause.*) Yeah! You look okay.

CLAUDE

> Would you pick me up in a bar?

MACK

> (*Surprised.*) What did you ask him?

KEN

> He's just if'n. If'n I was a woman, would I pick him up in a bar. Just if'n! You know what I mean?

MACK

> Oh! I see! If'n you was gay, would you pick him up in a queer bar? Is that what you mean?

KEN

> No way! I ain't no gay guy. Not even secretly.

CLAUDE

> You'd be the one in a gay bar, Mack. You'd be standing there in your original Wrangler jeans and those Tony Lama cowboy boots, trying to look super cool—you know, like some kinda stud in a beer commercial or something. You get the picture.

MACK

> Hell, yeah! I get the picture. Buddy, let me tell you something, I AM THE PICTURE! Beer companies copy off me for their commercials. America's always looked to guys like me as role models for their studs. It's just a fact of life. I mean to tell you!

CLAUDE

> Yeah, you'd be standing there offering old meat. You'd be trying to call it seasoned steak, but no one's going for it because America's had enough of seasoned steak and they know that all it really means is old, and in your case, shriveled up. Especially Ken, because he's already with me and you're just out of luck on this night, honey.

KEN

> Yeah, I'm with him. He's younger and way prettier.

Ken puts his arms around Claude, and they do a comical version of a two-step waltz.

MACK

> (*Looks nervously around.*) Be cool, guys. Don't be clowning around so much. They might see us. (*Beat.*) Act Indian!

CLAUDE

> What did you say?

MACK

> I said to be cool.

CLAUDE

> No—not that. What else did you say?

MACK

> Nothing!

CLAUDE

> You said, "ACT INDIAN!"

MACK

> So?

CLAUDE

> So what does that mean?

KEN

> It means act cool. (*Turns to Mack.*) Doesn't it, Mack? That's what you was saying, wasn't it?

MACK

> (*Looking disgusted.*) He knows what it means. He's just being an ass.

CLAUDE

> (*Pushing the issue.*) No I don't! I don't know what you mean. I bet if we went all over the country asking Indians what that means, we wouldn't find no two answers the same. No one knows what the hell that means.

MACK

> (*Stumped for a moment.*) ACT INDIAN? You don't know what that means? (*Pauses dramatically, winks at Ken.*) Oh yeah, that's right, you're a half-breed.

CLAUDE

> So where's the script?

MACK

> Script?

CLAUDE

> (*Laughing.*) I need the "Act Indian" script. You got one, Mack?

Ken, who has been shadowboxing behind Mack, goes into a silent version of a war dance.

MACK

> Don't act so stupid.

CLAUDE

> So who's got the script? Who wrote it? The BIA maybe! Is that who wrote it, Mack?

MACK

> Why don't you drop it?

CLAUDE

Act Indian! Don't act stupid! You mean, act like you! That's what you mean, ain't it? Well personally, Mack, I think you act like a jack-off. An Indian jack-off.

KEN

Come on, guys. Don't argue. Whatever it means to you, just do it, okay? I'm getting hungrier than a bear.

CLAUDE

(*Looks disgustedly at Mack.*) Whatever we got to do, we'll do it, okay?

Mack turns to Claude. He extends his hand to shake. Claude pretends to accept but gives him the go-ahead. Mack is undaunted and laughs. Extremely happy, he rubs his hands together.

MACK

Like he said, "we'll do what we got to," so let's go get them! This is what it's all about. This is excitement! I mean to tell you.

As they turn to approach the tent, Nora comes stumbling onstage as though she has just been pushed. She collects her balance and straightens her clothing. She looks up sheepishly, then speaks.

NORA

Welcome to our camp. I'm Nora Heart-Grave.

MACK

Morning. We're very happy to be here. My name is Harold B. J. Iron-Horse, but you can call me Mack. All my friends do.

NORA

They do, do they?

MACK

I would be honored if'n you would as well.

NORA

Okay. Welcome, Mack.

MACK

This here is Ken and that is Claude. He's a poet, and a good one at that.

CLAUDE

Of course Mack wouldn't know a poem from one of his hillbilly songs.

NORA

Perhaps they could be one and the same. (*Pause.*) So what brings you good gentlemen to our midst?

MACK

Drove nigh onto five hundred miles to get here. All the way from Chicago, in fact.

NORA

All that way just to hear some preaching? You must be truly devoted souls.

MACK

Indeed we are, my good woman.

NORA

I ain't your woman, Mr. Mack. In fact I ain't nobody's woman. (*Looks over at Ken.*) Not that I don't want to be. Pastor Simmons had an emergency and will not be available to preach.

Claude laughs a little, and Ken stops shadowboxing. They wait to see what Mack will do or say next.

MACK

No, no! It can't be. Is the pastor all right?

NORA

Fortunately, Rev. Turner is replacing the pastor.

MACK

Never heard of him.

NORA

(*Turns to Ken.*) What did he say your name was?

Ken is flustered and embarrassed by her attention. Claude grins. Ken fakes a punch in his direction. Claude dances away.

CLAUDE

Answer the lady. Well—tell her your name.

KEN

(*Shyly.*) I'm Ken Hops-Ground.

NORA

Well, Ken Hops-Around, you have a nice smile.

Claude starts laughing and begins hopping around in a circle.

KEN

No! Not Hops-Around. It's Hops-Ground. (*Turns to Claude.*) You better lighten up, boy.

NORA

I'm sorry, Ken Hops-Ground. You look famished. Would you like to eat? I'm the cook for this outfit.

KEN

(*Grinning broadly.*) Why, ma'am, you must have read my mind.

MACK

You've just made him a happy man. He loves to eat!

NORA

And I love to cook.

CLAUDE

A match made in heaven. You two should get along just fine.

NORA

I'm certain we will. Come along then. Let me show you the kitchen area. (*Takes Ken's arm.*) Mr. Mack, I'll tell the Reverend you're here. He'll be right with you, I'm sure.

Nora and Ken exit. Mack and Claude smile and wave. Claude makes a kissing gesture at Ken, who shakes his fist at him.

CLAUDE

(*Turns his attention to Mack.*) Okay, Geronimo, what's the game plan here?

MACK

Let me do the talking. I've done this plenty times before.

Rev. Turner enters stage. He has on a white suit and a big smile.

CLAUDE

(*In surprise.*) What's that? Jesus Christ himself!

REV. TURNER

Ah, my friends! I understand that the good Lord has guided you to our midst. We are indeed honored. (*Pause. Turns to Claude.*) I'm not Jesus Christ.

CLAUDE

No shit.

REV. TURNER

That language, young man, will have—

MACK

(*Reaches for his hand.*) Reverend Turner?

REV. TURNER

(*Does not shake hands.*) Yes, I am Reverend Turner. And you, sir?

MACK

I'm Mack. This young fellow is Claude. (*Pause.*) By your reputation, pastor—it is pastor, isn't it?

REV. TURNER

Yes, I am an ordained minister.

Claude walks around the pastor to get a better look. Rev. Turner notices and is slightly uncomfortable. Mack tries waving Claude away.

MACK

As I was about to say, by your reputation I'd have thought you to be an older man.

REV. TURNER

The Lord sometimes works in mysterious ways. (*Short pause.*) I understand from Nora that you were a friend of Pastor Simmons?

MACK

I'd like the opportunity to speak to you. Perhaps in private, sir. Would that be possible?

REV. TURNER

Of course . . . of course. We'll stroll. Nothing is as refreshing as this Georgia air. Great for the lungs, wouldn't you say?

MACK

I do agree.

REV. TURNER

(*Turns to Claude.*) You, my young man, may join Nora, my personal cook, and your friend. You look a little hungry too. Run along now, while I talk to your chief.

CLAUDE

My CHIEF?

TURNER

I said, your chief. He seems to be in charge, and he is older. I once heard that y'all Indians have a tendency to respect your elders—up until you become like a white man, and then you just toss them into old folks' homes. Have you reached that stage?

CLAUDE

Let me tell you something, mister, I . . .

MACK

(*Cuts off Claude.*) Go ahead and eat. I'll talk with the reverend.

CLAUDE

(*Gives a military salute.*) Yes um, big chief.

MACK

Just go on, would ya?

Claude exits. Mack looks around him as he studies the setup of the camp.

MACK

How many folks you figure to show up tonight?

REV. TURNER

I think the house will be full of people wanting the Lord's word tonight. I 'spect they'll be here in good numbers.

MACK

Full house? Did you advertise?

REV. TURNER

> Some flyers, a little on the Sunday radio. Most people don't read that much around here, so a lot of it gets spread by word of mouth. The Lord's word gets around, I assure you that much.

MACK

> I bet it does. They'll come looking for a good show, and you . . .

REV. TURNER

> (*Interrupts Mack.*) And the Lord has given me the privilege of supplying them just that.

MACK

> Yes, he has. I can see that you are indeed blessed.

REV. TURNER

> Really? How do you mean, sir?

MACK

> Well, you've certainly been blessed with good looks.

REV. TURNER

> Thank you.

MACK

> You have a good voice. Nice inflection. Yours is a voice that commands attention.

REV. TURNER

> Yes, that's true. You really are an insightful man.

MACK

> You're honest looking. Extremely important in your line of work, I would assume.

REV. TURNER

> In this case you might judge a book by its cover. I am honest. I believe that honesty is next to godliness.

MACK

> You're most definitely a sociable man. You probably can move about comfortably in any crowd.

REV. TURNER

> Oh yes. I've been told that.

MACK

> A just man of the Lord. Anybody can tell that much just by your appearance. You're probably very fair.

REV. TURNER

> Very much so. I try to be fair in all things. You must understand, though, being a preacher is at times trying. People come to you with such childish complaints.

MACK

> Are you a generous man?

REV. TURNER

To a fault!

MACK

Would you let me have a couple of hundred dollars?

REV. TURNER

(*Surprised.*) What? What did you say?

MACK

I'm in desperate need of some money. I asked you for some.

REV. TURNER

My good man—you don't just go around asking for money. Not in this day and age.

MACK

I'm sorry, Reverend, but you just look like the kind of person who would help a poor soul in need, and besides, you just said . . .

REV. TURNER

(*Cuts Mack off.*) Be that as it may, I don't have it right now— but perhaps after tonight's show. (*Pause as he thinks.*) Yes, yes—we should talk about tonight's show.

MACK

Okay.

REV. TURNER

You and Simmons go a long way back? Isn't that what you said?

MACK

I said I heard Simmons preach.

REV. TURNER

(*Leans closer to Mack.*) May I inquire as to where you heard Pastor Simmons preach?

MACK

In Chicago. At the Amphitheater.

REV. TURNER

In Chicago? Simmons at the Amphitheater in Chicago? Oh my Lord—that must have been something to see.

MACK

It was. Pastor Rev. Turner, it was a sight to see. I mean to tell you.

REV. TURNER

Was they talking in tongues?

MACK

Yes, yes. He had them speaking the Lord's talk.

REV. TURNER

That must have been interesting. (*Short pause.*) And just when was that?

MACK

>Not more than two years ago.

REV. TURNER

>This is extremely interesting. Extremely interesting indeed, but let's discuss our current situation.

MACK

>Yes—I need some money to get me and my friends back to Chicago. (*Pause.*) It must be nice to do what you do.

REV. TURNER

>I will admit it is nice to be doing the Lord's work. Very gratifying. However, it does have a down side, and foremost among those is the county committees. They are highway robbers in disguise.

MACK

>I can well imagine. (*Short pause.*) Do you think you'll be able to help?

REV. TURNER

>Let me point out that the Lord supplies what you need according to your efforts and devotion to his word. As I stated earlier, it is especially pleasing when the people are moved to speak in tongues. You understand, I'm sure.

MACK

>Oh you can count on it, Pastor Turner.

Blackout.

Scene Four

SETTING: In front of the revival tent.

As the curtain rises, Mack, Claude, and Ken sit at a picnic table eating.

MACK

>That Reverend Turner is a crafty one. This might not be as easy as I originally thought.

KEN

>What do you mean?

MACK

>Well, for one thing, he ain't just gonna hand over the money. He'll help us, but we got to earn it. We have to stick around for the show.

CLAUDE

>I don't mind. Should be some young Georgia peaches coming to the show. I wouldn't mind getting me some of that southern loving.

MACK

You be careful about that. Rev. Turner is a slick one. I mean to tell you.

KEN

That Nora sure can cook, though. She's great.

Claude and Mack both laugh as Ken shovels food into his mouth. Nora enters with more food.

CLAUDE

Oh hi, Nora. Ken was just talking about your cooking ability. He's absolutely right. You are an excellent cook.

NORA

Flattery will get you everywhere. I brought more. I'll tell you one thing about the pastor; he takes care to feed people good. Yeah, he takes care of that all right. Doesn't let anybody else do the buying but me. Insists that I get the best cuts of meat and the freshest vegetables. He's good about that, all right. Other ways he ain't so upright, though.

As she talks, she sets a plate in front of each of them, then sits down. She fusses a little over Ken's plate. Claude and Mack grin knowingly.

MACK

Really? Why I'd have believed him to be a saint.

NORA

Him a saint? Don't make me laugh. Why that man's the devil's right hand. Some of the things he's pulled—the devil wouldn't do as bad.

KEN

This food is scrumptious!

Nora beams and hands him a piece of pie.

NORA

You have such a way with words. Why, you can make me blush just like a young schoolgirl. I just love the way you do that. (*Beat.*) Do you like the pie? I baked it myself from scratch.

MACK

(*Impatiently.*) What kind of things were you referring to, Nora?

She looks around, then begins to talk quietly. Both Claude and Mack lean closer to hear it all.

NORA

Well—his wife, for instance. They were the perfect couple. Oh—they were so pretty to lay eyes upon. My husband, rest his soul, was convinced they were a couple made in heaven. She was so devoted to him until he got himself caught in a young girl's bed down in Boone County. The girl's father like to killed him. He was black and blue from the beating he took. Oh, that man has a weakness for pretty young women all right. He just can't resist them. His wife got wind of his shenanigans, and she left him. Started preaching on her own—under her maiden name. Was doing okay until he set her up to be arrested. Some say he paid an old lady to say that she'd stolen her life savings.

MACK

Unbelievable!

NORA

It's typical of him. Like I said, he likes the young ladies.

CLAUDE

Me too. Thanks for the food. It really is delicious.

KEN

D-E-L-I-C-I-O-U-S.

NORA

I'll be back to pick up the dirty dishes in a little while. Ken, take your time and enjoy your food. I have to check the stove.

Nora exits. Claude turns to Ken.

CLAUDE

That's spelled D-E-L-I-C-I-O-U-S.

KEN

So what did I say?

MACK

It don't matter none. She understood what you meant.

CLAUDE

Oh, I love these Holy Rollers with their holier-than-thou-attitudes. Don't you?

KEN

Nora told me that Simmons was his wife and she was supposed to preach here. Not him.

Mack drops his fork and grabs Ken by the shoulders. He begins shaking him.

MACK

What did you say? Did you say that she . . .

KEN

Hey, get up off of me! What's wrong with you?

MACK

Did you say she was supposed to be preaching?

KEN

That's what Nora said!

MACK

Jesus H. Christ! That sneaky creep. He knew all along, but let me go on. His ex-wife is M. Simmons.

CLAUDE

So? I don't get it. Why are you going ape?

MACK

Oh, you will, Poe.

KEN

Yeah, Mack—what's the problem?

MACK

I told him that I knew Reverend Simmons in Chicago. He knows I lied. He actually led me on. That sneaky bastard!

CLAUDE

The plot thickens.

KEN

I gotta go out to the car for a few minutes, then I'm gonna take a run to wear off this food.

MACK

You go ahead. I'll see you when you get back. Don't run too far, just in case we have to leave in a hurry. You never know what'll happen.

Ken exits. Nora comes in to pick up dishes.

NORA

Where's Ken?

CLAUDE

He went to work out. He's gonna take a run.

NORA

I admire that. Isn't he something?

A young woman walks across the stage. She doesn't say anything to them. Claude becomes visibly interested.

CLAUDE

Who is that?

NORA

She sings and plays the piano for Rev. Turner. Her name is Rose.

MACK

She looks part Indian.

NORA

And Black. She's hunting for her father. (*Pause.*) Rose isn't really all there. She hardly ever talks to anybody, but she sure can sing. Got the sweetest voice that I ever did hear.

Knows all the hymns. Rev. Turner told her when we get to
New York he'd help her get a recording contract. If I was
her, I wouldn't believe him. She sings and plays for her keep.

CLAUDE

So her dad was an Indian?

NORA

A full blood Choctaw. They say he was one mean son of a
bitch. Especially when he got to drinking.

CLAUDE

You mean to her?

NORA

No, no. He worshipped the ground that she and her mother
walked on. No, it was the others that caught that man's
wrath.

CLAUDE

The others?

NORA

Racists. He couldn't stand racists. He had problems with
white racists, black racists, and even other Indians that were
racists.

MACK

Would you two mind if I excuse myself? I have to talk to Ken.
We gotta work on the car just a little. He's a great mechanic
on a full stomach.

They nod okay and wave. Mack exits.

CLAUDE

As you were saying, he got himself into a jam.

NORA

Yeah. It was over in Union, Mississippi. He got into a fight
in a bar over a pool game. He beat some white guy with a
pool stick and stabbed another with his own knife.

CLAUDE

Did the guy die?

NORA

No. It was touch and go for awhile, but he recovered.

CLAUDE

You mentioned that she was looking for her dad. Why? He
couldn't have cared too much for her if he just took off like
that.

NORA

That's not necessarily true. Do you have any idea what
happens to an Indian who kills a white man in Mississippi?
(*Short pause.*) Claude, tell me a little about Ken. I find him
to be a fascinating man.

CLAUDE

(*Laughs.*) Ken? Fascinating? (*Pauses and thinks.*) I really don't know a lot about him. He used to be a boxer. I guess he was pretty good, too, according to Mack.

NORA

I think he's real good-looking.

CLAUDE

(*Laughs.*) Would you pick him up in a bar?

NORA

I know I would. I've done it plenty of times before.

CLAUDE

(*Laughs.*) What about Rev. Turner? Did you pick him up in a bar?

NORA

He's such a dog.

CLAUDE

A dog? Like a womanizer?

NORA

Will you excuse me? I must check on my ham. I don't want to burn it. Rev. Turner would flip if'n that happened. That committee will be here soon.

Nora exits. Claude sips on a cup of coffee. After a moment Rose enters.

CLAUDE

(*Looks up and smiles.*) Good morning.

ROSE

(*With a very soft voice.*) It's almost noon.

CLAUDE

You're right. One thing about being out here in the country, you lose all sense of time. At least I do. What about you?

Rose goes about pouring herself a cup of coffee. She ignores Claude. He continues talking.

CLAUDE

My name is Claude. (*Waits for acknowledgment.*) I said, my name is Claude.

ROSE

I heard you.

CLAUDE

So what's yours?

ROSE

I reckon Nora already done told you. She tells everything, that woman.

CLAUDE

You're right, she told me. (*Short pause. Waits for a response. None.*) I hear you can sing.

ROSE

Church songs. Nothing you'd like.

CLAUDE

Music is music. I like music.

ROSE

That's nice.

Rose sips coffee and nibbles on her toast. She doesn't say anything. Claude becomes fidgety.

CLAUDE

I'm a poet.

ROSE

So you're one of those uh . . . what is it they're called? Oh yeah, beat poets.

CLAUDE

Nah. I ain't like that. I don't wear shades.

ROSE

But you wear a choker.

CLAUDE

It's an identity thing. I'm not in a league with Kerouac or that guy Ginsberg. I don't got no goatee or beret and bongos. I just wear a choker, and I'm straight.

ROSE

That could be a matter of opinion. I don't talk to strangers.

CLAUDE

I'm not a stranger. You know something about me. Think about it.

ROSE

Well, I know you're part Indian. You wear a necklace that you insist is a choker. You recite poetry and—oh yeah, your name is Claude. So who are you?

CLAUDE

Who wants to know?

ROSE

I do.

CLAUDE

Okay. So now we're getting somewhere. My mother was a full-blooded Ojibwa. My dad was a lumber jack. I never knew him. They tell me he was French. I was told he was accidentally killed in British Columbia.

ROSE

I'm sorry for asking questions.

CLAUDE

Don't worry about it. This old Chinese guy told me once that one thing most people can be sure of is who their mother is. You can never be sure about who your father is.

ROSE

I know who mine was.

CLAUDE

Was or is?

ROSE

I sometimes wonder about that.

CLAUDE

So tell me, who are you?

ROSE

I once read somewhere that privacy is dignity. I kinda agree with that. I just simply don't want to be asked. At any rate, Nora told you. I'm sure she gave you all the facts.

CLAUDE

Nora told me the rumors. You tell me the facts.

ROSE

Are you sure you want to hear?

Blackout.

Scene Five

SETTING: In front of the revival tent.

As the curtain rises, three members of the county committee talk while they wait for a fourth member to arrive. They all look very country. Richmond has a flag in his hat.

SHERIFF SWAIN

As long as I can remember, we've been visited by a traveling show of this kind. It's a tradition. Why don't you just leave it alone? They don't hurt nothing, and they pay.

AMANDA

It's so . . . hillbilly in nature.

RICHMOND

(*Snaps to attention. Salutes.*) My group, Christian Business-men for a Better America, feels we need to protect our invest-ments from those who would undermine our system of free enterprise—of course, I speak about the evil thing called communism.

AMANDA

Communism? In this county? Mr. Richmond, is this heat getting to you?

RICHMOND

They're everywhere. We need to wipe them out. Them and the homosexuals, and the unions, and the environmentalists, and those militant Indians in South Dakota as well.

SHERIFF

Jesus H. Christ—listen to yourselves. Communism? Homosexuals? Unions? Environmentalists, Militant Indians? Hillbillies? Why hell, we're all a bunch of hillbillies and, what's more, most of us can find a Cherokee or a Blackfeet in our family tree when it serves our purpose.

RICHMOND

I don't understand why those Indians don't just admit that we did beat them fair and square. And those homosexuals! What other country would put up with what they do? Marching and all for equal rights . . . just like a bunch of Negroes.

Sheriff Swain gives Richmond a dirty look. Mack enters and stands quietly in the corner. Sheriff Swain notices him first.

SHERIFF

(*Points at Mack.*) Talking about Indians, I wonder who that fellow is?

DONNA

He certainly looks like an Indian. Better keep your eyes on him, Mr. Richmond. He might be a militant. In fact, I'm sure he is. (*She turns to Mack.*) Good morning, sir.

MACK

Good morning, and how are you?

DONNA

Are you Pastor Simmons?

MACK

No, I'm not.

AMANDA

I didn't think you were. Would you be a good man and fetch the pastor?

MACK

Fetch?

SHERIFF

I think introductions are appropriate here. We're the county committee. It is our duty to approve—or disapprove—any and all sideshows, including revival meetings, in the area. Do you understand?

MACK

Yes, I do.

SHERIFF

So would you mind fetching the pastor for us?

MACK

I'm not a dog. I don't fetch. You, being a Black man, should know . . .

AMANDA

Of course you don't. Let me rephrase that. Would you be kind enough to summon the pastor?

MACK

(*Starts to exit.*) I'll do it right now.

RICHMOND

One moment. I have some questions to ask you before you go.

Mack stops and turns to speak.

SHERIFF

Would you just let him go get the pastor?

RICHMOND

I only want to ascertain something about this man. After all, the safety of my fellow citizens in this county is at stake. I do have a right as an American.

MACK

(*Grinning broadly.*) Men like this fine-looking fellow stir the sense of patriotism in others. Makes us all proud to be Americans. Why, just look at him with that there flag ahanging from his hat. There's no mistaking what he stands for.

SHERIFF

Well, go ahead then. Just don't make a fool of yourself.

AMANDA

And please, Mr. Richmond, do make it quick. This heat!

RICHMOND

Are you a communist, sir?

MACK

No. I served in the navy during the Vietnam conflict.

RICHMOND

Are you an environmentalist?

MACK

Like all Indians, I feel a lot of respect for Mother Earth.

RICHMOND

Well, that doesn't necessarily make you bad. (*Pause. He studies Mack.*) Are you a union organizer, sir?

MACK

> I am not. Why? Are you having labor pains? I mean labor problems?

RICHMOND

> No, but we like to know whenever one of those leftist organizers is about. (*Short pause.*) Are you, perchance, a homosexual?

MACK

> Not unless the boys in your county all look like her.

Looks at Amanda in a suggestive way. She moves behind the Sheriff.

SHERIFF

> (*Grinning.*) Just answer the man's questions.

MACK

> No, I am not a homosexual.

Claude and Ken enter. They are amused by the questioning of Mack. They grin and slap each other five. Mack gives them a dirty look, which makes them get serious.

RICHMOND

> That's good, because we don't need that kind of perversion in this county. It's a threat to the very foundation of our free society. (*Pause.*) Now, Mr.—uh, I don't think I caught your name.

MACK

> I didn't throw it, but for your information, it's Mack.

CLAUDE

> (*Laughs.*) He's the HEAP BIG CHIEF! A purveyor of seasoned steak.

Claude and Ken laugh and slap five.

RICHMOND

> (*To Claude.*) Young man, this is of a serious nature. Your clowning isn't appreciated right now. (*To Mack.*) I need to ask you if you're one of those there militant-type Indians. The way you reacted to our request to go fetch the pastor makes me wonder.

MACK

> Well there, Mr. Richmond. That's what this pretty lady called you, isn't it?

RICHMOND

> Yes, it is. I'm Darrel Richmond, and I'm founder and president of (*snaps to attention and puts his hand on his heart*) Christian Businessmen for a Better America.

AMANDA
> He's the only member.

MACK
> Well, I don't fetch. I just don't do it. If that makes me a militant Indian, so be it.

CLAUDE
> Besides, he's the BIG CHIEF!

KEN
> A surveyor of seasoned steak. America's role model for beer commercial studs.

CLAUDE
> That's purveyor, not surveyor. Now we need another script. The "ACT LIKE A MILITANT INDIAN" script! Oh wow, this is getting heavy.

KEN
> And all we wanted was gas!

Ken and Claude laugh, slap five, then begin to shadowbox. Mack looks at them, totally disgusted.

SHERIFF
> All right, that's enough of this BS. (*Turns to Claude.*) You go get the pastor out here, and do it quick.

Claude hesitates a second, then changes his mind.

CLAUDE
> Yes sir, officer, I'm on my way.

KEN
> Me too.

Claude and Ken walk to the edge of the stage and signal for the others. Enter Rose and Nora.

SHERIFF
> Who the hell are all you people? Where is the pastor?

ROSE
> He said he'd be along shortly.

RICHMOND
> (*Looking at Claude and Ken.*) Someone in this group is a communist or a militant Indian or something. Look at them, Sheriff. Would you just look at them!

SHERIFF
> I'm alooking, Mr. Richmond. I'm alooking. Where the hell is the preacher?

ROSE
> I done told you, he said he'd be along shortly.

SHERIFF

Well, you go get his ass out here. Right now.

NORA

Yes sir, we will.

Nora turns to leave. The rest start to follow.

SHERIFF

I told her to go. The rest of you, I want to see some identification.

Mack, Ken, and Claude start to get out their IDs. Just then, Pastor Rev. Turner enters.

REV. TURNER

Ladies and gentlemen! Pastor Turner at your service.

SHERIFF

I assume you know who we are.

RICHMOND

For your information, sir, we are the county committee on special events. It is our duty to oversee all such happenings. As such we are a branch of the local government.

SHERIFF

(*Studies Rev. Turner with disdain.*) I'm sure he's aware of our function, and—I must add—why we're here. Am I right?

REV. TURNER

Yes, yes I do. Of course I understand. However, I was wondering about the separation of church and state. There is a fine line there, wouldn't you agree?

SHERIFF

(*Surprised and angry.*) You was wondering what? Let me make it perfectly clear to you. We have rules regulating sideshows in our county. Rule one is that you pay to be here. Rule two is if you don't pay, then pack your ass up and move your goddamned medicine show on down the highway. Is that clear enough for you?

REV. TURNER

You call the Lord's word a sideshow?

SHERIFF

You get snotty and you'll find your prissy ass packing on down the road.

Nora and Rose quietly start to leave the stage. Richmond notices them and reacts.

RICHMOND

Sheriff, Sheriff! Our prisoners are escaping.

SHERIFF

Mr. Richmond, they are not prisoners. Let them go. It's this guy I want to talk to. (*Turns to Rev. Turner as he reads a piece of paper.*) Where is this pastor Simmons? She filed for the permit. I don't see your name here at all.

NORA

Excuse me, Sheriff. Would you like a piece of fresh-baked apple pie? I'm going to pull it out of the oven right now.

ROSE

And while you're eating it I could sing for you, Sheriff. What's your favorite tune?

SHERIFF

Apple pie? Fresh baked? Hmm . . . sounds good to me.

MACK

I could go with her and fetch it for you.

RICHMOND

(*Focuses on Mack.*) I thought you said you didn't fetch. What is this? A cover-up of some kind? They're trying to create a diversion, Sheriff. I think the whole bunch of 'em should be arrested until we can check them all out.

NORA

Why, sir, that's not even the case. Y'all look so hot and flushed. (*To Amanda.*) Miss, would you like a tall glass of refreshing iced tea? I have some just as cold as if it came from Alaska.

RICHMOND

It may be poisoned.

NORA

Why, sir, do I look like I'd do something like that?

RICHMOND

You never know what a communist will do.

NORA

Do I look like a communist to you?

AMANDA

Mr. Richmond, why don't you shut up? (*To Nora.*) Everyone looks like a communist to him. In fact, a glass of iced tea would go down real nice.

NORA

Sheriff? Should I have Rose bring you a glass of refreshing iced tea?

SHERIFF

I will accept your offer.

RICHMOND

I, on the other hand, do not accept.

ROSE

(*Looks disgusted.*) Who offered?

Rose and Nora exit.

SHERIFF

Now, back to you. Where's Simmons? That's who we want to talk to, not you!

REV. TURNER

(*Grinning nervously.*) How very unfortunate. She is not available right at the moment. She got detained, but I'm sure she is with us in spirit. I'm terribly sorry about that fact.

AMANDA

Oh my. We do have a problem here.

RICHMOND

Are you licensed, by any chance?

REV. TURNER

Licensed?

RICHMOND

Every business has to have a license to be in business—otherwise they can't do no business. Not in this county. Do you have a license to preach?

SHERIFF

It makes no matter if'n he does, because he ain't got no county permit to hold no event.

RICHMOND

We check them out to see if'n they're communists. But for the moment, I say we all retire and discuss this situation.

AMANDA

For once we're in agreement. Once we've reached a decision or if we have any questions, we'll return.

The committee people exit.

REV. TURNER

I'll go see if I have anything the committee people want.

Rev. Turner exits.

MACK

Well, boys, ain't this something else? Isn't this making things more interesting?

KEN

Looks like the preacher is getting his ass into some kind of trouble.

MACK

You sure got that right. No show, no money, and that means no gas for us to get home.

KEN

> I'm getting worried. Now I'm hungry again. I think I'll go find Nora.

CLAUDE

> You're getting hungry? We just ate!

KEN

> What Mack just said has got me worried, and when I get worried—

MACK

> He gets hungry. Let him go. Nora will ease his troubled mind. Go ahead, Ken.

Ken starts to exit but the conversation pulls him back in.

MACK

> (*Turning to Claude.*) You and me got something to do. We gotta get our acts together so we can help the preacher-man out of this mess. I mean to tell you.

CLAUDE

> You wanna be in that sheriff's jail? Maybe we should just move on.

MACK

> He ain't letting us go nowhere. He's greedy. In fact, this whole bunch is. That may be what gets us out of this mess.

CLAUDE

> What the hell are you talking about?

MACK

> You just keep your ears and eyes open. You'll know what to do when I make a play. I have confidence in you.

CLAUDE

> You're the big chief.

KEN

> We ought to make a video about this trip.

CLAUDE

> Yeah—it could be a documentary or something.

Mack reacts and rubs his hand together. He looks like he's just found the solution to a major problem.

MACK

> Boys, you know that? You just came up with the idea that's gonna get us home. A documentary is just the thing.

KEN

> You got a plan, Mack?

MACK

> Now you boys listen up—this is the plan.

Mack gets them into a huddle. The reverend returns, and so does the committee.

REV. TURNER

> I hold a Doctorate of Divinity from the Heartland Christian College in Louisiana. However, with or without society's certification, I am a messenger of the Lord's word.

AMANDA

> Be that as it may, Reverend Turner, I am with the local church ladies' auxiliary, and frankly, I've never heard of your Heartland Christian College.

REV. TURNER

> It's very prominent in certain Christian circles. I can assure you of that much. I enrolled in their correspondence course.

AMANDA

> A correspondence course?

SHERIFF

> I personally have some reservations about the legality of such courses, but I really would like to see it, if I may.

REV. TURNER

> (*Smiling uncomfortably.*) Unfortunately, I did't bring it with me on this trip. My dear mother was to take it to a shop to have it properly framed. I trust you'll forgive my oversight.

AMANDA

> I have to question the ethical aspect of a correspondence preacher.

RICHMOND

> It seems so unpatriotic. Your politics, sir? I would most definitely like to hear about your politics.

AMANDA

> Not now, Mr. Richmond.

Rev. Turner takes out a hanky and wipes the sweat from his face.

AMANDA

> I'm afraid you'll have to leave.

REV. TURNER

> Is that your final answer?

RICHMOND

> I would suggest that we detain them and see if any of them are wanted by the FBI or any other agency that deals with national security.

AMANDA

> National security? Mr. Richmond, you are totally insane!

RICHMOND

> Make it official then, Sheriff, and give them the boot.

MACK

(*Steps forward.*) May I have the honor of speaking to this blue-ribbon committee of concerned citizens?

SHERIFF

Who the hell are you? What is your connection to this whole deal?

MACK

We are guests here. We came here from Chicago especially to hear Pastor Simmons preach. We are, of course, especially disappointed. We drove all night long.

SHERIFF

Mister, I asked you who you are. I'm used to being answered.

MACK

I'm sorry, Sheriff. Didn't mean to be disrespectful. My name is Harold B. J. Iron-Horse. People call me Mack for short.

SHERIFF

Okay Mr. Harold B. J. Iron-Horse, tell me this. What are you doing in my county? Why would anybody with a name like Mr. Harold B. J. Iron-Horse drive all the way from Chicago to hear some country-hick preacher preach?

TURNER

Sheriff, the Lord's word is not to be . . .

SHERIFF

You better shut up. Do you understand me?

Rev. Turner nods and continues to wipe his forehead with his hanky.

SHERIFF

Now, as I was going to say before I was so rudely interrupted, you drove all that way? It doesn't make sense.

AMANDA

I tend to agree with the sheriff, and besides—excuse me for being blunt, but you and your friends do not strike me as being especially Holy Roller types.

RICHMOND

You ain't whistling Dixie there. You look like militant Indians—the bunch of you.

SHERIFF

Nip it in the bud, both of you. (*Short pause.*) I want to hear what this man has to say.

MACK

Sheriff, Miss Amanda's right. We aren't here for the rivival. We have another reason for being here. Rev. Turner doesn't even know about it. You see, I work for a major TV network. I'm here partly to conduct a feasibility study. An informal one, you understand. You know what that is?

SHERIFF

> Of course I do. Go on.

MACK

> I'm traveling about looking for a good site to film a revival meeting. We want the real deal. What you people are doing here is exactly the kind of thing that would bring national attention to your county. Your concerns are just what I'm looking for. Do you follow me?

SHERIFF

> Of course I can verify what you tell me—that you work for a major TV network. Do you have a card or anything?

MACK

> Of course I do. (*Reaches in pocket, takes out wallet. Accidentally drops a long row of business cards.*) Let me see, where is that card? (*Looks at several.*) Ah, here it is. I like what I'm seeing so far. Something like this could be big.

As he talks he flashes the card to the group, but does not actually hand it to anyone. He returns it to the wallet.

RICHMOND

> What do you mean, big? (*Pause.*) This may well be of interest to the business community.

AMANDA

> Especially if it means money in YOUR pocket.

MACK

> That's exactly the point. It would mean an influx of people. You all know that people mean money.

The committee members look at each other and smile.

RICHMOND

> You are a most sensible man, Mr. Mack. With your disposition it's easy to overlook that mild air of militancy.

MACK

> I am so happy to hear that. Now, to continue what I was saying—

RICHMOND

> Please do continue.

SHERIFF

> Then don't interrupt the man.

CLAUDE

> (*Aside to Ken.*) That's our big chief, all right. He's just getting in gear, too. Just watch him operate on these hicks.

KEN

> Or get operated on.

AMANDA

And just how would it benefit the local churches? I'd be most interested in hearing that.

MACK

My dear Miss Amanda, the excitement of the revival meeting is not for everyone. Many prefer a more sophisticated mode of worship. In fact your churches may not be big enough to handle the overflow. Do you realize the possibilities that situation presents? Can you envision it?

AMANDA

Why yes, I can! We could have a bake sale and a bazaar.

MACK

(*Looks surprised.*) Why—I guess you could. (*Pause.*) People would be looking for mementos to buy. Key chains and those pencils with company names on them. What, Mr. Richmond, would that mean to you?

RICHMOND

Why—it would be a dream come true.

MACK

And that, my good friends, is all it'll be. A dream, unless you take steps to make it more. You can do that by letting this revival go on. Sort of like a practice run.

RICHMOND

But he doesn't have a permit. In this county we do not allow that sort of—

SHERIFF

Mr. Richmond, would you please stuff it in your starched underwear? That is a mere technicality. One this committee has the power to waive.

MACK

Think of it as a practice run. Preparation for the big day that could put you into a higher tax bracket. May I speak very bluntly?

The members of the committee all nod okay.

MACK

You people are in the unique position today to impact the welfare of this county for many years. What you decide right now will most certainly be discussed by others for years to come. Just think of the influence you'll wield then!

RICHMOND

I am! I am! We could take steps to get rid of the communists and those homosexuals. Yes, and the unions and the environmentalists. The militant Indians? Well, Mr. Mack, if they're anything like you, we certainly could use more of them.

As he talks, Claude and Ken mime his words: communists, homosexuals, unions, environmentalists.

CLAUDE

(*Aside to Ken.*) Isn't that an interesting twist?

KEN

(*Aside to Claude.*) You ain't kidding.

RICHMOND

I always said that the forefathers of this nation should have paid more heed to what they were being told by the Natives of this land. Why, had our ancestors listened to yours, Mr. Mack, perhaps we wouldn't have the problems we do now.

MACK

Probably not, Mr. Richmond, probably not.

RICHMOND

You know, of course, that I am speaking of the homosexuals, communists, and the womens' libers.

AMANDA

Watch your mouth.

RICHMOND

Women just like you, Amanda, would do like they used to and walk three steps behind their men. Oh, what a nation it would be.

KEN

I'd like to hear him tell that to Wilma Man-Killer or Char Teeters!

AMANDA

Indians respected their women. Gave them a place of power.

RICHMOND

That's what I always say. The Indian kept his womenfolks close to the tipi where they belonged.

AMANDA

Women had leadership power. (*Pause, frustrated by Richmond.*) Oh, what's the use?

CLAUDE

(*To Ken.*) We can write a script for that, too. Just picture it— *The Militant Indian!*

KEN

(*To Claude.*) America's Best Friend!

MACK

(*Scowls at the two.*) And just think about what else you could do. (*Hesitates.*) Why you could buy a new car for the sheriff. With the right equipment he could do a better job of protecting this county. Am I not right, Sheriff?

Takes the sheriff by the arm and walks him upstage as they talk.

SHERIFF

I need a radar gun!

MACK

Which, as we all know, would mean revenue for the county. It would reduce the need to increase property taxes and preserve the quality of life.

SHERIFF

And a two-way radio.

MACK

Communication with your main people. The most important of your citizens.

SHERIFF

A couple of high-powered rifles.

MACK

Protection!

SHERIFF

And one of those new-fangled fingerprinting machines.

MACK

Even more protection.

SHERIFF

And one of those riot guns!

MACK

A riot gun?

RICHMOND

A riot gun! What a great idea! We must attend to law and order.

MACK

(*Grinning.*) You took the words right out of my mouth.

RICHMOND

If'n we don't, the evil forces of communism will soon take over. A riot gun would be just the thing. How much cruisin' do you think those homosexuals would do if they knew we had a riot gun to pepper that itch up their—

AMANDA

Mr. Richmond! Don't let your imagination carry you away. I know you like to make the scene with your girlie magazines. Your ex-wife told us all about your collection of *Hustler*. Larry Flint is your guru, is what she said.

RICHMOND

Who cares what she said? I purchase it for the articles. I don't get weird about it like she said. She lied! I do not tie myself up or whip my own ass.

AMANDA

Right, Mr. Richmond—however, you do take advantage of yourself when you view those magazines.

RICHMOND

Masturbation is perfectly normal in our society.

AMANDA

So says you and Larry Flint!

SHERIFF

Jesus Christ what will they talk about next?

MACK

Can we get back to the issue? Now, folks, if I was a member of this blue-ribbon committee, I would make law and order a priority. That would be my first task.

SHERIFF

You are a sensible enough man. (*Turns to other committee members.*) Well we'd best get back to town. We have much to do. Amanda, you'll contact the appropriate people. That phone tree you women got together must be put into action.

AMANDA

(*To Turner.*) By six o'clock this afternoon everyone in town will know about tonight's event.

TURNER

Why thank you Miss Amanda, and so we end up doing the Lord's work together.

AMANDA

The Lord works in mysterious ways. I must go.

The committee members begin to exit, singing and skipping.

COMMITTEE MEMBERS

We're having a revival! We're having a revival!

TURNER

We're having a revival, all right. And I feel confident that they'll be Holy Rollin', and some might even be moved to speak in tongues. Ain't that right, Mr. Mack?

MACK

I mean to tell you.

Blackout.

ACT TWO

Scene One

SETTING: In front of the tent.

As the curtain rises, Ken and Nora sit at picnic table talking.

NORA

Mr. Mack sure is an eloquent fellow, and very resourceful. Does he really work for a major TV network?

KEN

He has a friend in every business. You want a riot gun for the sheriff, he can get it. What's more, he can get it at a discount.

NORA

But does he really work for a TV network?

KEN

He told me he did a consulting job with them once.

NORA

Consultant? On what?

KEN

Something about urban Indians.

NORA

But what about what he told that county committee?

KEN

Oh that! Wasn't that a beauty? He may have been shucking a little on that one.

NORA

Well, he saved Clyde Turner's ass with it.

KEN

Now you can hold your revival with their blessing.

NORA

You are coming, aren't you?

KEN

I don't think so. (*Hesitates.*) Maybe. We'll see.

Nora gets up and walks to a small side table with sugar and cream on it.

NORA

Didn't you tell me you were from Chicago?

KEN

I was born in Nebraska. I'm an Omaha Indian. I was brought to Chicago when I was eleven.

NORA

(*As she stirs her coffee.*) How'd you get into boxing?

KEN

CYO.

NORA

What's that?

KEN

A youth program. They had a boxing program. I signed up and liked it. Got pretty good at it, too. By the time I was sixteen, I was city champ.

NORA

What about girls?

KEN

I had girl friends, but nothing serious. I had to stay focused.

NORA

(*Stands at side table for a minute, returns to table.*) Do you find me attractive?

KEN

I do, but I wouldn't do anything about it because—well, I have my reasons.

NORA

Reasons? Am I too fat or something?

KEN

Are you kidding me? Too fat? You're just perfect for me.

NORA

What then?

KEN

You're white.

NORA

Fat would have been better! Ken—are you a racist? I never would have guessed that. (*She starts to get up.*) For your information, I do have some Indian in me too.

KEN

(*Reaches out and stops her.*) It's not that. It's like this—I met a girl one time and we really liked each other. She was white. We were walking home and a group of white guys attacked us. (*Pause.*) Someone hit me with a baseball bat and I was out. They beat her too, and she just quit seeing me. Wouldn't take my calls or nothing. I figured after that experience it wasn't worth it, and so white women became off limits for me. I only date Indian women.

NORA

Is there someone now?

KEN

Not really. I date a few women. Nothing serious. Mack says I'm better off like that. I guess he's right—he usually is.

NORA

> What does he know? You need a woman to take care of you. Cook and do those things a man needs done for him. Don't listen to anybody else. Follow your heart. I think you'd make some girl a swell husband. That's what I think.

KEN

> Now you're scaring me. Anyway, where would I find someone like that?

NORA

> (*Moves closer.*) Maybe closer than you think. That was one bad experience. Not everybody is so hateful. I think it would be a good thing between us.

KEN

> I agree.

NORA

> Well, Ken Hops-Ground, what are you waiting for? Get to hopping!

Blackout.

Scene Two

SETTING: In front of the tent.

As the curtain rises, Rose sits on a stump and listens while Claude talks.

CLAUDE

> It's simple. All you do is make up a line of poetry to whatever I just said.

ROSE

> Okay then—what's the topic?

CLAUDE

> Romeo and Juliet stuff. Okay—here goes! I see the curtain in your eyes move as you look me over.

ROSE

> Don't flatter yourself. (*Laughs.*) Okay—how about this one? It's those quiet guys that steal the precious moments and silence a young girl's reason. How was that?

CLAUDE

> Very good.

Rose extends her hand, and Claude drops to one knee and kisses it.

ROSE

> Oh my—you're so gallant, you take my breath away. Okay—your turn.

CLAUDE

But Rose, oh sweet Rose, you are so beautiful. I see a trans-
lucent glow in your innocence. (*Mack walks out of tent. Steps
back inside to listen.*) Your beauty sparkles like morning sun
rays on waves in a small pond. Sparkling like a million
diamonds, each a gift to my heart.

ROSE

Ah, you with the glib tongue and flashing eyes—how you
embrace life. Your warmest smile invades me with pleasure-
filled anticipation.

Mack, unseen by the two, steps out of the tent and listens more.

CLAUDE

Is mine a mind afraid to admit the truth? Have my emotions
become like a musician whose hands are arthritic? No, no,
sweet lady—the very sight of you strums softly on the
strings of my emotion.

ROSE

Oh, you gentle-souled man, you watcher of life with your
deep emotional attachment to pleasure-filled moments, will
you break my heart with your suave ways and magnetic
smile?

*Nora and Ken come out of tent. Mack signals them to be quiet. They
stand and watch as well.*

CLAUDE

Lady, oh lady, your brown eyes tell of a tender heart—an
instinct to love. Surely in the morning I shall be more smitten,
having tasted the sweet nectar of you.

MACK

(*With lots of energy and ridicule.*) Well, I'll be goddamned!
Would you listen to that poet, poetin' on the pretty lady!

Claude and Rose jump to their feet, embarrassed.

KEN

Sounded nice to me.

MACK

"I shall be more smitten?" I'll be goddamned! If I didn't hear
it with my own ears, I'd have never believed it. "Tasted the
sweet nectar of you!"

CLAUDE

Get lost, chump.

MACK

> You see that son of a bitch? Down on his knees slobbering all over the girl's hand. I got you now, Shakespeare! You ain't gonna live this down.

Ken and Mack slap five.

ROSE

> Mr. Mack, we were—

CLAUDE

> Don't pay him no mind. I mean, after all, he's the original American stud.

NORA

> Says who?

CLAUDE

> Himself.

NORA

> I bet he's the only one, though.

MACK

> Who are you to be talking like that to me?

NORA

> I'm sorry—I only meant it as a joke. (*Laughs.*) The idea of you as a stud!

Everyone else laughs too. Mack looks irritated. Turner enters and listens.

MACK

> Hey—I don't appreciate this. You don't know anything about me. So hold your tongue.

TURNER

> Mr. Mack, I realize that sometimes the woman can be very crass. There are times when she pushes me to the limits of my . . .

NORA

> You stay out of this, Clyde Turner.

MACK

> Maybe you should put her on a shorter leash.

NORA

> And just what is that supposed to mean?

MACK

> A bitch dog in heat should be . . .

KEN

> Mack! I won't tolerate that kind of talk to my friend.

MACK

> What you gonna do?

ROSE

Stop! Everyone just take a deep breath and count to ten. Come on now.

TURNER

That's not going to help matters any. Why don't you go take a nap before tonight's event? You'll need to be on your toes.

ROSE

A nap? Who do you think that you're talking to? I resent the implications of that statement. Hell no, Clyde Turner, I won't take a nap. I'm going to stroll by the river. Claude, would you join me?

MACK

He'd like nothing better. He can do some more slobbering.

TURNER

Please, ladies and gentlemen, all this bickering is trying my nerves. It is not conducive to the atmosphere of love and good spirits that we need to create for tonight's show.

ROSE

Everyone take a big gulp of air, shut your eyes, and think a nice thought. Come on, everyone has to do it. Do it together on three. One, two, three!

Everyone laughs and the mood changes.

TURNER

Ah—now that feels much better. Nothing is nicer than the children of the Lord having a good laugh together. Hallelujah! Hallelujah! Nora, I wonder if you'd be kind enough to drive into town to pick up some supplies?

Claude and Rose exit, hand in hand.

NORA

The ride would be nice. Ken can accompany me. (*Turns to Ken.*) Would you mind?

KEN

I'd love to.

Ken and Nora exit.

TURNER

Mr. Mack, I haven't yet had the opportunity to properly thank you for intervening on my behalf with the committee. You changed their minds.

MACK

Well, I need that money to get back to Chicago. It was no big thing.

TURNER

Nonetheless, your resourcefulness saved the day. That was
a great story you came up with. They went for it—hook,
line, and sinker.

MACK

How do you know it's not the truth?

TURNER

Oh come on, Mr. Mack. I'm not a child, nor am I exactly
gullible. Why, my good man, that was as believable as—
Simmons at the Amphitheater in Chicago.

They both laugh.

MACK

No hard feelings?

TURNER

Of course not.

*Mack doesn't say anything, but grins and raises his fist in a Power to
the People sign.*

Blackout.

Scene Three

SETTING: At a picnic table outside of the revival tent. Night.

*As the curtain rises, Ken and Claude sit with Nora and Rose. Church
music plays softly. Turner can be heard offstage, preaching.*

TURNER

(*Off stage.*) Remember, ladies and gentlemen, God so loved
the world that He gave His only begotten son . . . (*Turner
fades out. Music continues.*)

CLAUDE

Rose and I have something we want to share with you two.

ROSE

(*All aglow.*) I wouldn't have believed it myself four hours
ago, but I'm going to Chicago with Claude—as a couple. If
you know what I mean.

They all laugh and celebrate.

KEN

Well, congratulations!

NORA

And you, young lady—you didn't even give me a hint.

ROSE

You've been so preoccupied with Ken.

NORA

I have, haven't I?

Richmond dances onstage with a sign that says, "God hates Communists."
He dances backward offstage when they boo him.

KEN

You know what's so strange? I mean, it's real weird that
you two decided that, because—well, you tell them, Nora.

NORA

What Ken's saying is that we're going to go to Chicago to
open a restaurant.

CLAUDE

No way! He'll eat up all the profits.

ROSE

It is strange indeed! Just think, we'll all be there together.
That's great! (*Pause.*) I think. (*Looks at Nora, then smiles. The*
two women hug.) We'll have so much to see.

NORA

We can get together for movies and stuff like that. Oh—it
will be fun.

CLAUDE

We'll be partying down, pal. It'll be a regular hoot.

KEN

I heard that.

Mack enters. He looks at the two couples, both of whom are embracing.

MACK

So what the hell is this? A love-in or something?

CLAUDE

Rose and I are hooking up, Mack.

MACK

Doesn't surprise me any, the way you was slobbering all
over her forearm. I wonder what Turner will have to say
about that?

ROSE

What can he say?

MACK

(*Seriously.*) What if you have kids?

CLAUDE

Don't even go there. I know what that's all about. I'm a
breed, remember? You sound like some kind of racist, Mack.

KEN

Hey—slow down there, pal. He ain't said nothing like that.

ROSE

In my mind, no kind of racism is acceptable. We need to see each others' character, not skin pigmentation.

MACK

Oh yeah? Listen to this. The world should be all peace and love, right? Well, it's not. It's about a lot more than skin color, doll. It's about character and values and quality of life. When others try to strip me of my rights to the kind of life I want, it makes me mad. I have a right to my beliefs just as much as you do.

KEN

Well, Mack, I got some more news for you.

MACK

I don't want to hear it right now, okay?

KEN

Nora is coming to Chicago with me to open up a down-home type restaurant in the uptown area.

MACK

Oh no! What's wrong with you two, anyway? We just stopped for some gas (*looks at Ken*), and some food (*looks at Claude*), and a little—well, whatever else.

CLAUDE

Yeah—but we found more. (*He puts his arm around Rose.*) A lot more, Mack.

MACK

Listen, Ken, maybe you don't want to do that. What I mean is, you don't know everything about that woman. Either of you. You guys just met these two women. You don't know shit about them—and there is shit to know, according to Turner.

NORA

I feel like it's my responsibility to clarify what he's talking about. I wasn't always like I am now.

KEN

I don't care about before.

NORA

Nonetheless let me finish. I'm not proud of my past, especially now that I've met you. (*Ken tries to put his arms around her, but she pushes him away.*) All I need is a chance to make things right. What I'm trying to tell you all, and especially you, Ken, is that I used to be . . .

MACK

She used to be a hooker. A whore.

Nora starts crying. Ken takes her in his arms. They all stand quietly. Turner can be heard preaching in the background.

MACK

I don't want you to get hurt, Ken, because you're my friend. I wish there was some other way of . . .

CLAUDE

You're full of shit, Mack.

MACK

I don't want my friend getting burned by some country whore.

KEN

Say that one more time and I'm going to kick your ass.

MACK

Over some streetwalking whore?

Ken lunges at Mack. Claude and the two women step between them.

MACK

Come on, then—I'll fight you.

Mack begins removing rings and other jewelry, talking as he does.

NORA

He's an old man.

MACK

You think so, huh? I'll give him a boxing lesson.

ROSE

Oh—would you all stop this nonsense! Fighting will solve absolutely nothing. It can only result in more trouble.

Mack is finally ready. He assumes a boxing stance.

MACK

Come on, then.

NORA

Mr. Mack! Would you act your age?

MACK

Shut up, whore!

Ken loses it. He comes after Mack. Mack takes a swing. Ken ducks under the punch and counters with a hook to Mack's jaw. Mack goes down. The fight is over quicker than it started.

CLAUDE

Oh shit—you knocked him out.

ROSE

>Now look what's happened. I told you, fighting never solved a thing. What are we going to do?

NORA

>We need water. Come with me, Rose.

The women exit. Ken and Claude kneel down to check on Mack.

KEN

>I didn't mean to do that.

CLAUDE

>I know that.

KEN

>You think she's a whore?

CLAUDE

>Maybe in her past, but not now. (*Looks down at Mack.*) You know, he thinks he's protecting you. Once he understands how you feel about her and how she feels about you, he'll come around. You know how he is.

KEN

>Yeah—he sure is something, ain't he?

CLAUDE

>If I had an old man—a dad—I'd want him to be just like Mack.

KEN

>Really?

CLAUDE

>This old bronco rider is real cool. I love the son of a bitch.

KEN

>I do too. Man—he is gonna be pissed off.

CLAUDE

>He'll be talking much shit. Could be a long ride back home.

MACK

>And you'll both deserve everything I have to say. (*Gets slowly to his feet. Turns to Claude.*) You okay, Ken?

CLAUDE

>I'm Claude—Shakespeare—the poet. Remember?

MACK

>Oh yeah! (*Turns to Ken.*) I didn't hurt you, did I?

KEN

>(*Amazed.*) I'm all right. Are you?

CLAUDE

>(*Laughing.*) You didn't even hit him.

MACK

>Bullshit, too! I hit something. My knuckles are sore as hell.

CLAUDE

You hit the floor when you fell.

MACK

I was listening to what you two were talking about. I love the both of you, too. You're like sons.

KEN

So you're not mad?

MACK

Hell yeah, I'm mad, but I love you guys. Where is Nora? I owe her an apology. Hey—what the hell—families get into fights all the time. That's what we are. We're family, us three, and we got to stay that way even if I got to kick the shit out of you now and then.

They all laugh and hug. Turner enters.

TURNER

What, may I ask, is going on out here? (*Goes to Mack.*) Are you all right, Mr. Mack? You look a little shaken.

Nora and Rose return with a pitcher of water and a towel. They make a big deal about cleaning Mack up.

MACK

Ken and I had a little spiff about him and Nora getting hooked up. She wants to go to Chicago with Ken. They plan to open a joint together.

TURNER

Ken and Nora? (*Turns to Nora.*) What is this?

NORA

It's true, Clyde. I'm leaving with Ken. (*Pause.*) Look, Clyde. It's best that way. We only made each other miserable.

TURNER

That certainly is true. I am, however, just a little concerned about you running off with the likes of him. You were doing so well. Reformed yourself, so to speak.

NORA

Oh, Clyde, you are so full of it. Come here and give me a hug. Ken is a good man. I know a good man when I meet one.

TURNER

(*To Ken.*) Young man, you are getting a good woman. Maybe better'n you rightfully deserve. Remember now, there's an old saying: "A retired whore makes one hell of a wife." You count your blessings, young man.

Everyone laughs as Turner hugs Nora and shakes Ken's hand.

ROSE

   Why, pastor—what kind of language is that for you to use?

TURNER

   (*All smiles.*) Sometimes, my dear little songstress, the language and sentiments that come from the lower echelon of society are most deft. I truly believe that Sister Nora will make him a good wife. He's a lucky man. She's experienced in many ways. Most of them unmentionable, of course.

ROSE

   You think I'd make a good wife?

TURNER

   You would be a blessing to any man's life. (*Richmond dances onstage with a sign that says, "God Hates Art." Turner points his thumb at Richmond.*) Even him.

ROSE

   Not likely, pastor, but what about Claude?

TURNER

   Him? Make a good wife? Certainly not for Mr. Richmond. They'd argue.

ROSE

   You know what I mean, Clyde Turner.

TURNER

   You too? You're going too, aren't you?

Rose nods and puts her arm around Claude. Turner stands back and views the couple.

ROSE

   Well?

TURNER

   Although it saddens me, I must admit you make an attractive couple. You're suited to each other. You're both so— what is it I am looking for here? Oh yes! The word *hippie* comes to mind. You'll make a nice-looking hippie couple.

MACK

   I mean to tell you. A poet and a pie-an-o player.

TURNER

   Which reminds me. We better get the show on the road here. My flock awaits the Lord's word. Come on, Mr. Mack. You too, Mr. Richmond. Let's go pray for a miracle.

RICHMOND

   What's the miracle going to be?

TURNER

> Brother Mack has one leg shorter than the other. We'll pray that they even out.

RICHMOND

> Could I have just a moment before we proceed?

Richmond uses a magic marker to alter the sign he has from "God Hates Art" to "God Hates Short Legs!"

TURNER

> How appropriate! Come along, now. Ladies, are you ready to do your stuff? In the name of the Lord, proceed.

They all exit except Claude and Ken. Claude looks at Ken and shrugs. He takes out a pencil and works on a poem. Ken shadow boxes and occasionally goes to peek into the tent. Meanwhile, offstage Turner can be heard preaching. He asks the people to pray for Mack's short leg.

TURNER

> (*Off stage.*) Brothers and sisters, the Lord has sent us a sign. Oh, I tell you the spirit is in our midst. Hallelujah, thank you Jesus! We have Brother Mack who the Lord has sent all the way from Chicago, Illinois. That's right, brothers and sisters, all the way from the big windy city. I want you all to pray for Brother Mack. He has been bothered all his life with an ailment. His left leg is shorter than his right leg. I want you to join me in asking Jesus to enter Mack's body and make him well. Hallelujah, Jesus, hear our prayer.

CHORUS

> (*Singing.*) We need a miracle! We need a miracle! Oh yeah.
> (*Sing several times. Turner keeps preaching as chorus is sung.*)

TURNER

> Is there anybody who would like to join me as I begin? Welcome Sheriff, and Miss Amanda. Jesus bless their souls! Step right up here, Brother Richmond, and pray. Yes, Rose, and you too, Nora. Pray, sisters, pray! The spirit of Jesus is with us tonight! Hallelujah! Hallelujah! Can you feel it? Let us pray, brothers and sisters, let us pray!

CLAUDE

> Listen to that. They're praying for Mack right now, and he's—why, the son of a bitch is talking Indian.

KEN

> I thought he was supposed to talk in tongues. What's he saying, anyway?

CLAUDE

> Quiet! I can't hear.

KEN

Reckon he's acting Indian?

CLAUDE

Big time, buddy, big time.

AMANDA

Oh, Brother Mack. The spirit is in you. It's a miracle. After
the meeting we must get together. We must.

KEN

There he goes again. What's he saying?

CLAUDE

That son of a bitch!

KEN

What?

AMANDA

Say it again, Brother. Let the Lord's spirit in and say it again.
Speak to me, my brother! (*Pause.*) Oh—share it with me,
Brother Mack. Such a delight. Oh yes, yes, Brother Mack—
such an experience. So wonderful.

*Claude is practically on the floor from laughing. Ken begs him to tell
him what Mack is saying.*

CLAUDE

That bastard is talking some dirty-assed Indian to that
woman. First he said— (*Pulls Ken to him and whispers in his
ear.*) Then next he told her that she could—(*Whispers again.*)

KEN

No, he wouldn't say that. Not Brother Mack. (*Pause.*) Well,
on second thought—maybe he would. Should we go in
there and stop him?

CLAUDE

Why?

KEN

I'll be damned. We can't just let him go on? That's against
the Bible or something, ain't it?

CLAUDE

I mean to tell you. Don't worry about it.

Rose and Nora enter stage. They are all excited and sweating.

NORA

That's the best I ever heard Clyde preach. He moved Mr.
Mack very quickly.

ROSE

He sure was hot.

NORA

You sang beautiful tonight. So much passion.

ROSE

It was the preaching—and Mr. Mack talking in tongues to Miss Amanda. The spirit was moving. It was beautiful, wasn't it?

NORA

It was like Clyde knew this would be our last time together, and he wanted to make it special. I'd really like to tell him how special he was tonight—both him and Mr. Mack.

KEN

I'd like to tell them something too. Both of them are really—

CLAUDE

Great! What Ken means to say is that when we heard him preaching and Mack responding like he did—well hell— we were moved too. Ain't that right, brother Ken? RIGHT?

KEN

In ways you'd never expect.

NORA

Listen! There they go again. They make a good pair.

KEN

You ain't just kidding, either.

Both couples pair off onstage. Claude is highly entertained. Ken does some shadowboxing but stops often to listen. Nora watches him in admiration.

TURNER

(Off stage.) Is the Lord speaking to you, Mr. Richmond?

RICHMOND

(Off stage.) Yes, He is. Yes indeedy! He says to change my ways—to love everyone.

MACK

(Off stage.) Everyone?

TURNER

(Off stage.) The environmentalists?

RICHMOND

(Off stage.) And the union man and the artists.

TURNER

(Off stage.) The homosexuals?

RICHMOND

(Off stage.) I shall judge not my brother in the spiritual way. *(His voice changes back to his ordinary voice.)* However, my own plumbing prefers . . .

TURNER

(Off stage.) We get the message, Mr. Richmond

MACK

(Off stage.) And you feel the spirit?

RICHMOND

(*Off stage.*) Ah yes! The SPIRIT! Yes, indeedy! I do feel the spirit. I do! I do!

AMANDA

(*Off stage.*) That, Mr. Richmond, is not the spirit you're feeling. That is my derriere, and if you do not remove your hand immediately I will slap you into kingdom come itself. Has this heat gotten the best of you? Mr. Richmond, I said (*pause*)—oh, Mr. Richmond.

TURNER

(*Off stage.*) Would you look at that, Mr. Mack!

MACK

I mean to tell you!

TURNER

Thank you, Jesus. Hallelujah!

AMANDA

You are indeed touching the spirit. Oh, Mr. Richmond! Ohhhhh, Mr. Richmond.

RICHMOND

Amen! Amen! And I am happily feeling the spirit—what a spirit it is!

AMANDA

The spirit is everywhere. Can you feel it too, Reverend Turner? Brother Mack, it is indeed the spirit you are feeling. Ohhhh! Speak to me in tongues, my brother. In tongues!

TURNER

Hallelujah! Hallelujah! The spirit is spreading, Miss Amanda. Hallelujah!

MACK

I mean to tell you!

Blackout.

EPILOGUE

SETTING: Outside of the tent.

As the curtain rises, farewells are being made.

SHERIFF

Whoopee! This was sure one hell of a weekend. I'm very happy we didn't send you packing after all. Miss Amanda and Mr. Richmond will make certain we keep the spirit alive and well. Won't you, Mr. Richmond . . .

RICHMOND

> We sure enough will, Sheriff. I mean to tell you.

MACK

> Hey—that's my line.

TURNER

> You guys take care of my girls, you hear?

Sheriff, Amanda, and Richmond exit. There is a moment of silence as the rest look at each other.

MACK

> Well, guys, I guess this is it. (*Turns to the women.*) You know Ken likes to eat a lot and Claude there needs his quiet times to write poetry—other than that they aren't too bad.

CLAUDE

> You going to be okay?

KEN

> I'm worrying about you too, and when I get worried . . .

MACK

> You get hungry. I think Nora can handle that for you. Hell yeah, I'll be all right. I'm going to work with Clyde to arrange a TV special about his work.

TURNER

> We'll make a great team.

NORA

> I'm sure you will.

CLAUDE

> Well then, we better get rolling. Chicago is waiting our arrival. We got us a Greyhound to catch. Next stop, Chicago—all aboard!

MACK

> Yeah, I guess you're right. Come here, the two of you. (*He hugs both of the men.*) Don't forget the stuff I taught you— and don't you forget to act Indian.

They all laugh. The guys pick up the women's suitcases and exit. Turner and Mack watch them depart.

TURNER

> Are you ready for the next county, Mr. Mack? Are you ready for the next, Miss Amanda? Does your leg feel all right?

MACK

> Hell yeah, I'm ready for anything. I mean to tell you!

Blackout.

While lights are out, Neil Diamond's revival music is brought up very loudly. Cast reenters and bows.

Chili Corn

A PLAY IN TWO ACTS

Characters

VANESSA (CHILI) CORN: Eighteen to twenty-five years old. Dresses in a very modern and street-smart way. An urban-raised Chippewa with roots in the Duluth/Superior area.

BENNY RED-BEAVER: Ojibwa, twenty-five to thirty years old. Intelligent, philosophical. Director of the local Chicago AIM chapter. Some half-finished artwork can be observed in his apartment. Lives alone and has girlfriends. He was born and raised in Canada in the woods. Has spent most of his adult life in Chicago except for some time on the road. Moved to LA but came back to Chicago to attend the University of Illinois. Has a very modern, stylish haircut.

GABRIEL PEOPLES: A thirty- to forty-year-old Menominee from the Green Bay, Wisconsin, area. The "street lieu-tenant" for AIM—a behind-the-scenes organizer. Totally committed to AIM, he is statewide coordinator. His hair is long and he wears a beret with an eagle feather attached to it. A Vietnam veteran who was awarded medals for bravery, he wears the medals on his beret.

ROSARIO CHAVIS: A mestizo from Mexico. Twenty-five to thirty-two years old. Pretty, intelligent, committed, quick tempered. Dressed in an interesting blend of traditional Mexican and modern clothing. Although she can speak English, she does so with an accent.

SCENE: Chicago.

TIME: Around 1975.

PROLOGUE

SETTING: A bare stage, dimly lit.

As the curtain rises, a red spotlight comes up slowly to reveal a young woman sitting on a stool. One after another she is joined by the other cast members as they come onstage, saying a poem.

ROSARIO
> She took it until her broken bones
> And broken heart
> Ached like an old woman's.

BENNY
> The Anishanobae Quae . . .
> The sister warrior's spirit pushed her forward

GABRIEL
> In recovery from the war
> That was strapped to her back
> And drilled into her brains . . .

CHILI
> Kicked and choked and socked,
> Trying to comprehend
> The nature of my enemy,
> My tormented tormentor.
> I'm staggering, but not down.

Chili stands, then exits. Other cast members follow her. Three drumbeats and a rattle fade away.

Blackout.

ACT ONE

SETTING: An apartment in uptown Chicago.

Scene One

As the curtain rises, lights come up on a living room. Benny and Chili enter from stage right. Benny carries a suitcase. Chili has a makeup case. She stands surveying the apartment. Benny takes the suitcase to a table.

BENNY
Well, Miss Corn—this is it.

CHILI
Call me Chili. (*Looking around.*) You live alone?

BENNY
Yeah, but I'm hardly ever here. The AIM thing keeps me busy. (*Indicates suitcase.*) I'll put this in the bedroom.

CHILI
I don't want to put you out. The couch is okay. Beggars can't be choosers.

BENNY
Hey—it's okay. You're not a beggar—you're a guest. You take the bedroom.

CHILI
You sure?

BENNY
Like I said, I'm gone most of the time.

Benny carries the suitcase into the bedroom. Chili sits at the table. Benny reenters.

CHILI
I'm very embarrassed about this whole deal. It would be different if I knew you.

BENNY
Embarrassed? Why?

CHILI
You know. Coming here to hide out.

BENNY
Beats getting yourself killed. Anyway, it won't be for long. The police will catch him. He'll screw up. They always do.

CHILI
He's such a pig. Always bragging about everything.

BENNY
Bragging?

CHILI

Like just the other day, we were watching the news on TV and they were talking about a gang-banging thing over by Ravenswood.

BENNY

Yeah, I saw that. Wasn't that on Channel 7?

CHILI

Some kid got killed. Waabooz jumped up and started laughing and saying that he'd done it. What do you think about that?

BENNY

It doesn't take much to shoot a person. Not that I've ever done it, but it seems like it . . .

CHILI

You think he could have done it?

BENNY

I don't know the guy. What do you think?

Chili gets up from table and looks out of the window.

CHILI

What if he finds me? You know, he's not exactly a dummy.

BENNY

Don't worry.

CHILI

What is this place, anyway? (*Looks around again.*) Is this, like, a hideout?

BENNY

It's a safe house.

CHILI

And just what is that? (*Pause. Looks around the room. Picks up a flyer and reads it.*) A-I-M? (*Holds it up in the air.*) What's this?

BENNY

American Indian Movement—AIM for short.

CHILI

What does AIM do?

BENNY

We try to serve our people. Our mandate is to protect our community.

CHILI

And this is one way? Hiding women from their crazy boyfriends? (*She rubs her face.*)

BENNY

(*Nods.*) That's one way, but there are lots of others too. (*Pause.*) You all right?

CHILI

You get paid for doing that? (*Benny shakes his head.*) You don't? Then why do it?

BENNY

Because it's the Indian way.

Chili looks at Benny suspiciously.

CHILI

You aren't going to try taking advantage of me are you? Try making me sleep with you or something? If you are, I'll tell you right now that—

BENNY

I wouldn't do that. (*Pause.*) Not that I don't find you extremely attractive. I would be more than happy to hop into the bed with you. (*Short pause.*) If you asked me nicely.

CHILI

Fat chance of that. You don't have to worry. After Waabooz, men are off limits for awhile.

BENNY

Yeah, right! You're an Indian woman and looking good too. I'm an Indian man, honey. (*He looks at her, waiting for an answer—she shrugs her shoulders.*) Like I said, I'm an Indian man.

CHILI

(*Touching her eye.*) So is Waabooz.

Benny is caught off guard. He nods an answer. They stand and look at each other. He takes her face in his hands and inspects her bruises. She is embarrassed.

BENNY

Chump ought to be shot. (*Pause.*) I have a few errands to run. I'll only be gone a few hours. Don't answer the phone—let the machine do it. Understand?

CHILI

You have one of those answering machines. Boy, that's really modern. (*Laughs.*) An electronic warrior.

BENNY

It's necessary.

CHILI

Did you go to college?

Benny nods yes.

BENNY

There's food in the fridge. Pots and pans are in the pantry. (*Laughs.*) Do you know how to cook?

CHILI

> Very funny. (*Smiles.*) I can cook most anything. I come from a big family. If you didn't cook—you didn't eat.

BENNY

> Can you cook fry bread?

CHILI

> No.

BENNY

> You can't? (*Short pause.*) You want to catch a good Indian man you gotta cook good fry bread. No other way. (*Pause.*) Well, wait—there is one other way.

CHILI

> You can keep that information to yourself. (*Pause.*) Are you one of the leaders of AIM?

BENNY

> Dog soldier. (*Turns to exit.*) I gotta run.

CHILI

> Wait a minute. What's a dog soldier?

BENNY

> (*Starts putting on his jacket.*) Bottom of the ladder. Servant to the people. I got a real important appointment. I'd tell you all about it, but I got to dash.

Benny leaves. Chili moves about the apartment. Nervous and agitated. She walks to the window and looks out for awhile then goes back to the mirror to comb her hair. She walks over to the bookshelves and gets a book then goes to the couch and sits down. Phone rings three times. She sits and stares at it. The answering machine kicks on. Chili listens.

ANSWERING MACHINE

> Hello! Please leave a brief message and I'll get right back to you. Thank you very much. (*Beep.*)

VOICE

> Eagle flies over the valley tomorrow. It's me and you to pick her up, so be ready and packed. This isn't no panty raid, college boy—this is the real deal. A recon mission, pal. (Pause.) You know what? In Nam they used to always stick us Skins on point. Every time we'd go out on patrol. Like we had better ears and could see in the dark. Goddamned boy-scout syndrome or something. That's what that was and still is. (*Pause.*) Be ready. Later, bro. (*Click.*)

Chili takes a drink of pop and stares at the phone.

Blackout.

Scene 2

As the curtain rises, Benny enters, nervous and agitated. Chili watches him as he fusses around the apartment.

CHILI
> You had some calls.

BENNY
> Anything sound important?

CHILI
> (*Nonchalantly.*) Something about life not being a panty raid. Guy didn't leave a name.

BENNY
> (*Cusses under his breath.*) Gabriel. He's coming over. When he gets here I want you to make yourself scarce. Get busy in the kitchen. Okay?

CHILI
> No problem. (*Pause.*) Is Gabriel the boss?

BENNY
> Boss? There really aren't any bosses. Each chapter's autonomous, but yeah—he's heavy into the AIM thing. (*Pauses, searches for and finds a book on bookshelves.*) Oh yeah, I need to know where I can find Mr. Charming—your boyfriend. Waabooz?

CHILI
> He'd shoot you quick as look at you.

BENNY
> Yeah, well, there's ways we can help him too—counseling, legal aid. Resolve this thing peacefully if we can.

CHILI
> Why bother? He's more into being a gangster than he is an Indian. (*Pause.*) You can find him over at Clark and Montrose. That's where he hangs out at.

Benny sits down and begins to read the book. Chili sits at the table. There is a loud, authoritative knock at the door. Chili jumps. She looks at Benny with fear in her eyes.

BENNY
> Relax. That's Gabriel.

He goes to open the door. Enter Gabriel, very militant looking. Chili is obviously impressed, but perhaps a little intimidated.

GABRIEL
> (*Sees her and frowns.*) Who's this?

BENNY

Chili Corn, meet Gabriel.

Chili sort of bows, then stops and starts to salute. Gabriel laughs and takes her hand, bows to kiss it. Chili is flattered and flustered.

GABRIEL

It's a pleasure to meet you, Chili Corn.

CHILI

I'm the one who should be honored, sir.

GABRIEL

We gotta talk, college boy. (*Turns to Chili.*) Excuse us?

CHILI

Of course. I was just about ready to go fix something to eat anyway. You want I should fix you something?

Both men shake their heads no.

BENNY

Unless it's fry bread and—ummm? (*Snaps fingers like he's trying to remember.*)

CHILI

(*Laughing.*) You guys go ahead and have your meeting.

Chili exits into kitchen. Gabriel and Benny comes to front of stage to talk.

GABRIEL

What the hell is she doing here?

BENNY

I can explain.

GABRIEL

And it better be good. (*Throws his hands in the air.*) College boys!

BENNY

She came looking for protection from an abusive boyfriend. Remember, that's what we do.

GABRIEL

I thought Norma handles the woman stuff.

BENNY

Norma is in Milwaukee with her sister.

GABRIEL

Well, get rid of her. This isn't any college ice-cream social. Okay?

BENNY

She stays until Norma gets back.

GABRIEL

I'm the statewide coordinator.

BENNY

> Exactly! Coordinator, not dictator. You have no say in this chapter—we're autonomous.

GABRIEL

> (*Walks to bookcase and picks up book.*) You college boys kill me with that shit. You mess things up and I'm holding you responsible. I'll have you in front of that council.

BENNY

> Actually, Gabriel, I'd like nothing better. (*Pause.*) So tell me, what's so big?

GABRIEL

> I'll tell you when it's time.

BENNY

> Why so ambiguous?

GABRIEL

> What?

BENNY

> (*Impatiently.*) Why are you keeping me in the dark?

GABRIEL

> (*Tosses book on the table.*) I got some real heavies coming in. What I need from you is to be ready on a minute's notice.

BENNY

> Ready for what?

GABRIEL

> Something that will put your chapter on the map. (*Goes to the phone.*) You mind?

BENNY

> (*Looks doubtful.*) No. Go ahead.

Gabriel dials a number.

GABRIEL

> Frank—Gabe here. You got your guys ready? (*Pause. Listens.*) Frank, everyone will know that Chicago AIM means business. They won't be calling us a tennis-shoe Mafia anymore. You guys just be ready to rock and roll. See you in a bit.

Gabriel hangs up the phone and dials another number.

GABRIEL

> Niij. Frank's got everything ready. You got some good wheels? (*Pause.*) No, we need something fast. (*Pause.*) Funny, pal. Real funny. We gonna rock and roll.

Gabriel hangs up phone.

BENNY

> Did this come through the council?

GABRIEL

(*Throws arms in the air.*) There you go with that structure stuff again. Look—we're in a war, college boy.

BENNY

I don't believe I'm hearing this. (*Points finger accusingly at Gabriel.*) You're doing this on your own.

GABRIEL

(*Paces as he talks.*) Don't point. Didn't they teach you that in college? Now, did I say they didn't know about it? No, I didn't. The key people know all about it.

BENNY

What? I'm not a key person?

GABRIEL

Of course you are. You're central to everything. (*Pause.*) Do you have any idea what it's like to be statewide coordinator for this outfit? It's a headache, I'll tell you that much. (*Puts his hand on his forehead.*) You gotta worry about all kinds of stupid little arguments. (*Becomes more emotional.*) I gotta hear all this stuff—stupid stuff—like this guy in Peoria isn't a real Indian. Some guy down in Springfield is complaining about who that AIM leader is sleeping with. Like it's their business, right?

BENNY

It comes with the job. I thought you knew that.

GABRIEL

And then there's some woman feels like she's an Indian by injection. Isn't that about a bite on the butt? She been sleeping with Indians for the last ten years, I heard. A real tipi creeper at the powwows. Now she's trying to act like she's a chief— a bleached blonde chief. Jesus Christ—can you imagine that?

BENNY

(*Sits indifferently at table.*) Wannabes. It's part of this whole thing—something we have to live with.

GABRIEL

Now dig this—I got four people right now who say they were adopted into the Sioux Nation by some fast-talking fool who passed through East St. Louis. Each of them paid this clown $139.50 to be adopted—(*pause*)—and another $99.95 for an Indian name.

BENNY

(*Grinning.*) Well you know how them Sioux are. (*Chuckles.*) Sounds like a good deal to me.

GABRIEL

This is serious stuff. A major issue! Now get this—I found out the clown isn't even Lakota. He's a full-blood Ojibwa—

just like you, who went to college—just like you—and
majored in marketing. An Ojibwa selling Sioux citizenship!
Ain't that about a bite in the ass? You got any idea what that
would do to a bunch of full-blooded Lakotas? It could put
us back 150 years. We'll be at war again. (*Throws his hands
in the air.*)

BENNY

An Ojibwa in marketing with nerve enough to sell Sioux
citizenship? Interesting. You got his number?

GABRIEL

Would you get serious? (*Pause.*) And that's not all, Benny.
There's this nut in Bensonville who won't pay his taxes
because he heard Indians don't have to pay taxes. Wanted
one of us as an expert witness. Said we owed it to him
because he donated a box of used clothing to the Indian
Center. What the heck is that?

BENNY

A lot of people think like that.

GABRIEL

To top that off, this school downstate has this mascot—
supposed to be an Indian dancing at football games. Chief
Illino—dick or some goofy shit.

BENNY

That's Illinowek! I-L-L-I-N-O-W-E-K. Illinowek.

GABRIEL

Yeah—whatever. Got everybody all excited.

BENNY

Say it—Illinowek—

GABRIEL

Damn it college boy, you know what I mean.

BENNY

It's an Indian word. You should be able to say it.

GABRIEL

How's it gonna affect my life if I could?

BENNY

It's the principle.

GABRIEL

Principle? Yeah, right! Well, it ain't my tribe, but it sure as
hell got everybody excited.

BENNY

It should get people excited.

GABRIEL

Oh shit—it's crazy. Real crazy. Now, what I supposed to tell
these bunch of cranks? (*Pause.*) I really don't need any crap
from you.

BENNY

> I'm not trying to give you none, Chief, but there has to be some procedures.

GABRIEL

> (*Gets serious. Tries more of an appeal.*) We got us a big chance to make a difference, brother—and we can't let it slip by us. We'll go down in history as patriots. Our names will be right up there with Geronimo, and Crazy Horse, and (*pause, as he searches for another name*)—and Lenny Big Belly.

BENNY

> Who the hell is Lenny Big Belly?

GABRIEL

> (*Shrugs.*) That's not the point. You just gotta trust me? Okay? Did I ever steer you wrong? (*Pause.*) Well, did I?

BENNY

> I can't say that you have, but you know we can't have any loose cannons running around out here. Everything has to be approved by the council.

GABRIEL

> That's another thing. This council stuff. Does everything have to be discussed by a thousand long-winded Indians? You know how long it takes to get anything done? Heck, young blood—we're the cutting edge of our people's sword. All this discussion makes it hard to keep a secret. I heard you say that yourself.

BENNY

> Yeah, I said that, but it's done and we gotta—

GABRIEL

> Hello Benny! As AIM leaders we have to make moves on our own. It'll be all right, believe me. Why, when I was in Nam . . .

BENNY

> So it didn't come through the council. You better know what you're doing. You can't just go off demonstrating against this and that—especially if you're gonna use violence.

GABRIEL

> College has made you think like a white man sometimes. (*Pause.*) And that haircut! I swear, you remind me of Wally from *Leave it to Beaver*.

BENNY

> Don't even go there.

GABRIEL

> You look like a teenybopper Beatles fan! What's up? Is there a lice epidemic I ain't heard about?

BENNY

> Ha ha. Very funny. Now you sound like a white person accusing Indians of lice.

GABRIEL

> Look here, college boy, if you don't have the guts to do this . . .

BENNY

> I didn't say that.

GABRIEL

> Willard said that statue gotta go. It's a violation of the Illinois State Constitution—their own law.

BENNY

> According to whose interpretation?

GABRIEL

> Oh, aren't you something? Just listen to you! Whose interpretation ,you ask! Read the Constitution. It's right there in Article—I forget what article, but Benny, it's there—believe me.

BENNY

> The people at the Chicago Historical Society already agreed with that. They admitted it. At least in principle.

GABRIEL

> (*Emphatic again.*) See? You sound just like a white man. What the heck does that mean? At least in principle. (*Pause.*) Anyway, Willard said . . .

BENNY

> I don't give a hoot what Willard said. I got a thousand things to do, including watching over that girl. I don't see his butt out here working with the people. Who does he think he is, anyway?

GABRIEL

> No, no Benny. Who do you think you are?

BENNY

> (*Emphatic.*) I call the shots in this chapter. Not Willard!

GABRIEL

> (*Grabs Benny by the shirt front.*) Let me set you straight about something, college boy. You are operating this chapter only because the powers that be are letting you.

Chili enters and stands at the door. They don't see her standing there.

BENNY

> (*Pushes Gabriel away.*) You forget that we're on the same side. Don't be grabbing me like that, or we'll be boxing.

Gabriel and Benny have a short staredown.

GABRIEL

I'd like nothing better.

BENNY

I organized that Historical Society thing.

GABRIEL

(*Straightens Benny's collar.*) Don't get me wrong about this. You do a good job. Everyone knows that. Benny my boy, you have a career with this organization, but you got to give respect where it's due. You don't . . . well, you know what can happen. (*Pause. He moves away from Benny.*) There's not a lot of time. Things are already in motion. This is big, Benny (*moves back to Benny*)—I can tell you that much. Don't rock the boat. Need I say more?

BENNY

No, you're perfectly clear. (*Long pause.*) What about that girl from Mexico?

GABRIEL

She's part of the whole deal. (*Leans closer to Benny.*) The expert, in fact. You work with me, and AIM chapters all over the country will have your name on their lips. It's that big.

BENNY

(*Looks doubtful.*) You're sure about this?

GABRIEL

Yes, I'm sure. We have to pick her up in twenty minutes. You still have that piece?

BENNY

Yeah. I got it stashed in the bedroom.

Gabriel removes a gun from his jacket pocket and checks it as he talks.

GABRIEL

Well, get it—just in case—and let's get going. Time's awasting. (*Gabriel points gun toward the door and assumes a shooting position.*)

They notice Chili at the door as Benny moves to exit.

GABRIEL

How long have you been there?

CHILI

I just stepped out of the door. Why?

GABRIEL

What did you hear?

CHILI

(*Grins.*) I heard you tell Benny to get his gun.

GABRIEL

This ain't no joke. What are you doing here? Maybe you should go elsewhere.

CHILI

Maybe I should. I didn't know there'd be nuts running all over the joint with guns. (*Turns to Benny and points to Gabriel.*) Billy Jack here got a point—maybe I should go. I didn't mean to be no trouble.

GABRIEL

Who's Billy Jack?

CHILI

(*Grinning.*) Go look in the mirror.

GABRIEL

What you grinning about, anyway? (*They stare at each other. Chili doesn't flinch. Gabriel grins at her.*) Ain't you about a bad little lady. (*Turns to Benny.*) I'd feel better if she was gone.

BENNY

BS. She stays.

GABRIEL

Anything goes wrong—she turns out to be a fed or an informant—

CHILI

A fed? An informant? Boy, you are a real work of art—and I thought you were something a few minutes ago! You sound like Waabooz. I think I'm gonna leave.

BENNY

I run this chapter.

CHILI

Really? You could have fooled me.

GABRIEL

This is on you, Benny. I'm holding you responsible.

BENNY

I say she's okay. I'll put my reputation on it.

GABRIEL

What reputation? (*Pause. Smiles to himself.*) Well, come on then. If you insist. We got things to do.

CHILI

I don't know, Benny. The guns and all. FBI? Informants? I don't need that kind of thing.

BENNY

Trust me, okay? Everything will be all right. I promise you. (*He takes her face in his hands and looks at her bruises.*) Okay?

CHILI

(*Smiles shyly.*) Okay—for you, then.

GABRIEL

Let's go, Prince Charming. (*He starts to exit, throws arms in the air.*) Goddamned college boys. You gotta be more like me, Benny! No dame turns my head.

CHILI

Be careful, Benny. Real careful.

Benny winks at Chili, then exits.

Blackout.

Scene 3

As the curtain rises, Chili Corn paces nervously between couch, window, and bookshelves. She dusts and cleans up. Phone rings. Answering machine plays message.

VOICE

(*Big Indian accent.*) Benny? I hate machines. Just as much as I hate treaties. All this technology. It ain't Indian. Ha-ha. This is Carl. Call me tonight. Don't forget Indian bowling is tomorrow night. Be lots of sisters there. (*Click.*)

CHILI

(*Echoing voice.*) Be lots of sisters there. I bet that old Benny is really interested in the "lots of sisters" part, all right.

She continues to clean up the apartment for a few minutes, then phone rings a second time. Chili reacts by looking impatiently, but she listens.

VOICE

(*Very sexy.*) Hi, Benny boy. This is Donna. I'm sorry we missed each other. I was really looking forward to being with you. (*Chili sits up and takes notice.*) I just love the way you talk. So passionate. Don't forget about Friday night. I've got my wagon train in a circle, and my black teddy is ready. I'm wanting to be a naughty girl. You get my drift, doll? Remember this? (*Voice starts to sing.*) Oh Don Dooley, I love you truly. You like me to sing that, Benny? Bye!

Chili mimes the voice and prances around like she has on a teddy. She is very much amused by all of this.

CHILI

I got my wagon train in a circle—I'll bet you do, honey. Wagon train in a circle, huh? Don Dooley? Teddy ready? That's not all that's ready. I bet you that much, honey.

Benny enters from the kitchen. Chili doesn't see him. He looks somewhat shaken. She sees him and is embarrassed, but he doesn't notice it.

CHILI

> You scared the shit out of me. Ever try knocking?

BENNY

> I didn't mean to scare you, but it is my house.

CHILI

> Where's your pistol-packing pal?

BENNY

> You wouldn't believe what I been through. I hate this cloak-and-dagger shit.

CHILI

> He doesn't really believe I'm a spy, does he?

BENNY

> With him you never know. I'll tell you one thing, though; he's for real about AIM.

CHILI

> I hope you don't let him drag you into something stupid.

BENNY

> Don't misjudge Gabriel. You know the dude was in Nam. A lot of guys got messed up real bad—you know—in the head.

CHILI

> I'm pretty sure he's one of them.

BENNY

> Naw. Man, I mean some guys got all screwed up. You know when they got back some of them hippies was calling them baby killers and all sorts of negative things. Society turned on them. It was different with skins, though.

CHILI

> How?

BENNY

> It's the way they were looked on by society. In our communities, veterans are held in honor. You know—they're given a place of respect. They're right up front in the grand entry with the flags at every powwow. You know that. You been to a powwow, haven't you?

CHILI

> Yeah, I been to a few.

BENNY

> A lot of the vets went through a purification ritual. It helped them get their heads on right. Put them back in balance.

CHILI

> You think he really suspects I'm a spy.

BENNY

I know you're not a spy. (*Pause.*) Did I get any calls?

CHILI

Oh, you sure did! A couple in fact. Some guy named Carl.

BENNY

And?

CHILI

Oh yeah—this one may be important to you. (*Pause.*)

BENNY

Well?

CHILI

Some woman named Donna who loves Don Dooley truly. (*Chili laughs. Benny blushes.*) She said she gots her wagon train in a circle. Oh yeah, and she has her teddy ready, and (*giggles*)—I would guess, other things too. Sounded kind of kinky.

BENNY

She is kinky!

CHILI

Talking about kinky, where's Gabriel?

BENNY

That's what I meant by cloak and dagger. He wanted to make sure no one was following us—like the FBI. He's coming in the back way. (*Pause.*) Now this other stuff has come up too.

CHILI

What's that?

BENNY

Aw, it's no big thing. (*Pause.*) Well, it is in a way.

CHILI

So tell me. What is it?

BENNY

It's this big-assed statue of a white woman getting scalped by an Indian. At the Historical Society. I organized a demonstration against it.

CHILI

I bet that don't make you any too popular with them people over there.

BENNY

I suppose not, but what the hell? I was totally freaked out when I saw what kind of damage it was doing.

CHILI

Damage?

BENNY

A busload of kids was running about—you know, from this day camp. When they see us standing there they looked really scared and went way around us. At first I was wondering to myself, what's wrong with these little guys? Then I spotted the statue and this cabinlike thing. We went over by it.

CHILI

What was in it?

BENNY

There was this sign that said, "American Indians—Friend or Foe?" Then they showed a few farming implements and a whole wall full of weapons. Now, you ask yourself what would that make a little kid think?

CHILI

Man, you talk about your racist statements!

BENNY

No jokin', Sherlock. Some hippie came up with the idea that it's actually against the Illinois constitution to have a statue like that because it incites hate against Indians. It's potentially a hot issue.

CHILI

Why would they put up such a thing? The Historical Society leaders should have thought about that.

BENNY

It's a symptom of institutional racism.

CHILI

They oughta trash that kind of shit, ennit?

BENNY

I think Gabriel feels the same.

They hear a knock at the back door. It's like a code. Three soft, two loud.

BENNY

That's them now. I'll go let them in. You be cool.

Benny exits backstage into kitchen area. Gabriel enters, followed by a woman.

GABRIEL

This is a friend. A warrior for her people's cause. She'll be here for a few days.

CHILI

Welcome to Chicago. You got a name?

ROSARIO

My name is Rosario.

CHILI
>Where you from?

ROSARIO
>Mexico.

CHILI
>I didn't know they had Indians in Mexico.

ROSARIO
>(*To Gabriel.*) Somehow, I just knew that you wouldn't know
>that.

*Rosario studies the medals on Gabriel's beret. She gets closer so she can
get a better look. Gabriel sees her studying him and reacts by assuming
a pose. Both Chili and Benny notice the two of them reacting to each
other.*

ROSARIO
>(*Sees the medal on Gabriel's beret.*) For bravery, no? Is it yours?

GABRIEL
>I got it in Vietnam.

ROSARIO
>So you're a military man?

GABRIEL
>(*Stands at attention.*) In the people's army, now.

*Rosario looks impressed. She touches Gabriel's arm in a signal of admir-
ation. Their body language suggests that they are attracted to each other.
Chili and Benny look at each other. Chili rolls her eyes.*

ROSARIO
>I'd like a word in private with you, if I might.

GABRIEL
>Of course. (*Turns to Chili and Benny.*) Would you two mind?

Chili and Benny exit to kitchen.

ROSARIO
>How well do you know these people?

GABRIEL
>Benny's okay. He's hooked up with us. Heads the local
>chapter. (*Pause.*) Chili? I don't know much about her. I under-
>stand she's hiding from an abusive boyfriend. We have a
>program.

ROSARIO
>They always stay here? With Benny in this apartment? She
>doesn't like me.

GABRIEL
>What does it matter?

ROSARIO

Seems odd to me. Does Benny really know her?

GABRIEL

No, but I get the feeling that he's going to. He sometimes thinks with his pecker instead of his brain. He's young.

ROSARIO

And vulnerable.

GABRIEL

I doubt that. He can't be compromised. He doesn't know anything, really. (*Pause.*) Rosario, I have everything I was told you'd need. We can start whenever you're ready. Get some rest and we'll start making it.

ROSARIO

Yes, of course. What is it that we're making?

GABRIEL

You know—the thing. What do you people call it? An explosive. Explosivo?

ROSARIO

Explosives! Uno momento, amigo!

GABRIEL

But José said you were an expert.

ROSARIO

An expert? At what?

GABRIEL

Explosives. You know, el bombo!

ROSARIO

You think I make bombs?

GABRIEL

Well, that guy Juan said . . .

ROSARIO

Juan? Do you know what he does?

GABRIEL

He's part of your organization, isn't he?

ROSARIO

No, he isn't. He's a smuggler. But he did give me a package to give to you.

GABRIEL

A package? Did he say anything else?

ROSARIO

He said it's real powerful. The best around.

GABRIEL

How big of a package?

ROSARIO

I have it in my bag. I'll get it for you.

GABRIEL

Let me have it. No—wait a minute. (*He looks into the kitchen, acts conspiratorial.*) Okay go ahead.

Rosario goes into her bag and pulls out a package. She shakes it.

GABRIEL

Be careful with that! Please! You want to blow us to kingdom come?

ROSARIO

What is it?

GABRIEL

A bomb.

ROSARIO

A bomb?

GABRIEL

Yeah—a bomb. You know, KER-BOOM! They told me you were going to make one, but hell—this is better yet.

ROSARIO

Well, I don't know anything about that. I don't want it around me.

GABRIEL

It's not very heavy. I wonder what it's made of.

ROSARIO

Horseshit, if I know Juan. What did José say?

GABRIEL

I asked him if he could get me some real dynamite, and he recommended Juan. Let's open it.

ROSARIO

Are you crazy? We have to be real careful with this. You never know about these things. They could go off at any minute.

GABRIEL

Lady, I spent a lot of time in Nam.

ROSARIO

I don't care where you were. Don't you open that. Not while I'm around.

Rosario takes the bomb from Gabriel and hides the package under the table. Gabriel tries to get it, but she pushes him away.

GABRIEL

(*Laughs at her.*) Well, you know this is some real heavy shit that's going to be happening. (*Looks at his watch.*) In fact, it's all going down in a couple of hours.

ROSARIO

What?

GABRIEL

Watch the news, lady. (*Grins at her.*) You'll see. Look, I don't want you to say anything at all about this to Benny. Promise? (*Rosario nods okay. Gabriel and Rosario stand looking at each other for a moment, then he turns to walk to the kitchen door.*) Hey, Benny. Let's roll.

Benny and Chili come back onstage.

GABRIEL

(*Very happy.*) You ready to make history, Benny my boy?

BENNY

Oh—now I'm your boy?

GABRIEL

Let's go. Okay, ladies, you're on your own.

Gabriel and Benny exit.

CHILI

Well we're stuck here together—I suppose we should try to get along. (*Chili reaches out her hand. Rosario ignores her.*) Who learned you to speak English?

ROSARIO

I was taught in school. That's who LEARNED me. I went to college. Mexico City.

CHILI

Touché!

ROSARIO

Touché indeed.

There is a very long uncomfortable silence as Rosario goes about digging in her bags. Chili watches her with a look of contempt on her face. Phone rings.

CHILI

Don't answer that!

VOICE

Hi! This is Donna again. Look, a friend of mine is coming in from Florida and I won't be able to see you. She's spending the whole weekend. I'll miss you so much. Remember now, my wagon train is in a tight circle. Come over on Tuesday night and I'll get real naughty for you. Do those things you really like. (*Starts singing jingle again.*) Oh Don Dooley, I love you truly. Bye!

Chili reacts by laughing. Rosario is half shocked.

ROSARIO

Weird!

CHILI

Indeed, and kinky.

ROSARIO

Do you know this song?

CHILI

I don't have a clue. Not yet, anyway.

ROSARIO

I didn't mean to be rude before.

CHILI

Sure you did.

ROSARIO

You're very astute. I guess you're right. I'm usually not like that. (*Pause.*) So what are you doing here?

CHILI

You wouldn't want to know.

Rosario studies Chili for a moment.

ROSARIO

Gabriel told me. Man trouble?

CHILI

Asshole wants to kill me. You know what I mean?

ROSARIO

Unfortunately, I do. My mother was in a situation like that. She had a boyfriend who was mean to my whole family. (*She points to a scar on her arm.*) He tried to kill us when he was drunk. Stabbed me here.

CHILI

I'm sorry. (*Pause.*) So what's it like where you come from?

ROSARIO

It's beautiful.

CHILI

So what's your tribe?

ROSARIO

You ask lots of questions.

CHILI

Only trying to make conversation. You don't want me to speak to you? Fine with me.

ROSARIO

Now it's my turn to be sorry.

CHILI

This cloak-and-dagger stuff keeps people on their guard. It gets in the way.

ROSARIO

In answer to your question, in Mexico we're referred to as Mestizos. Not really Indians, because we don't speak the language. Yet I consider myself Indian.

CHILI

Lots of Indians around here can't speak their language, but they're still Indians—if only in their hearts. (*Pause.*) So what did you do that was so wrong? Kill somebody or something?

ROSARIO

I was identified as a supporter of the Indian cause. It's a long story, but I went from Mexico City with a group of students to help organize the Indians in Chiapas. That was in 1968. That year they went crazy and killed a whole bunch of demonstrators during the Olympic Games.

CHILI

Who?

ROSARIO

The police, the army.

CHILI

So you went to Chiapas to organize against what?

ROSARIO

Against the landowners who were trying to take over more Indian land.

CHILI

Why?

ROSARIO

You know, timber . . . minerals . . .

CHILI

And for that you had to flee your country?

ROSARIO

Big money is involved. They're putting student organizers in prison. Many have been exiled. Some have been murdered. It's getting worse.

CHILI

I can see why you got your ass out of there. I don't blame you.

ROSARIO

Things are very bad there for Indians. I think they'll revolt soon. Too much oppression! (*Pause.*) Benny Boy has some interesting friends. How did he meet you?

CHILI

My aunt. She knew about this program. It's like a safe haven for women in abusive situations. I didn't know it was AIM.

ROSARIO

So he really doesn't know you?

CHILI

> Not really.

ROSARIO

> Did he do a background check on you?

CHILI

> Why?

ROSARIO

> Did he ask you any questions?

CHILI

> He asked me if I could make fry bread. Did he do a security check on you? I think Gabriel is willing to take care of the other part. You two are so obvious.

ROSARIO

> (*Exasperated.*) You're a foolish girl if you think that I'd—I need to take a shower and change clothes.

CHILI

> (*Grins.*) Go ahead—it's in there. (*Pause.*) You sound just like Gabriel. Is he gonna be your man or something? You sure you ain't one of those mail-order brides?

ROSARIO

> (*Beginning to exit, stops.*) Hardly! I am committed to the cause.

CHILI

> I don't doubt that. But you and Gabriel—I see something else.

ROSARIO

> Really? And what do you think you see?

CHILI

> Mutual attraction.

ROSARIO

> I'll admit I do find him to be attractive, but I like military men. Always have.

CHILI

> He likes you too.

ROSARIO

> I wouldn't be so sure of that! I think he's a little disappointed in me. He thought I was a bomb expert, but I'm not—I don't know anything.

CHILI

> The way you move when he's around. Your body language
>   . . .

ROSARIO

> Would you stop? Forget it!

CHILI

I'm surprised he doesn't grab you and drag you to his bed right now. Like a caveman or something. That's how interested he is in you.

ROSARIO

Let's stop this crazy talk. I said, forget it!

CHILI

Can you?

ROSARIO

I haven't got time for this.

Exit Rosario. Chili sits down to read. Suddenly Rosario rushes out half dressed.

ROSARIO

I saw someone—a man, looking in the window.

CHILI

Are you sure?

ROSARIO

Yes I am! Of course.

CHILI

(*With a grin on her face.*) Was he a dark man?

ROSARIO

(*Irritated.*) Maybe. I don't know. Yes, I think he was a dark man.

CHILI

How can someone be looking in the window? We're three floors up in the air, for Pete sakes.

ROSARIO

Listen. Do you hear that? (*A rubbing and banging sound can be heard.*) What do you think that is? Do you believe me now?

Chili picks up a baseball bat that sits in the corner by the front door. With Rosario behind her, they edge toward the bedroom door.

CHILI

Don't crowd me. I can hear it real clear now. Someone's trying to get in. Listen.

ROSARIO

What are we going to do?

They stand at the side of the door. She holds the bat at ready. Suddenly the phone rings. Chili jumps. They stare at the phone.

Blackout.

Scene 4

As the curtain rises, Benny is talking to the women. Both are upset with him. They've taken the stereo set and pushed it against the bedroom door. Rosario still has on panties and bra, but has wrapped a tablecloth around herself.

BENNY

Don't worry, ladies. I said I'll take care of it.

CHILI

That was Waabooz on the phone. I know it was.

BENNY

(*To Rosario.*) Are you sure there was somebody there? Maybe your imagination. When things—

ROSARIO

I know what I saw! Don't you say it was my imagination. It was your responsibility to make sure that—

BENNY

Would you mind wrapping yourself better? I don't need to see everything you got.

ROSARIO

Keep your mind on the job. That's part of your problem. You tend to think with your . . . your . . . you know what I mean. Gabriel told me about you.

BENNY

(*Grins.*) He did, did he? He's coming over in a bit.

ROSARIO

Thank God. We need a warrior.

BENNY

What am I? Chopped liver or something?

They have a short stare-down. Rosario wraps the table cloth around herself tightly. Chili stands with hands on her hips watching to see the result of the stare-down. Rosario averts her eyes first.

ROSARIO

You're young. (*She turns her back toward Benny with a smug look.*) Oh yeah. Your hillbilly called. She sounds young . . . and horny . . . and—oh, to be sure, kinky.

BENNY

A horny, kinky hillbilly? (*Looks at Chili with a grin.*) Sounds interesting.

Chili laughs. Rosario is disgusted.

ROSARIO

That's what Chili said.

CHILI

Said you been replaced for the weekend.

BENNY

Okay, Chili—you can cut with the teasing.

CHILI

My way of handling all this stress. I'm sorry if you find it offensive.

BENNY

(*Looks at her for a long time.*) No, no—I'm the one who should be sorry.

CHILI

No big thing. I appreciate everything you're doing. You're one of the nicest guys I've ever met. No, no, I take that back—you are the nicest. But she DID say that. (*Laughs and turns to Rosario.*) Right?

ROSARIO

She also said she loves you.

BENNY

You two ain't got nothing better to do than listen to my messages?

CHILI

Actually . . . we haven't got a choice, do we?

ROSARIO

Benny, would you please go in there and check? I want to get dressed.

Benny goes into the bedroom. The phone rings again.

VOICE

Is this the chinese chicken place? I want to order some Chinese food. I want a large order of Chinese chicken-fried rice, some chop suey, and some Chinese egg rolls, and oh yeah—you got Chili there, right? I want some Chili. (*Pause.*)

CHILI

(*Yells.*) Benny, its Waabooz!

VOICE

(*Voice sings out.*) I shot the sheriff, but I didn't shoot the deputy. Ha-ha! But I did shoot that punk from across the tracks. Ha-ha! Think on that, Chili Corn . . . you too, Chief Yahoo. (*Silence.*) Have a good day. I'll see you later. (*Benny runs to get on the phone. He's too late.*)

CHILI

(*Rushes to the window to look out.*) That was Waabooz! See! I told you he was crazy! God, how did he find me again? I thought you said—

ROSARIO

> I was promised a safe place—what's this? Men peeking in windows. Telephone calls. You are really some kind of—

BENNY

> I'm some kind of what?

ROSARIO

> Incompetent! That's what you are.

CHILI

> Oh, would you go get some clothes on!

Rosario leaves in a huff.

BENNY

> Are you all right?

CHILI

> What do you think?

BENNY

> I'm gonna get that punk. (*He starts to walk into the bedroom. Rosario screams. He backs out real quickly.*) Shit! She's butt-assed naked.

CHILI

> (*Grins.*) Now you've seen it all, huh? (*Smiles, then gets serious.*) Benny, maybe I should have a gun. What do you think? Just in case.

BENNY

> I'm not sure about that, but you know, she's right. I am screwing this thing up. (*Sits on couch, dejected.*) Gabriel's gonna have plenty to say about it. Maybe I should just get out of the whole deal. Go back to painting pictures.

CHILI

> (*Sits next to him.*) It wasn't your fault. Don't beat yourself up about it.

BENNY

> (*Looks around his apartment.*) Would you look at my pad? It's a mess.

CHILI

> Don't worry about it. Rosario and me can get it back in shape.

BENNY

> I'm kinda funny about that. I like everything in its place. (*Pause. Looks around again.*)

CHILI

> It's not just the apartment being wrecked. It's more. (*Beat.*) What?

BENNY

> (*Hesitates.*) I can't stand the way he keeps implying that I'm not really committed.

CHILI

> Yeah, well he kind of messed up too. He thought Rosario was a bomb expert.

BENNY

> Her? A bomb expert? So that's what he was talking about, huh? He's trying to get his hands on a bomb. He is crazy—this confirms it in my mind.

CHILI

> Don't let him know you suspect anything. She doesn't know anything about bombs. Your pistol-packing friend just bombed out.

BENNY

> How do you know all this stuff?

CHILI

> (*Winks.*) I got my ways. (*Gets up and walks to the window.*) What are we going to do about Waabooz?

BENNY

> I'm going after that punk.

CHILI

> I don't want you to leave me here alone. Especially with those two.

Someone knocks.

BENNY

> That's Gabriel. (*Gets up to let him in.*)

Gabriel enters, obviously very irritated.

GABRIEL

> What's going on here?

BENNY

> I can explain.

GABRIEL

> And it better be good! We're gonna have a talk about this. Believe you me. Now what's this about a peeping tom? Where's Rosario? I want to talk to her.

Chili points to the bedroom. Gabriel heads for it.

CHILI

> I wouldn't go in there. (*Gabriel ignores her.*) She's not dressed.

Rosario lets out another scream.

ROSARIO

>(*Yells loudly.*) Would you mind?

Gabriel rushes out.

GABRIEL

>Why didn't you tell me she was undressed?

BENNY

>She tried. (*Beat.*) Oh, by the way, did those heavies get here yet? I wanna put this AIM chapter's name on everyone's lips. You know, become a household word?

GABRIEL

>Not now, Benny. Forget about it. Everything's on hold.

BENNY

>I can't imagine why.

Rosario enters.

ROSARIO

>What are you? A bunch of perverts? A woman can't even get dressed.

GABRIEL

>I want to talk to you, now!

Rosario looks concerned.

CHILI

>Let's go in the kitchen.

BENNY

>Yeah, let's do that.

Chili looks at Rosario and rolls her eyes. Benny and Chili exit. Gabriel watches them leave and then turns on the radio. He first finds a pop station and then selects a station with Mexican music on it.

ROSARIO

>What are you doing?

GABRIEL

>Listening ears.

ROSARIO

>(*Swaying to the music.*) You wished to speak to me?

Gabriel nods yes. He watches Rosario swaying to the music.

ROSARIO

>You like this music?

GABRIEL

>Yeah. It's nice.

ROSARIO

>Do you dance?

GABRIEL

    No, I came here to talk.

ROSARIO

    What did you wish to talk about?

GABRIEL

    About your plans for the future and about the way that I'm feeling. You've had a strange effect on me. You are a beautiful woman.

ROSARIO

    (*Smiling, moves closer.*) Thank you. Flattery will get you everywhere. I too am being strangely affected by meeting you. It feels like I've known you all my life, and yet we just met. It's crazy.

GABRIEL

    I'll tell you something, this is not me. I don't just jump into relationships, but I do want to know a lot more about you. Can you understand?

They look into each other's eyes. They start to kiss, but suddenly they pull apart.

GABRIEL

    I'm sorry.

ROSARIO

    Me too.

GABRIEL

    I don't know why I did that.

ROSARIO

    We were just caught up in the music. (*Fans herself and smiles.*) It was the mood.

GABRIEL

    Yeah, you're right.

ROSARIO

    Would you excuse me?

GABRIEL

    Of course.

Rosario exits. Gabriel walks to the window. Benny enters. Music is soft.

BENNY

    What's up?

GABRIEL

    I'm not sure.

BENNY

    What's wrong with you?

GABRIEL

(*Looks around, a little dazed.*) Nothing's wrong, Benny. Nothing at all. Can I ask you something?

BENNY

Sure. Go ahead.

GABRIEL

You know how you're always playing the field. With this woman and that woman. (*Pause.*) You ever been in love?

BENNY

I fall in love every weekend.

GABRIEL

No, not like that—with a nice girl.

BENNY

Like I said, every weekend. With some real nice girls. (*Draws a girl's figure in the air.*) Real nice. You know what I mean?

GABRIEL

Do you believe in love at first sight? I mean the real thing. Not just a night in bed, but in love with someone who you know would be perfect for you.

BENNY

I suppose it could happen. Why? You got the hot chili peppers for that Mexican girl, don't you?

GABRIEL

I was only talking hypothetically.

BENNY

Bullshit, too.

GABRIEL

You say anything about it and I'll bust your skull.

BENNY

Yeah, right. Gabriel, I think it's great. I didn't think you had it in you.

GABRIEL

What the hell is that supposed to mean?

BENNY

I never seen you pay much attention to any other women. You're always all about business. The serious guy.

GABRIEL

See—that's what's so weird. At one level I know what needs to be done—an officer doesn't fraternize with troops—but then there's that other level . . .

BENNY

Hold it! Hold it! Squad halt! We're not in the army. Damn, Gabe. It's okay for you to be turned on by her. I mean, look at her. She looks like a hot tamale if you ask me. She got a nice set of . . .

GABRIEL

Now you hold it! I won't tolerate any demeaning talk about her. Let's not get talking dirty here.

BENNY

Man, you got it bad, pal. I didn't mean to talk bad about her, but I did see it all, and pal, let me tell you . . .

GABRIEL

Don't go there, Benny! I'm warning you!

BENNY

Okay! Okay! (*Laughs.*) She's in the kitchen.

GABRIEL

Huh?

BENNY

Go ahead. Go in there and be with her. Take it easy though, and don't you go trying to put your hands on that set of . . .

GABRIEL

I was serious, Benny. Don't be talking to me like that about her. Okay?

BENNY

Okay, you got it pal—but go on and be with her.

Gabriel exits. Chili enters.

BENNY

Wow! What's going on with them two?

Chili laughs and makes kissing sounds.

BENNY

I know, but he's not normally like that.

CHILI

These aren't exactly normal times.

BENNY

You can say that again.

CHILI

How did Waabooz find out where I was?

BENNY

I'd like to know that too.

CHILI

You know he's going to be back.

BENNY

We'll be ready next time.

CHILI

Why won't he just leave me alone?

She sits on couch.

BENNY

> Ain't nothing going to happen to you. I give you my word as an Indian man.

Chili looks at him doubtfully for a minute. Noise of chair falling over from kitchen.

BENNY

> I better go check.

CHILI

> I wouldn't do that.

BENNY

> Well what are they doing? It's gotten so quiet.

CHILI

> (*Starts laughing.*) I swear, sometimes you're like a little boy. I like that.

BENNY

> Let me tell you something, lady. I happen to head up one of the biggest, most active AIM chapters in the country. Not bad for a little boy, huh?

Suddenly the sound of shots rings out. Benny pulls Chili to the floor. Gabriel rushes out with his gun drawn, but trips and falls. His gun bounces across the floor. Rosario dashes out and picks it up. She runs to the window. Several more shots ring out, and she ducks down. When the shots stop she jumps to the window and shoots once. They hear Waabooz hollering.

WAABOOZ

> (*From offstage.*) I told you I'd be back. I'm gonna get you, Chili—you too, Yahoo. Nobody messes with my woman and gets away with it. You hear me?

Rosario jumps up and takes another quick shot. Waabooz lets out a scream of pain.

GABRIEL

> You got him!

CHILI

> I hope you killed the bastard.

GABRIEL

> Nice shooting! (*Gets up, rubbing his butt.*)

Rosario pukes into a wastepaper basket. Sound of police siren gets louder and louder.

Blackout.

ACT TWO

SETTING: The apartment.

Scene 1

As the curtain rises, Rosario and Chili sit at the table. Chili comforts Rosario, who is crying. Benny peeks out of the window. Gabriel has his gun in his hand as he tries to make phone calls. He tries several times and is becoming angry.

GABRIEL

I can't get a dial tone. (*He impatiently pounds on the phone.*)

BENNY

Hey, hey, don't do that! You know how much those things cost?

GABRIEL

(*To Benny.*) What are the pigs doing out there?

BENNY

They're just sitting like before. (*Looks out again.*) No wait. An ambulance is coming.

ROSARIO

I'm going to be sick again. (*Grabs the wastepaper basket.*)

CHILI

A warrior for her people? (*Gabriel gives her a finger. She returns it.*)

GABRIEL

This damned phone. (*He bangs it again.*) There—it's working now.

BENNY

Is it necessary to beat on that? (*To Chili.*) See the guy beatin' on my phone? Look at him. (*To Gabriel.*) Hey, that's not an ax or something, you know. Who are you calling?

GABRIEL

The press.

BENNY

What? Why?

ROSARIO

Don't call them! I gotta get out of here. (*She heads for the door. Benny grabs her.*)

BENNY

You can't go out there. They'll arrest you.

She starts struggling with Benny as she tries to escape. Benny has to slap her to make her stop. Gabriel hangs up the phone and goes after

Benny. He tries to pull him off of her. Chili jumps on Gabriel and the four struggle. The phone rings. They all sit on the floor and stare at the phone.

CHILI

> It's Waabooz. I know it is.

ROSARIO

> God, please, let it be him.

GABRIEL

> (*Answers phone.*) Hello. (*Pause.*) Frank. Police have surrounded us. (*Pause.*) It's probably the FBI. (*Pause. To Benny.*) The FBI got the AIM office under surveillance. (*Back to phone.*) What do you think about alerting the media now?

BENNY

> Don't even think about that. Give me that phone. (*Grabs phone from Gabriel.*) Listen, Frank. See what you can find out about a guy named Waabooz. (*Pause.*) Okay then—bye! (*Hangs up the phone.*)

GABRIEL

> What do you think you're doing? I wasn't finished talking to him.

BENNY

> Oh yes you are. There's gonna be no media.

GABRIEL

> Damn it, Benny, use your head for more than a hat rack. The FBI is sitting in front of the office.

BENNY

> So what! They've been there for months! We live with it!

GABRIEL

> The police have this place practically surrounded. Something's coming down, Benny.

CHILI

> We got what? Three or four little wee pistols—and her (*points to Rosario*)—a warrior for her people. (*Pause.*) What chance do we have?

GABRIEL

> (*Ignores Chili.*) You know what they're going to do to us? (*Pause.*) Like they did to Fred Hampton and the Black Panthers.

CHILI

> Maybe we should just go out there with our hands up. Deal with them in a court of law.

GABRIEL

> You can leave anytime, Chili Corn.

CHILI

Yeah, right! Get real, Gabriel. I'm not going anywhere.

ROSARIO

I could be shipped back to Mexico, and I believe in my heart that they'll kill me . . . just like they did to that other girl.

GABRIEL

What other girl?

ROSARIO

Nobody. I was mistaken.

GABRIEL

What girl are you talking about? I'm not playing with you, woman. I want the truth. (*Gabriel pulls his gun out again. Rosario starts to cry.*)

CHILI

Just like Waabooz. Big man with a gun. Put the goddamned thing away.

GABRIEL

Shut up and stay out of this, Chili. I mean it. How do I know you ain't a spy?

CHILI

There he goes again. (*Gets in Gabriel's face.*) How do we know that you aren't a spy?

BENNY

Okay, okay, you two. Let me handle this before it gets out of hand. Okay, Rosario. Tell us what happened.

ROSARIO

When we were crossing, the border police spotted us. They told us to stop, and one guy started shooting at them. They opened fire on us and she was hit in the neck. She died very quickly.

CHILI

Who? What are you talking about?

ROSARIO

Before she died she handed me a bag with some papers. All she said was, "deliver this at all costs."

BENNY

Go on.

ROSARIO

I ran for hours and hours. It was dark, and I didn't know where I was. Finally, I found a church and slept on the steps. In the morning I found these papers with your phone number.

GABRIEL

Why didn't you tell me that? What the hell were you thinking about, anyway?

ROSARIO

I wanted to . . . but I thought you wouldn't help me.

GABRIEL

That's it! That's it! I'm calling the press. They're gonna blow us away!

CHILI

Would you relax, you pistol-packing . . .

GABRIEL

What? What did you say? I am relaxed.

ROSARIO

Please don't let him die. I did not come to America to be a murderer.

CHILI

Take it easy, Rosario.

ROSARIO

I thought he had shot Gabriel. I was very angry.

GABRIEL

(*Ignores Rosario's comment.*) What are they doing outside, Chili?

CHILI

Did you hear what she just said? (*Gabriel ignores her.*) Hey, Billy Jack, did you hear her?

GABRIEL

(*To Benny.*) It won't be long now! (*Gabriel begins loading his gun.*) Yeah, Chili—I heard what she said. Forget it. I don't need you in my conversation with her, okay?

BENNY

What do you call what you're doing?

GABRIEL

We have to be ready. (*Pulls another pistol from his boot, then one from his jacket pocket, absorbed in his task.*)

CHILI

Jesus Christ! Would you look at that? What are you doing with all those guns?

GABRIEL

Standard procedure!

CHILI

Standard procedure? You're as crazy as Waabooz! (*Turns to Rosario.*) If I was you I'd stay away from him. He probably has guns under his pillow.

ROSARIO

God don't let Waabooz die.

CHILI

(*Throws her hands into the air.*) I need this like a hole in the head.

Gabriel starts to move the furniture around. He then signals to Rosario to help him.

BENNY

What the hell are you two doing? Would you look at him!

GABRIEL

Building a blockade. Like a fort. I'm going to blast them.

BENNY

Jesus H. Christ! I don't believe this!

CHILI

(*Laughs nervously.*) You sound like you're expecting company. They wouldn't come in here shooting . . . would they? (*She starts looking for a place to hide.*) You think they would?

GABRIEL

What planet did you just fall off of? This is Chicago.

BENNY

Hey, don't do that! You're wrecking my pad. For Christ's sake, Gabriel, WOULD YOU STOP?

Blackout.

Scene 2

As the curtain rises, Gabriel talks on phone. Chili and Rosario sit at the table. Rosario is crying. Chili tries to comfort her. Benny is at the window. The furniture has been rearranged to look like a blockade.

ROSARIO

I don't know if I killed him or not. (*She reaches for the waste-paper basket again.*)

BENNY

Why does she keep puking? My wastepaper basket is spoiled. Would you just look at my apartment?

GABRIEL

Come here, Rosario. Sit over here by me. (*Rosario comes and sits closer to Gabriel.*) Now, look. Crying isn't going to change nothing. You got to be strong. If by any chance you killed that dumb asshole, we'll say that I did the shooting. He probably deserved it anyway.

Rosario starts crying even harder.

BENNY

Now what did you do?

GABRIEL

I didn't do anything.

ROSARIO

(*Hugs Gabriel.*) You would do that for me?

CHILI

That was mighty white of you, Gabriel.

GABRIEL

Ain't anything white about me. I just want her to stop crying. (*To Rosario.*) I want you to stop crying. It drives me crazy. Would you stop?

ROSARIO

This is what you wish?

GABRIEL

Yes, it is. It really, really is.

ROSARIO

Okay. (*She picks up a pistol.*) Now we will prepare to die together. (*Dramatically.*) Such is our fate.

GABRIEL

(*Ignoring the drama.*) Benny, what's happening out there?

BENNY

It looks like there's more of them. Two more cars just pulled up. They're getting ready for something dramatic. Maybe you're right. Gabriel.

Phone rings again. Benny answers it.

GABRIEL

It better not be that crank. I'm tired of her.

BENNY

Hello. (*Pause.*) It's Frank for you. (*Hands phone to Gabriel.*)

GABRIEL

What's up? (*Pause.*) Okay. Okay. I'm going to try. Later, bro. (*Hangs up phone.*) I gotta try to get out of here.

CHILI

What about the rest of us? You bastard!

GABRIEL

Screw you, Chili.

CHILI

Not in this lifetime.

Gabriel picks up the bomb and puts it into his bag very carefully.

BENNY

Where do you think you're going?

GABRIEL

The statue! We plan to blow it to kingdom come.

BENNY

> Don't be crazy. You won't be able to touch that thing. It's made out of solid . . . I don't know . . . steel, brass, marble . . . something.

GABRIEL

> Is there any way out of here?

CHILI

> You mean you're just going to leave us holding the bag? (*Chili stands in front of the door.*) Thanks.

GABRIEL

> Don't you get started, Chili. I mean it. Get out of my way.

CHILI

> And what if I don't? You gonna shoot me, big man? You're not leaving us holding the bag. I go down and you're going down too.

GABRIEL

> I'm leaving. I got to. Try to understand.

CHILI

> What I understand is that you're cutting out on us.

ROSARIO

> I am coming with you.

BENNY

> There's no way you can get out of here.

GABRIEL

> What about the roof?

BENNY

> I never been up there. Maybe. What's in the bag?

GABRIEL

> A bomb.

BENNY

> You had a bomb in my house? With all of these people around? What is wrong with you?

GABRIEL

> I have a mission, Benny. I can't be concerned about anything else. This is bigger.

BENNY

> If I get out of this—when I get out of this, I'm taking your ass in front of the council. You can count on it.

GABRIEL

> I don't care. That statue has to go.

BENNY

> At all costs? Is that all you can think of?

GABRIEL

> This is for the cause, Benny. It's bigger than all of us.

BENNY

You're crazy, you know that?

GABRIEL

One day you'll understand, brother!

BENNY

Don't call me your brother. (*Pushes him against the door.*)

GABRIEL

Jesus Christ—would you be careful, Benny, or I'll blow your ass away. (*Pulls out his pistol.*) I'm warning you. (*Cocks the gun and points it at Benny.*) I'll do it, man.

CHILI

Stop this crazy shit.

ROSARIO

Don't leave me, Gabriel.

BENNY

You gonna shoot me? (*Pause. They stare at each other.*) I don't think so.

GABRIEL

You're an AIM brother . . . and I love you for that, but college boy . . . you don't know who you're messing with.

BENNY

Then go ahead and shoot me. Do it! Do it now!

Gabriel steps toward Benny with a wild look on his face.

GABRIEL

Don't you even think I won't!

Phone rings. Chili runs to answer it.

CHILI

Hello. (*Pause.*) This is Chili Corn. Who's this? (*Pause.*) Yeah, they're both here. Wait a second. Gabriel, it's some guy for you. It's really important. Come on. (*Pause.*) Put the gun up and talk to him. It has to be important.

Gabriel backs away from Benny, toward the telephone. He takes the phone but keeps his pistol pointed at Benny.

GABRIEL

Hello. (*Pause.*) Don't say that, Frank. This cannot be happening to me. (*To Benny.*) They moved the statue already.

Rosario goes to window and peeks out.

ROSARIO

They're coming in.

Benny rushes to the window. He pulls Rosario to the floor then peeks out.

BENNY

> (*Starts panicking.*) They have a battering ram. (*To Gabriel.*) You were right. They ain't playing.

GABRIEL

> Frank, it's coming down. Just like I figured. Gotta go. (*Hangs up the phone.*) Everybody be calm. Get behind something. Benny, you have to work with me on this. (*Benny nods his head.*)

CHILI

> I don't know, Benny. Maybe we shouldn't do this. Maybe we should just go out there peacefully.

GABRIEL

> What you gonna do, Benny?

CHILI

> Don't be stupid.

BENNY

> I got to explore my options here. On the one hand, Chili might be right . . . but on the other hand . . .

GABRIEL

> COLLEGE BOY! What are you going to do?

BENNY

> (*Tips over table and draws gun.*) Gabriel is right. We fight!

Gabriel kneels behind the overturned couch. Benny turns over the table and positions himself there. Both draw out their guns. Chili hides next to Benny. Rosario joins Gabriel. They point their weapons toward the door.

Blackout.

Scene 3

As the curtain rises, Benny (with shirt off), Chili (wearing a headband), and Rosario sit on the floor. Gabriel has crawled into the kitchen to see what's happening in the back.

BENNY

> What is he doing in there? Hey, Gabriel— what's up with you, man? (*No answer.*) Jesus—what is going on with him? Hey, Gabe!

ROSARIO

> I'm going to see if he's okay. (*She starts to crawl toward the kitchen.*) I'll be right back.

BENNY

> I don't believe this. If they're gonna come, why don't they do it? It's already been fifteen minutes.

CHILI

> (*Looks at watch.*) More like eight minutes.

They sit thoughtfully for awhile.

CHILI

> You know, I been thinking about things.

BENNY

> I thought I smelled something burning.

CHILI

> Jeez—see how you are? I'm trying to be serious.

BENNY

> Okay, I'm sorry. (*Pause. Looks at Chili quietly.*) About what?

CHILI

> About my life. About AIM. You. About Waabooz.

BENNY

> Did you love him?

CHILI

> I suppose I did in the beginning, but the point is, I placed him above myself. I don't think that's very healthy.

BENNY

> I suppose not, especially if he's treating you bad.

CHILI

> And he treated me real bad. I actually started listening to what he was telling me. Like I was stupid and worthless. That no one else would want me because I was dumb.

BENNY

> You're a pretty woman. Other guys had to be hitting on you, or at least . . .

CHILI

> I ended up with such low self-esteem. I didn't feel very pretty . . . or desirable. (*Pause.*) You understand? (*Pause.*) Sometimes I even felt like I deserved it when he'd beat me up. (*Pause.*) Then one time he stuck his gun in my mouth. He had removed the bullets, but I didn't know that. He pulled the trigger, and I fainted. When I regained consciousness, he was raping me.

BENNY

> Punk needs to be horsewhipped.

CHILI

I was so afraid that I . . . He was getting pleasure out of torturing me. He was raping me, and he . . . (*There is a long silence.*)

BENNY

He comes near you and he's dead.

He takes her into his arms. She puts her head against his shoulder. He holds her for awhile. She lets out a small laugh.

BENNY

What? What's so funny?

CHILI

I'm not laughing at you.

BENNY

What are you doing then?

CHILI

I'm laughing because I believe you.

BENNY

Why would that make you laugh?

CHILI

Don't get sensitive on me now, college boy.

BENNY

Would you mind not calling me that? You know, because of Gabriel.

CHILI

(*Nods to Benny.*) Boy we sure are in a big mess, aren't we? I mean, here we are in a standoff against the cops, just like Bonnie and Clyde or something. You know what I mean? It's crazy.

BENNY

I'm sorry. I didn't mean to get you into this.

CHILI

Don't flatter yourself. I'm here by choice right now. I'm in control of my life again, and it feels good.

BENNY

Do you know how beautiful you are when you smile like that? I just feel like I could kiss you.

CHILI

(*Somewhat shyly.*) You could if you wanted to.

BENNY

Well, I want to.

CHILI

You do?

BENNY

Yes, very much.

CHILI

Well, shut up and do it then.

Chili shuts her eyes and waits for the kiss. Suddenly there is a crashing sound from the kitchen. Rosario screams.

CHILI

Oh my God! They must be coming in.

BENNY

Gabriel?

Laughter can be heard from the kitchen.

ROSARIO

We're okay.

GABRIEL

We just knocked a pitcher off the table.

Enter Rosario on hands and knees followed by Gabriel. Both are grinning.

BENNY

You scared the shit out of us.

GABRIEL

Sorry about that, pal.

CHILI

What's that all over your face?

GABRIEL

What?

BENNY

He's got lipstick smeared all over him. What were you doing in there?

Both Chili and Benny turn to look at Rosario. She has a big smile on her face.

CHILI

I know what they were doing.

BENNY

(To Gabriel.) You were in there playing Prince Charming.

CHILI

More like Romeo.

BENNY

You were trying to get you some before we get arrested.

ROSARIO

No, he wasn't. I was.

CHILI

Look at that grin on his face, and hers too. Something happened.

Benny goes to the window.

BENNY

Well, I guess if you gotta go to jail, you might as well go freshly f . . .

GABRIEL

Watch that mouth, boy! We get the message. About shooting it out with them . . . I've rethought that. We better not.

BENNY

(*From window.*) Maybe it's too late. There are more of them out there now.

ROSARIO

What should we do?

CHILI

We can't just stand around with our hands in the air. Can we?

BENNY

Gabriel? What do you think?

GABRIEL

I don't know. I never surrendered before.

CHILI

Here's what we have to do. We'll kneel with our hands on the back of our heads. They'll see that and know what's up.

GABRIEL

When this is over, I'm going to move back up north. I've had it with Chicago.

ROSARIO

I'm going with him.

CHILI

What'll you do up there?

GABRIEL

My parents have a business. They're getting old. I think I'm going to get my ass back in school. I think I'll go to college.

BENNY

You? A college boy? Will wonders never cease?

ROSARIO

We can both enroll at the same time. (*Pause.*) As Mr. and Mrs.

CHILI

You're kidding, right?

GABRIEL

No, she's not.

BENNY

Just like that?

GABRIEL
> (*Nods and points to window.*) What's going on out there now?

Benny crawls over and looks out the window.

BENNY
> Holy shit! Here they come. A bunch of them. Shit! This is it, man!

CHILI
> Everybody just lay their guns in a neat pile by the door and assume the surrender position. Stay calm.

BENNY
> What about the bomb?

GABRIEL
> Oh shit, that's right. I'm going to put it with the guns.

They put the guns and the bag with the bomb in it in a pile by the door and kneel with their hands on the back of their heads.

ROSARIO
> I'm afraid.

GABRIEL
> Remember, I did the shooting. I shot Waabooz. Everybody remember to say that. Okay?

CHILI
> (*Smiling.*) You're something else. You aren't even scared, are you?

GABRIEL
> Actually, I'm shitting in my jeans, Chili. Here they come. Stay strong for our people.

The sound of footsteps running can be heard. There are a lot of them. The phone rings.

BENNY
> What the hell?

Phone rings.

VOICE
> If there's someone else, she could come and we could make it a threesome. Wouldn't that be fun?

The machine shuts off with a loud click.

CHILI
> A threesome?

GABRIEL
> That is one horny, kinky woman.

The four of them laugh nervously.

CHILI

Okay, this is it. For our people!

The four brace themselves for the onslaught. Lights change to red. The sound of footsteps approach the apartment door, get even louder then pass by. Lights change back to normal.

BENNY

What the hell?

GABRIEL

(*Jumps to feet.*) Hey! We're in here.

CHILI

Don't call them back.

ROSARIO

They're going to be very angry when they realize their mistake.

GABRIEL

Damn cops. I wonder what's going on?

The sound of footsteps again. Voices and radios can be heard.

VOICE

(*On walkie-talkie, from outside of apartment.*) Okay we got them all. Ten four.

BENNY

Jesus—what the hell is going on here? (*Looks out the window.*)

Phone rings again. Chili picks it up.

CHILI

Hello. Who? Benjamin? Oh—you mean Benny! Yeah, he's here. One moment. Benny, it's for you. Some guy. (*Hands phone to Benny.*)

BENNY

Hello. (*Pause.*) Ruben. What's up? I been trying to reach you for hours. (*Waves his hand for quiet.*) Where were you all day? (*Pause.*) No shit? A dope-house? (*Pause. Benny laughs.*) Bowling? You want to go bowling?

GABRIEL

Well, what did he say?

BENNY

(*Ignores Gabriel.*) Yeah, I'll be there with my buddy. You remember Carl, right? He says there'll be lots of sisters around. (*Pause. Laughs.*) Hey—don't forget you're a public servant now. I'll see you then. Bye.

Benny hangs up the phone and grins at his friends.

GABRIEL

What did the guy say, for Christ's sake?

ROSARIO

Did he say anything about Waabooz?

CHILI

Is he dead or what?

BENNY

He's dead all right.

ROSARIO

Oh no! (*She grabs wastepaper basket again.*)

BENNY

But you sure as hell didn't kill him.

CHILI

That's not cool at all, Benny. You shouldn't play with her head like that.

BENNY

Okay! Okay! He had a very slight wound. Not more than a scratch, but he signed a confession about shooting some kid over by Ravenswood.

CHILI

I can't believe this is happening.

GABRIEL

I don't believe this. Why were they outside like that?

BENNY

Oh, that. Listen to this. They were getting ready to raid the dope-man's house, but someone told them they had a cache of weapons inside. They didn't find anything except some people in la-la land.

GABRIEL

(*Looks out of the window.*) You mean all that noise was about some freaked out junkies?

BENNY

That's right. It wasn't about us at all.

Gabriel walks over to the pile of guns and looks at them.

GABRIEL

What are we going to do with these?

CHILI

We could turn them in and say we found them.

GABRIEL

Benny? What do you think?

BENNY

>I don't know. Chili, what do you really think we should do?

CHILI

>Stash them just in case you ever really need them.

GABRIEL

>Yeah, I agree. You never know.

CHILI

>What about that bomb? What are you gonna do with the bomb?

Gabriel picks up the bag and gets out the package.

CHILI

>For Christ's sake, Gabriel. Would you be careful with that? You wanna blow us all to hell?

Both Benny and Chili head for the door.

GABRIEL

>(*Opens package.*) What the hell kind of bomb is this? It got a damned worm in the bottom of it.

Chili and Benny stand by the door to watch.

BENNY

>Gabriel, be careful with that thing.

GABRIEL

>This ain't a bomb.

Rosario takes it from Gabriel, holds it up to the light. Unscrews the cover.

ROSARIO

>(*Laughs.*) It's dynamite to drink, though. It's mescal. (*Hands it to Gabriel.*) Take a taste.

GABRIEL

>(*Hands it to Chili.*) I don't want it. I don't drink.

CHILI

>I sure as hell ain't gonna drink it.

BENNY

>Come on, go ahead and try it. It can't be that bad. You chicken?

CHILI

>If I do, will you?

BENNY

>Yeah, I will. In fact I'll take twice as much as you do.

ROSARIO

Benny, you better be careful. How's that saying go? (*Pause.*)
Don't let your mouth overload your butt hole. I heard a
tourist say that once.

*Chili slowly tips up the jar and takes a swallow. Her eyes open wide; she
lets out a screech.*

CHILI

Holy H. Christ! What is this? (*Still gasping for breath.*) No
wonder them Mexican guys go pssst, pssst. It's their vocal
chords reacting. They can't say anything else.

BENNY

It can't be all that bad. Give me that. (*Benny takes the jar.*) I'll
show you how a man does this.

GABRIEL

You mean a foolish man. I wouldn't do that if I were you.

CHILI

Remember what you just said. Twice as big as mine.

*He tips the jar up and takes a big swallow. Like Chili his eyes open wide.
His mouth does the same thing. He can't speak as he does a short jig step.
Finally he coughs. He hands it back to Chili.*

BENNY

Son of a oh—man!

CHILI

Don't give me this. (*Hands it to Benny.*) Take it to your kinky
girlfriend.

ROSARIO

Oh yeah! The horny hillbilly. Two shots of this and you'll
be riding high, Benny boy.

GABRIEL

All right, tell us about her.

BENNY

Okay, then. I met her at the Saxony Lounge one night. It had
been one of those bad days. We started talking . . . we talked
about everything. She was real nice . . . a good listener. Well
I ended up going to her house after a few drinks. Man, then
she really got freaky.

ROSARIO

How?

BENNY

I'll tell you how, but you may not believe it. She wanted me
to tie her to the bed, paint my face with her lipstick—you
know, like war paint.

CHILI

No way! Did you do it?

BENNY

Yeah. I did it just to make her happy.

ROSARIO

What more did you do?

BENNY

She wanted me to take her with an ardent yell. (*Pause and shakes his head.*) I wasn't sure what an ardent yell was, so I let out a holler and jumped her bones. (*They laugh again.*) I must have done a good ardent yell, 'cause she liked it. We did it over and over.

GABRIEL

Now he's bragging.

Everyone laughs again.

BENNY

Truth be known . . . well, I . . . like, you know . . . I was getting into it, until the neighbors threatened to call the cops.

They all have a healthy laugh. Without realizing it they stop and look around at each other. The moment is broken. The mood changes. Everyone realizes it's over.

CHILI

It's been one hell of a day hasn't it?

ROSARIO

One I'll never forget—or any of you.

The four embrace.

GABRIEL

Well, I have to get going. (*Looks at Rosario.*) I mean we.

ROSARIO

(*Putting arm around Gabriel.*) And don't you forget that.

GABRIEL

I won't. (*Turns to Benny.*) I guess you two will probably hook up, aye.

The men shake hands. The women hug each other. Gabriel and Rosario exit. Chili and Benny look at each other nervously.

CHILI

I guess everything turned out all good.

BENNY

I guess so. (*Pause.*) What'll you do now?

CHILI

Oh, I don't know. Get my life back on track.

BENNY

Can I help?

CHILI

You already have.

BENNY

You could stay here. Roommates!

CHILI

How long do you think that would work? (*Pause.*) Don't think that I don't find you attractive. Hell, Benny, on a scale of one to ten, you're right up there at a two and a half. At least. I'm just teasing.

BENNY

So we can't be roommates? Well what about . . .

CHILI

(*Stops and studies Benny.*) I'm sorry. Don't think I'm not tempted.

BENNY

We had some magic going, Chili.

CHILI

(*Laughs.*) Well, college boy, I guess this is it.

BENNY

I guess it is. (*He steps forward, kisses her on the forehead.*) The one that got away.

The phone rings. They stare at each other.

CHILI

You better get that.

BENNY

Hello. (*Pause.*) Donna? Would you hold on, please? (*Cuffs the phone and talks to Chili.*) It's my friend.

CHILI

The one with the teddy ready? (*Benny nods.*) Are you going to her place?

BENNY

(*Hesitates.*) What do you think? What would you do? (*Chili smiles and nods.*)

CHILI

Just don't get arrested for disturbing the peace.

Chili smiles and walks out. Benny stands looking at the door. Through the telephone Donna can be heard singing Don Dooley.

BENNY

> (*Speaks to the door.*) CHILI CORN! Oh boy . . . what a woman. (*He remembers the phone. Puts receiver to his mouth.*) Baby doll! So what you got in mind? (*Pause.*) You're a bad girl. (*Pause. Listens and grins.*) You say strawberries and whipped cream? (*Grins.*) I'll be right over there.

Blackout.

Coyote Sits in Judgment

A PLAY IN ONE ACT

CHARACTERS

NARRATOR

COYOTE: A grumpy Coyote addicted to Starbuck's coffee and Whitman poetry. Also likes to surf the Internet. Sometimes visits the porno pages, but doesn't know why—there are so many of them. Irrelevant to this tale. He was out late the night before he was summoned. He had a date with a hot-looking Coyotette. He didn't score.

BUSINESS: Slick, seductive. Also known as big bucks.

TECHNOLOGY: Feels put upon by Business. Exploited and becoming angry, but also very much a partner with Business—unwilling, though.

SETTING: Deep in the forest, a fog-filled meadow. The sun has just come up.

As the curtain rises, low lighting. Center stage, Narrator sits on a stump.

NARRATOR

> (In a radio-personality voice.) Coyote has been summoned by the powers that be to sit in judgment of a court case. The dispute is between Technology and Business. Each blames the other for problems in the environment. There are no time constraints to this story, which means that it could be long ago . . . now . . . or maybe it's to be in the future. The only relationship to time is the one that you as a listener attach to it. Remember, this is a collaboration between you and the people on this stage so please be careful . . . be considerate . . . be open-minded . . . and above all, be happy!

SETTING: A meadow in the forest somewhere.

As the curtain rises, lights up full. Coyote walks around the small meadow. Lifts his leg and sprays various objects. He finds a stump and sits on it. The two disputers approach Coyote. Coyote wears a fur coat. Technology wears a box over his head with blinking Christmas lights. Business wears a crown of dollar bills.

COYOTE

> We'll start this proceeding by stating your names, and please do be quick about it. I'm not interested in long explanations, and I'm not interested in your grandmother's history. (*Points to Business.*) We'll start with you.

BUSINESS

> My name is Business. (*Makes a slight bow.*) My function is to fulfill the material needs of mankind. To see to it that his comfort level is maximized.

COYOTE

> (*Turns to Technology.*) I see! And you are?

TECHNOLOGY

> They call me Technology. (*Does a curtsy.*) My function is to help fulfill the needs of mankind. It is my work, your honor, that tends to meet mankind's material needs. (*Very dramatically.*) Not Business, as he would have you believe.

COYOTE

> Who, may I ask, tends to the spiritual needs?

BUSINESS

Not I, although I generally leave mankind in a better mood. (*Bows to Technology*.) My flea markets do that.

TECHNOLOGY

Greed at a sickening level. If I may interject, it's my inventions that cause good spirits. Case in point—flush toilets and Charmin tissue. Prior to that, it was outhouses in unbelievable weather conditions and either a corncob . . .

BUSINESS

Interesting concept, a corncob.

TECHNOLOGY

(*Looks at Business with an evil eye*.) . . . or the Sears catalogue.

COYOTE

We can dispense with the theatrics. (*Pause as he eyeballs both parties*.) So we have a case of parallel functions?

TECHNOLOGY

Yes, except that . . . (*short pause*)

COYOTE

Except what? Well, speak up. I haven't had my Cheerios nor my Starbuck's yet. As a result, I am not in the best of spirits.

TECHNOLOGY

Every time I make some headway in my altruistic search for knowledge, Business always seems to jump in and exploit me. I study those problems mankind faces long and hard, and when I come up with a solution, it's sold away by Business. I can't take it anymore. This must be settled.

COYOTE

Yes, I see. Business, what say you?

BUSINESS

Needs! Mankind has needs. It's simple mathematics. Supply and demand. Surely that cannot be wrong?

COYOTE

You do make a point. (*Turns to Technology*.) And you?

TECHNOLOGY

Oversimplification! (*To Coyote*.) He does make a point, but . . .

COYOTE

But what? Come on speak up. My instructions were to be curt, be concise, and be quick. My stomach is growling. I need food—caffeine! Hurry.

BUSINESS

If I may, please? Your exact words were . . .

COYOTE

Never mind what my exact words were. You know what I meant. (*Turns to Technology.*) Please continue, but be brief, and you (*to Business*)—do not try my nerves.

TECHNOLOGY

Mr. Coyote, it's never like that—greed enters.

COYOTE

How so?

TECHNOLOGY

They start to cheat each other. Happens every time. Man A extracts more than he needs . . . a little something extra for a rainy day, so to speak.

COYOTE

And Man B?

TECHNOLOGY

Same thing—and it gets worse.

BUSINESS

Oh, so dramatic—really, Techy! And what's with that primitive farm implement you carry around? Is that supposed to represent something to someone?

TECHNOLOGY

Business takes my knowledge and reshapes it. I am manipulated to become weapons—arrows and spears, and more recently rockets and missiles and those there smart bombs that are used against mankind. That I really do resent, not to mention that other small piece of transaction . . . in the name of Business. It should be stopped—a moral deterioration!

COYOTE

A noble sentiment I must admit. (*Turns to Business.*) Business, what say you for yourself in this matter?

BUSINESS

Business is Business. Business does not kill. Technology is the murderous soul.

TECHNOLOGY

My innocence can be attested to by the many good things that I do for mankind. The wheel, for instance, or radar—even nuclear power, and (*stands at attention with a grand motion*) those little rubber things. Those are all good things. (*Points accusingly at Business.*) It's you who should be prosecuted as an enemy of the state—a common criminal.

COYOTE

Stop! The dramatics are becoming overwhelming. Pretty soon we'll need shovels.

BUSINESS

I must protest! Robert's Rules clearly spell out . . .

COYOTE

Robert's Rules? I'm starving and you want me to heed some abstract procedures? At any rate, Robert's Rules of the Road don't count in these . . .

BUSINESS

Rules of the Road, sir?

COYOTE

Okay, okay. Robert's Rules . . . strike the road part. Robert's Rules don't count in these procedures. Only in meetings, not courtroom proceedings.

TECHNOLOGY

Actually, it's quite scientific.

COYOTE

(*Becoming very angry.*) The two of you be quiet.

TECHNOLOGY

I demand a ruling!

BUSINESS

Me too.

COYOTE

Okay, okay— but just give me a moment, please. Does anyone in this place have an extra bagel or some fries? Anything! I can't do this on an empty stomach. This ain't as simple as deciding between an apple or an orange. Just one moment, let me consider. (*Turns back to the two and speaks to the audience.*)

The creator made the world
in perfect balance, but humans turned away
from moral and spiritual principles.

BUSINESS

What about Technology?

TECHNOLOGY

(*To Business.*) If you hadn't exploited me, especially with that Ford thing . . .

COYOTE

(*Speaking to audience.*) Mankind did not follow Nature's rules. They misused their spiritual powers for selfish purposes.

TECHNOLOGY

Thus came Business—the bad seed of greed, masked as progress.

BUSINESS

Cultivated by the Hoe (*points thumb toward Technology*), known as Technology, I might add.

TECHNOLOGY

> You better be speaking of this (*holds up hoe*) when you say Hoe!

BUSINESS

> And those little rubber things that you were speaking of with that moralistic tone are gaskets. Spelled G-A-S-K-E-T-S! Used to control the flow of liquids.

TECHNOLOGY

> What kind of liquids, and what are they attached to, may I ask? That's the issue here—or at least it should be!

COYOTE

> (*Turns quickly to face them again.*) Silence! I'm thinking! Harmony between human beings and Nature is being upset.

BUSINESS

> (*Points accusingly.*) By Technology!

TECHNOLOGY

> That is pure nonsense. It's your greed!

COYOTE

> Silence! Mankind is violently extracting natural resources faster than they can be replaced. Life cannot be sustained without limits and moderation. (*Pause.*) Does anybody have some pizza?

TECHNOLOGY

> My sole function is to meet mankind's needs. His comfort is mine to see to.

COYOTE

> Give me some pizza, then.

BUSINESS

> I can't.

Coyote looks at Technology.

COYOTE

> And why not, may I ask?

TECHNOLOGY

> You're not a human.

BUSINESS

> Unless you have some redeemable value. Do you? (*Steps closer to Coyote to inspect him. Coyote lifts his leg. Business bends over to look, then jumps away.*)

BUSINESS

> You pissed on my hand!

COYOTE

> There must be balance, and me thinks that this can only be achieved through equalizing the natural world with the supernatural world. Life taken must be restored.

BUSINESS
What?
TECHNOLOGY
Please, Coyote, do elaborate.
COYOTE
Case in point—the greenhouse effect.
TECHNOLOGY
Oh yes! The greenhouse effect. We are only beginning to comprehend, but as usual Business refuses to listen.
BUSINESS
There's big bucks involved. Major investments that must be shielded.
COYOTE
The greenhouse effect is the result of humans changing things.
TECHNOLOGY
Please elaborate.
COYOTE
I am too hungry to elaborate, but they are messing with the natural order of things.
BUSINESS
For instance.
COYOTE
Changing the natural pattern of vegetation and polluting the atmosphere.
BUSINESS
But let me point out that land is being developed.
COYOTE
Making the earth warmer.
BUSINESS
A small price. Mankind needs more land to grow essentials.
COYOTE
But you gotta stay within the narrow range needed to support life. You don't, and zap—you're outta da game, pal. You can't be violating the natural laws.
BUSINESS
Economic demand, sir! What of economic demand?
COYOTE
If I may continue. The natural laws which, if I may point out, are there to protect all species so that they can live together in harmony and balance. Every species must be considered. Every aspect must be looked at. I mean everything.
TECHNOLOGY
Such as?

Business takes out a calculator and starts figuring as he inspects Coyote again. Coyote lifts his leg, and Business runs back to his original place.

COYOTE

History. How many times has this very argument come up? Must mankind continually repeat old sins?

BUSINESS

(*Looks up from calculator.*) Excuse me, but did I miss something?

COYOTE

I missed my breakfast. I'm not really all that happy. You listen to me. All of the world was one land once—no?

TECHNOLOGY

That could be true. Scientific evidence seems to . . .

COYOTE

(*To audience.*) Natural laws were ignored and a separation occurred. Then came the Ice Age and still the natural laws were violated, but the creator was generous and let a few survive to repopulate.

BUSINESS

(*Irritated.*) What, may I ask, is the point?

COYOTE

Does anybody even have a slice of baloney? Even the county-jail kind would go over good right now. I am so starved.

TECHNOLOGY

The issue! Would you please stick to the issue.

COYOTE

I'd like a little something to stick to my ribs. (*Pause.*) Where was I, now? Oh yeah. Then there was a third chance (*turns to the audience*), but once again, mankind chose to ignore the rules. Again, they gambled with spiritual principles and, well—you all heard of the big flood.

BUSINESS

Yes, it's mentioned in the history and mythology of many nations.

TECHNOLOGY

It is being studied. Scientific evidence . . . well, these things happened a long time ago, and real conclusive evidence is hard to establish.

COYOTE

But the natural law, that which connects us all, is every-where. The evidence is observable. In the beginning we were all linked.

BUSINESS

So what do you think we should do? I came here for a ruling.

COYOTE

I cannot tell you what to do. It is not within my powers. I can only suggest.

BUSINESS

Well, would you suggest then? Time's awasting and time means money, my friend. Would you hurry? Like, ándale, amigo.

COYOTE

All right then! The rain forests.

BUSINESS

Are you still harping on that?

COYOTE

Reducing the destruction of the tropical rain forests would help to alleviate the greenhouse effect.

TECHNOLOGY

(*To Business.*) Scientific evidence does illustrate that trees do a lot for humanity.

BUSINESS

Trees are pure profit. Very easily harvested and much needed by mankind. Easily marketed to the Japanese for toothpicks and those there eating sticks.

TECHNOLOGY

Chopsticks. Simple Technology. (*Cleans fingernails.*) An example of my early work, I might point out. Your suggestion!

COYOTE

Mankind should pray and promote the welfare of all living things and strive to preserve the world in a natural way.

BUSINESS

Yeah, right! But what of commerce?

TECHNOLOGY

And science? We must progress.

COYOTE

I'm tired of this. I'm hungry, and you are trying my nerves. It's simple. The exploitation continues despite overwhelming scientific proof that the consequences are drastic and increasingly clear. We are headed for disaster!

BUSINESS

So profit must be made quickly. Techy, this is where you come in. Your shining hour, if you will. You must devise a way that we can rape the world at twenty times the current pace. Are you up to the task?

TECHNOLOGY

Yes, I believe I am . . . why, over at the DuPont labs they are doing wondrous things. The test tubes are glistening and scientific exploration is the buzz word, but we must have a new order! An enlightened way of looking at things.

COYOTE

This new order must be one that preserves all of nature and restores balance.

BUSINESS

That's a new economic order? It's old thinking!

TECHNOLOGY

Saw-and-ax ideology. Mule skinners and Paul Bunyon. No good, Coyote.

COYOTE

Attention to the spiritual balance must factor in.

BUSINESS

(*To Technology.*) Maybe you can clone workers, and I'll upgrade all work schedules. We must have production.

TECHNOLOGY

Yes—I'll clone everything—sheep, then sheep herders. Just think—just think. Hail to the new order!

BUSINESS

It's you and I, Techy, that are the driving forces.

COYOTE

Remember—what you do to Mother Earth, you do unto yourselves. Now, does anybody have anything to eat? Anything at all?

BUSINESS AND TECHNOLOGY

We function to fulfill man's needs, not yours, Coyote!

NARRATOR

(*In a radio-personality voice.*) Coyote was mad. He left and hunted down a rabbit, enjoyed a Waabooz burger, and sat under a tree contemplating his shrinking habitat. Then he got a severe stomachache, because the rabbit had been contaminated by having eaten the leftovers from an old neon-sign-making company. He started a scandal by posing as a hound and moving to Lincoln Park, where he seduced yuppie dogs and killed rats. Then Coyote posed as the president of the U.S.A., kept seducing yuppie bitches, and was eventually exposed by Republican rats. He signed Asinine Option Nine, a major attack on American forests, and then he disappeared. It was all over the news, because Arafat, a master terrorist, came to America to visit with him. Arafat returned to the burning sands, laughing. Coyote? Well, we'll see, ennit?

Shattered Dream

A PLAY IN TWO ACTS

CHARACTERS

LUKE FRAMBEAU: Anishinaabe, late twenties. A leader of the resistance movement.

NORMA GRAY WOLF: Anishinaabe, mid-twenties. Older sister to Teresa Gray Wolf. An artist type. A leader of the resistance movement.

TERESA GRAY WOLF: Anishinaabe, early twenties. Wife of Luke Frambeau.

DAN O'MALLEY: Clean-cut Indian, mid- to late twenties.

MONIQUE PEPIN: Half-breed, late teens to early twenties.

BRENDA MCGINNIS: White, mid-twenties.

JUNE BEAVER-HEART: Anishinaabe, in her late fifties.

JACKSON BREYER: Gay Anishinaabe, mid-twenties. (Played by same actor who portrays Two Kill.)

HENRY LICORICE: Early to mid-thirties. Head of security.

HARVEY TWO KILL: Anishinaabe, mid-twenties. (Played by same actor who portrays Breyer.)

OFFICER MURRAY AND OFFICER ERICKSON: (Played by same actors who portray Breyer and Licorice.)

THREE TERRORISTS: (Played by same actors who portray Frambeau, O'Malley, and Two Kill.)

NEWSCASTER

SCENE: Chicago; Atikokan, Ontario, Canada.
TIME: 1996.

ACT ONE

Scene One

SETTING: Union Station in Chicago, represented by two chairs and the sound of a railroad station that is piped in.

As the curtain rises, a young man and woman sit on the bench waiting for a train. He is in his late twenties and she in her mid-twenties. They sip on coffee from paper cups.

BRENDA
Have you ever been to Canada?

DAN
A couple of times. Why?

BRENDA
How'd you like to go there for a short stay?

DAN
I have to find work.

BRENDA
Don't worry about that right now.

DAN
(*Sits back and feigns shock.*) Brenda McGinnis! Are you suggesting that I become a kept man?

BRENDA
Daddy says that when you're ready you can come to work for him. He needs a dependable, hardworking assistant. Someone who will have a vested interest. And Dan, I think you do have a vested interest. (*Nestles closer.*) Don't you?

DAN
Brenda, we've been through this before.

BRENDA
But Dan, it would be a great chance to . . .

DAN
Be a high-paid messenger boy. No thank you!

BRENDA
That's not true. And I don't understand why you continually insist that would be the case. Why, just this morning we talked, and Daddy has something he'd like you to do for him.

DAN
And what's that?

BRENDA
> He'd like to hire you as a consultant to the Hydro Project.

DAN
> He has an office full of experts. What could I possibly do there?

BRENDA
> He's made a generous offer, Dan O'Malley.

DAN
> Really? How generous?

Brenda writes a figure on a napkin. She hands it to Dan. He looks at it and whistles.

DAN
> That's a generous piece of money. (*Pause.*) And what exactly would I be expected to do?

BRENDA
> We! I'm in this too.

DAN
> Okay. What would we have to do?

BRENDA
> Convince a tribe of Indians to accept his proposal to dam a small river on their tribal lands. It's simple, really.

DAN
> Are they opposed to the project?

BRENDA
> Some are.

DAN
> Why?

BRENDA
> Daddy said he'd have some stuff sent over for us. Copies of plans, complete with projections and environmental impact evaluations. There's also some testimony. We can look them over. (*Short pause.*) Will you accept?

Brenda points to the napkin.

DAN
> It does sound tempting. Yes, I'll consider it. I have to read the whole thing first. I'd have to consider the finer points.

BRENDA
> (*Becomes enthused.*) If we can convince those Indians, we'll be bringing electrical power that will make life more comfortable for virtually millions of people. It's mind-boggling, Dan. It really is!

DAN
> I guess it is.

BRENDA

> YOU GUESS! Hello, Dan! This project is huge. It could put us on Easy Street. My father picked you because he believes in you—and so do I. He feels that those Indians will relate to you because you're an Indian like them.

DAN

> He does? (*Pause.*) I wonder about the opposition. There has to be a reason.

BRENDA

> Do we really care, Dan?

DAN

> I do.

BRENDA

> Well! Unfortunately, they don't understand the implications. People are afraid of change, and ultimately, Dan, change is what this is all about.

DAN

> But change has to benefit people.

BRENDA

> Exactly! Daddy's vision on this is right on the mark. Do you realize that this project could completely upgrade their lives? They're dirt poor, and until Daddy went to see them they didn't even realize they're sitting on one of the world's most needed resources. They need this project, Dan. We'll really be helping them. Just think about it. You and I have an opportunity to do some really good work up there. I get all emotional when I think about it.

DAN

> It does sound good.

BRENDA

> It is good. With the wealth they will get because of this project, they could live like the rest of us. Dan, we would be helping to bring them into the twenty-first century. I feel very passionate about this, Dan. This is a win-win situation, and you and I will have made it possible. I'll do whatever I have to to make Daddy's dream come true! I will, Dan! I will!

Blackout.

Scene Two

SETTING: In front of the Community Center.

As the curtain rises, Luke Frambeau sits on a block of firewood. Teresa Gray Wolf sits on the ground. He has a bottle of orange juice that he shares with her.

LUKE

I don't know how I existed before you came into my life.

TERESA

We've known each other all our lives, Luke.

LUKE

I know that. I meant since we been in love. What I'm saying is . . .

TERESA

I know what you're saying. (*Reaches over to kiss Luke on the cheek.*)

LUKE

I only wonder what you see in me. Why do you love me?

TERESA

Because I know what's in your heart. So do the people. Look at how all the young guys look to you for leadership. Everytime we have a rally they ask you to be our spokesman.

LUKE

(*Laughs.*) Because I got a big mouth, aye.

TERESA

Every deer season they want to go hunting with you.

LUKE

We actually hunt a little and play around a lot. We're like a bunch of kids out there in the bush.

TERESA

There's nothing wrong with that. Every one of you gets a deer.

LUKE

I don't try to be no leader, aye.

TERESA

But you are, and I'm proud of you.

LUKE

You're gonna give me a big head with this leader stuff.

TERESA

It's the truth! You deserve it because you take care of the people.

LUKE

Come on—I do what I think needs to be done. You know, I'm just trying to live right. The Indian way . . . if there is such a thing anymore.

TERESA

> People know that, and they reward you with leadership. That makes me so proud to be in love with you, Luke. (*Pause.*) I think you should run for chief in the next election.

LUKE

> Are you insane? Me? A chief? I'm a dog soldier at most.

TERESA

> I could see it happening. I really can, Luke. (*Pause.*) Would I make a good "first lady?" (*Twirls around for Luke to see.*) Think of what honor you could bring to our families if you were chief. We have to think about that, Luke. I want that for us. In fact I'm already planting the seeds. I'd be the first lady of our tribe.

LUKE

> Yeah, but you know the first lady of this tribe got to make the best fry bread around.

TERESA

> Are you saying that I don't make good fry bread?

LUKE

> No, no! Would I say that? You think I'm crazy or something? (*Laughs and hands her the juice.*) Better take a drink of this before you blow away. I didn't know you felt like that. I didn't know you had political ambitions. Who'd vote for me anyway?

TERESA

> You have more support than you think. Then the Hydro Company would have to deal with you. The people are already talking, Luke. It's been three generations since any of our family has served as chief. You'd be perfect. You've changed so much, and the people see it.

LUKE

> Without you my life was a mess. Remember? You made things better for me. I got you to thank for that.

TERESA

> I love you, Luke. I want this for you . . . for us. Luke Frambeau—the chief. Sounds so good. It's always been my dream to be the wife of a chief. Aye!

Teresa hands him the bottle. He drinks.

LUKE

> This Hydro Project got me worried, though. This reserve is in a big mess. Some of these people don't seem to care.

TERESA

> They care, Luke, but they don't know what to do. We have to force the company to keep their promises.

LUKE

They're saying it doesn't make sense to go on until the second phase is underway. Something about another feasibility study.

TERESA

Feasibility study?

LUKE

All they do is make proposal after proposal.

TERESA

Do you think the tribal council will pass this expansion proposal?

LUKE

They'd be crazy if they did. It's hard to tell, aye. You never know.

TERESA

People are confused.

LUKE

It's pathetic. People are getting drunk all the time. Life has really gotten bad around here. Kids are doing drugs. You know how it is.

TERESA

Yes I do, and I know that it's really hard on the elders. They're afraid of the council. They're never consulted about any of this stuff. Did you read that flyer they distributed about how the Hydro Company will raise the standard of living? What a piece of shit that was! I wonder who wrote that?

LUKE

Yeah sure, aye! They'll change our lives, all right. Because of their influence, family values are under attack and eroding—dying out. Our tribal government is some kind of gutless wonder. Nobody even wants to serve on the council anymore, it's so corrupt!

TERESA

It's those new people they're bringing in. They're really bad news. They have totally different values than we do.

LUKE

And that's why I'm so worried. Sometimes, when I'm walking down by the water, I think I can hear the moaning of our ancestors. This damming business is bad. It's bad.

TERESA

We need to keep the pressure on them, Luke.

LUKE

You're right, as usual! It's you who are the real leader around here. I don't know what I'd do without you. (*Pause.*) It's about half and half now, right? With the people, I mean.

TERESA

> A lot of them are undecided. You have to keep working. Don't stop! You understand me, Luke Frambeau? The people need you.

LUKE

> I won't, honey. I won't. You can count on it, aye.

TERESA

> I have some other news to tell you.

LUKE

> What's that, aye?

TERESA

> You're gonna be a daddy!

LUKE

> (*Excitedly.*) That's what we need to do! We need to repopulate. (*Pause as he laughs.*) Let's go home and work on another one!

TERESA

> Oh, you! That's all you can think of? You're gonna be a daddy! (*Pause.*) Well, let's go work on another one just for fun, though.

Lights begin to go down and you hear Luke let out a happy whoop.

Blackout.

Scene Three

SETTING: Inside the Community Center.

As the curtain rises, Norma, Monique, and Jackson set up the room for a meeting. Monique and Jackson banter back and forth as they work.

JACKSON

> Girl, you should have seen him. I mean this guy was gorgeous, aye. I tell you, girl, I would do that man like he ain't never been done.

MONIQUE

> You're such a whore!

JACKSON

> Watch it, now! Girls who live in glass houses shouldn't throw stones.

MONIQUE

> So you fell in love?

JACKSON

> I don't fall in love. I fall in lust. You would have too. He was "all-night sex" personified.

MONIQUE

I could use an "all-niter" right about now.

NORMA

Would you two stop the chattering and get busy? We have to have this place set up by six, and people are already starting to get here.

JACKSON

Listen to you! Just worrying, aye. What's going on in your life? Who's creeping into your wigwam lately?

MONIQUE

No one. That's why she's being such a bitch.

NORMA

What do you know? You don't know nothing about my love life.

JACKSON

She's so private, ennit?

MONIQUE

(*Laughs.*) I know about Harvey Two-Kills!

JACKSON

Mr. Moneybags? Oooh! Do tell, girl friend.

NORMA

We're just friends.

JACKSON

So—has he hit on you, or what?

NORMA

Not really! He brings me presents and stuff.

JACKSON

(*Gets more interested.*) Like, what kind of presents?

MONIQUE

(*Laughing.*) Oh, does he ever!

NORMA

Don't you dare!

MONIQUE

(*Still laughing.*) A bag of beans and some coffee.

NORMA

Don't forget the flour! Last time I'll tell you anything, big mouth!

JACKSON

He gave you a bag of beans? How tacky! These Indian men, I swear!

NORMA

(*Laughing.*) But it was a real big bag.

MONIQUE

She was eating beans for six months.

NORMA

You! I gave them away to people who really needed them.

JACKSON

Listen, girl friend, you hold out for a diamond.

MONIQUE

That would be a gas! (*She laughs.*) A gas? You get it? Beans? Gas?

Norma rolls eyes at the sky. Jackson and Monique slap five, then twiddle fingers at each other.)

JACKSON

(*Laughs.*) Not to change the subject, but I hope this meeting turns out okay.

MONIQUE

Oh, by the way—did you hear that young girl from Chicago is here again? Her dad owns the Hydro Company or something.

JACKSON

Yeah, I heard that. She brought her main squeeze. I heard he's supposed to be something. Real cute and a sharp dresser.

NORMA

I have a bad feeling about her. She's trouble, mark my words! (*Short pause.*) Well, anyway, this room looks okay. We should get this show on the road. We'll wait five minutes. (*Teresa enters.*) There's Teresa. She'll make the introductions. Come on, Monique, let's go get Luke and June.

Monique and Norma exit.

JACKSON

I heard! Congratulations! How'd Luke take the news he's gonna be a father?

TERESA

It blew him away.

JACKSON

He'll be a good dad. You know, I got a good feeling about this meeting. Something good is gonna happen here. I just feel it in my bones.

TERESA

I think so too. It's like this baby is gonna make good things happen.

JACKSON

(*Hugs Teresa.*) For all of us too. I'm thinking about quitting drinking so I can be a better example. You don't realize how great it will be to have a baby around. I'm so happy for you!

(*Short pause.*) Oh, by the way—did the company send anybody?

TERESA

They said they've already made their position known to the council. They don't recognize us as being a legal group. They said they don't deal with radicals, aye.

JACKSON

Arrogant bastards! We'll show them radical. (*Short pause.*) Well, I better go get these people seated.

Jackson exits. Teresa prepares the table for the meeting. She puts water glasses where the speakers will sit. When she's done, she bangs on the table.

TERESA

Can I have your attention, please! I want to thank you for coming here tonight. We have several speakers lined up who will talk to you about the Hydro Company's latest proposal to dam the Sapawe River. We invited the company to send a spokesperson, but, in typical style, they declined. We're gonna get started in a minute, so please bear with us.

The speakers come onstage. They go to their chairs.

TERESA

Well, here they are, ladies and gentlemen. It's my pleasure to introduce Luke Frambeau—my man! My good friends Monique Pepin and June Beaver-Heart and, last but not least, my sister Norma Grey Wolf.

VOICE

What is this? A family affair?

TERESA

(*Laughs.*) Come on folks, let's give them all a big hand. (*Teresa claps.*) The first speaker is Luke Frambeau. You all know him.

LUKE

Before I get wound up, I'd like to make an announcement. One that makes me very happy and proud. (*Pause.*) Teresa's pregnant! We're having a baby. I'm extremely proud to . . .

VOICE

You bragging or complaining, Frambeau?

LUKE

(*Does a little fancy-dance step.*) You figure it out, Andy. (*Everyone laughs and claps.*) It's something, ain't it? (*Looks thoughtfully around the room.*) I'm glad to see that there are many white brothers and sisters in this crowd too, because

I think every one of us stands to lose something. (*Crowd claps.*) Well, I better get going here. Time's awasting. (*Pause.*) Five years ago the Hydro Company came to us, and they made a lot of promises. They said they would build us a school and a hospital if we let them go ahead and dam the Atikokan River. Well, we do need a hospital and a school here. We thought it was a good idea, so we said okay. We needed work for the men around here, both Indians and whites. But as it turns out, none of us had the skills they were looking for. Then they told us they would build us a new road, because their trucks and all that heavy equipment were doing major damage to the one we already had.

Well, here we are five years later. They got their dam, but so far there's no road, no school, and no hospital. The unemployment rate is higher than it ever was around this area. Now they want permission to expand their project. Now they want to dam the Sapawe River too. We all know that's where most of the walleyes around here spawn. They must think we're stupid, aye. (*Short pause.*) Their first dam is already poisoning the fish with mercury, killing the beaver, and displacing a lot of game. That dam has totally disrupted the local ecosystem for miles around. Mother Earth has been totally shocked by this project. NOW they ask us for even more. (*Long pause as he collects thoughts. People in audience respond by leaning forward in interest.*)

I say we tell them to get off of our land. It's ours, aye, and we want to keep it like it's supposed to be. Like it has always been! (*Pause.*) Our ancestors taught us to respect this land. We don't go changing it all around to suit our purposes. (*Begins to get more passionate. Audience cheers.*)

I say, by God, we tell them to go. No more flooding! No more of their genocidal projects! No more whiskey! No more drugs! I say we tell them to stick their project where the sun doesn't shine. (*Audience claps and cheers.*)

I look out at you people and I see guys, both Indian and white, that I've known all my life. People I see out on the lake, and we always smiled at each other and asked, "How's the fishing?" Sometimes we'd pull up and lie to each other about the big bugger that got away, aye. And we had good hearts toward each other. (*Pause.*) I see Dougie Siegfried sitting out there. Hell—we played hockey together. Remember the time we kicked Kenora's arse? We've always respected each other. What's happened to us now? Now we look at each other suspiciously. Our hearts are confused. We have to stop this. We've had ENOUGH! (*Everyone cheers.*)

We have to stand up and fight for our land just like we always have. Everyone in this room knows this is all about money. We could all live together—Indians and whites—but it's the special-interest groups that mess us all up. Wherever big Business wants natural resources, they first turn us against each other. (*Pause as audience claps.*) Indians against Indians, whites against Indians, whites against whites. Shit! I say we're all victims. We're all being ripped off. Everyone in this room—and that's a fact that we all have to face up to.

(*Pause for a moment as audience cheers.*) Because we are the thinking species, we have the responsibility to fight for our animal relatives too. We have to! It's our responsibility! (*Long pause.*) I have spoken from my heart. Thank you for listening with yours. Miiqwech!

Luke sits. Audience cheers loudly, then gets quiet as Monique stands to speak. She is obviously very nervous.

MONIQUE

I just want to say that I'm against the Hydro Project because I know it's not good for our people. (*Short pause.*) I have always thought that people should stand for what they believe in. Especially Indians, because they got so much going against them. You know. (*Pause.*) Sometimes it feels like the only way out of it is to get drunk. And . . . so that's what I did. (*Pause.*) But I know that's not the answer. (*Glances around and looks out of a window.*) It's like a windstorm, ain't it? No, no—I guess not, aye? (*Stands very still for a moment.*) I'm on the wagon now! I'm trying to stay straight, and it's one day at a time for me.

VOICE

One day at a time, honey!

MONIQUE

Thanks! (*Peers into audience.*) Who is that? (*Short pause.*) Oh—it's you! Bohunk! It's the first time I ever seen you when you're so . . . Feels good to be sober, ennit?

VOICE

Not always!

MONIQUE

That's why I'm so actively involved in this fight against the Hydro Company. It doesn't feel very good either. It's worse than a hangover. You know, I'm, uh, trying to go back to the old ways now. (*Very nervously.*) I'm starting to feel stronger every day. I really believe you have to go back, because that's where the strength is for us Indians. Every day I pray and offer tobacco like June Beaver-Heart told me to do. I really do. I thank the Great Spirit for life. (*She stops and looks up at the ceiling, hands in pockets.*)

I know I started drinking because I was confused and stressed. I lost hope! But I'm lucky. I have my dad. He took care of me like I was his little baby again. But I know it takes more than that. He taught me that it takes the Great Spirit's help too. (*Pause.*) I'm so ashamed of some of the things I did while I was drinking. (*She starts to cry.*) I feel so bad, because I brought shame on my family and on you people. That's all I have to say. I'm sorry—I just can't talk no more.

VOICE

We're with you, honey.

MONIQUE

Thanks, Bohunk.

Monique sits down. Audience cheers loudly and people call out support. Luke dries her eyes. Norma gets up to talk.

NORMA

(*Very slowly and deliberately.*) My mom was born and raised here. She never left. She was against this Hydro Project from the start. She was afraid this would happen. It doesn't take a rocket scientist to tell she was right. She didn't need no impact study to tell her. Those old Indians know more than we think they do. We need to listen to them more. The fish and game that we always depended on as a people are dying out, and there seems to be little we can do about it. But that's not the truth. Like Luke said—it's our obligation. (*Crowd claps politely.*)

As a woman of this tribe, I am really concerned about the well-being of our people. I see how unhappy the men are. I feel their pain in my heart. We all do—and, it's not only Indians. You can see it in their eyes. The Hydro Company promised them jobs so they could feed their families. They promised training. Well, the truth is there was no training and there weren't any jobs. The men all got buggered real good, every last one of them. They were lied to . . . again! It has to stop, and now is the time. (*Crowd gets more animated in their response.*)

Our people are in trouble, and it's because of what the Hydro Company is doing. It's affecting everyone. The price for what they call progress is too high. As a women of this tribe, I'm ready to do whatever is necessary to put a stop to this. I want to live my life like my grandmother and my mother did. I don't want to be redefined. (*Pause as audience cheers loudly.*) I should not feel unsafe on my own land. The price for what they call progress—and I'll say it again and again—is way too high. We need to get ourselves together and put a stop to what the Hydro Company is trying to do up here. We cannot let them run over us. (*Pause as audience cheers loudly.*) They owe us a school, a hospital, and a road. Why haven't they paid us? That's all I got to say. Thank you for hearing me talk. Mrs. Beaver-Heart will be the next and final speaker.

Norma sits down. Audience cheers. Luke helps June Beaver-Heart to her feet.

JUNE

I've seen so much change around here. I can remember when we were a happy people. The men went fishing and hunting, and we lived on the land. This place has been good to us. It gave us everything we ever needed. (*Pause.*) Luke, would you mind helping me again. (*Luke jumps up to help her out of her chair.*) Now where was I? When you get old it's hard to remember sometimes. (*Laughs.*) Oh yeah, I was saying about how life used to be around here. Sure, life was hard, but we were always laughing. Luke, I'm sorry, but would you help me sit back down? I can't stand too long. (*Luke helps her sit down.*) Thank you. You know, we Indian people laugh a lot. We're always making jokes. Sometimes we tell dirty jokes. (*People laugh.*) That's the way we used to be. (*Crowd cheers.*)

Things started changing for us, though. They came with guns and took us kids away. They loaded us on trains and took us to Kenora to an Indian School. I remember how sad I was, because one day I heard two nuns talking in their German language to each other. They wouldn't let us talk Indian, and they punished us if we did. I asked them, why didn't they talk English like they were making us do? One of those nuns turned around and slapped me so hard that I seen stars. I was scared for a long time to speak my language. Other kids were too, and sometimes we'd all be crying together. That's all in the past now, but we better never forget about it. When they took our language like that, it was the start of our sadness.

All the way up until now the rich white people took our land, piece by piece, and now they want even more. These young people are our future, and they're fighting the Hydro Company with all they've got. Boy—it makes me feel young again to be around them. I joined them because I feel like they do about this. It makes my heart swell with pride when I see them making their signs and getting people to sign them there petitions. I feel good when they ask me to lead them in prayer. They treat me with respect just like they're supposed to do. They do things in the old way. I'm gonna fight this thing as long as it takes. (*Pause. Audience cheers.*)

I'm an Indian and I'm proud of it. I offer tobacco every day and pray for these young people. We don't need no dam. They should just get away from us. Sometimes I feel like this is a bad work of a Windigo. I hold my medicine bundle to my heart and pray the Hydro Company will go away. They should just take their greedy asses off our land. (*She turns to the other speakers.*) Come on, kids. Off our land! Off our land! (*Rest of Cast joins her. They stand with their fists in the air and chant. Audience cheers loudly.*)

Blackout.

Scene Four

SETTING: Interior hotel scene with three chairs. Very bare room.

As the curtain rises, Dan, Brenda and Harvey Two Kill are in a meeting.

BRENDA

Harvey is going to run for tribal council. Naturally he'll have the backing of the company. We need a man with his vision there.

HARVEY

As a council member, I'll be able to do more for my people. That's the most important thing to most Indians. (*Pauses, looks closely at Dan.*) Dan, are you an Indian?

DAN

Yes, I am.

HARVEY

I thought so. An Indian can always tell another one. Besides, you're darker than this white woman here. (*He laughs somewhat loudly.*) So we're both on the same side, huh?

DAN

In one sense.

HARVEY

(*Laughs good-naturedly.*) I hope in the right sense. Time will tell. It's always good to . . .

BRENDA

(*Interrupts Harvey.*) Let's get down to business here. We have a lot of ground to cover. The way I see it is that we need information and lots of it.

DAN

And where will we get that?

BRENDA

That's where Harvey comes in. (*Dan looks suspiciously at Harvey.*) He's agreed to keep us posted on any suspicious activity.

DAN

(*Surprised.*) So you've already made an agreement?

HARVEY

Last week.

DAN

Last week? How'd you make an agreement last week? Brenda, I thought you told me we were partners. You should have . . .

BRENDA

(*Rudely cuts him off.*) Let's get back on track, gentlemen. Shall we? With the information that Harvey can furnish us, we have a place to start. We get a feel for what they are up to. Example one: they had a meeting, a town-type meeting, just last night. Now, I hear tell they were able to do quite a bit toward unifying the town people and the Indians. We don't want that! That's a no-no! Do you both understand? We have to do something to sway them to our side or else totally discredit them in everybody's eyes. Agreed?

DAN

(*To Harvey.*) I don't know that it's that drastic. Tell me, Harvey, what do the people feel about this dam?

HARVEY

Some for, some against. Most are just undecided. Some don't even care.

DAN

Who's against it?

HARVEY

Mostly younger people, but that's starting to change. Those young ones have dreams.

BRENDA

Not rooted in reality, I can assure you of that. Dan, there's no point of getting into it.

DAN

> If we hope to understand, we have to consider their viewpoint. They may have valid reasons for it.

BRENDA

> But our mission is to . . .

HARVEY

> Dan, it's really complicated. I'll explain, but right now I have to rush off. You know how business is. Big boxcar sale on canned Spam in town.

BRENDA

> You go ahead, Harvey. I'll fill Dan in on the details.

HARVEY

> That works for me. Oh yeah, Miss McGinnis—do you have that?

BRENDA

> (*Hands Harvey envelope.*) Of course. Here—you've certainly earned it.

Harvey opens envelope, looks inside.

BRENDA

> It's all there.

HARVEY

> I'm sure it is. I just like the feel of it, you know?

BRENDA

> (*Laughs.*) I sure do. I love the feel of money too.

HARVEY

> (*More seriously.*) Remember, cash . . . every time! No checks. Those can be traced.

Brenda nods okay. Harvey shakes Dan's hand, then exits.

DAN

> I don't trust him. Something doesn't ring true.

BRENDA

> He likes money. I know how to handle him . . . and get what I want.

DAN

> So what's the game plan?

BRENDA

> (*Hands Dan some folders.*) Dossiers on everyone involved.

DAN

> You don't fool around, do you? I'm impressed. Where'd you get these?

BRENDA

(*Smiles proudly. Kisses Dan.*) Internalize the information. We need to identify those that might cooperate, then offer them a deal they can't refuse.

DAN

(*Holds up a folder.*) Is this legal? You're talking about bribing people.

BRENDA

(*Unbuttons her blouse behind Dan.*) Call it what you want, but it has to be done. And, my dear (*kisses Dan over shoulder*), you're elected.

DAN

(*Sarcastically.*) Thanks!

BRENDA

Look, Dan—we have a job to do, so let's just get it done so we can get our butts the hell out of here.

DAN

You're right. I stand corrected. (*Pause as he reads.*) Did you say useful information?

BRENDA

That's right! (*Brenda has removed her blouse.*)

DAN

(*Turns to hand folder to her.*) Look at this. (*Startled as he notices she's undressing.*) Jesus H. Christ, woman. The curtains are open. Put on a robe or something, would you?

BRENDA

(*Laughing. She doesn't take the folder.*) You old fuddy-duddy.

DAN

(*Reading from file.*) Jackson Breyer is known to frequent gay establishments? So what? Sounds kind of homophobic if you ask me.

BRENDA

(*Brushing her hair.*) Maybe he doesn't want anybody to know. (*Short pause.*) You know we have to work fast.

DAN

Why?

BRENDA

Because I'm going back to Chicago. My Aunt Rebecca is having a party, and I simply must be there. Social obligations. You'll be all right. Just keep yourself busy, and you won't even miss me.

DAN

I was hoping we could rent a canoe and explore the lake this weekend.

BRENDA

Forget it, Dan. I'm not the outdoor type. I'd be utterly miserable.

DAN

I suppose you're right.

Brenda comes up to Dan and puts her arms around him.

BRENDA

Remember what's at stake here, Dan. OUR FUTURE! Dan, it really depends on us getting the job done right. Daddy doesn't like screw-ups. There is no such thing as failure to him. Remember that, Dan.

DAN

I love you, Brenda.

BRENDA

And I love you. I love you so much.

Blackout.

Scene Five

SETTING: In front of the Community Center.

As the curtain rises, Norma sits on a bale of hay reading a book. Dan comes onstage and watches her for a minute. She is startled.

NORMA

Who the hell are you?

DAN

I'm sorry. My name is Dan O'Malley.

NORMA

Dan O'Malley? (*Pause.*) Oh yeah, the company man. What do you want?

DAN

And your name is?

NORMA

Norma Gray Wolf. I asked you what you want?

DAN

To talk to you about the Hydro Company and their proposal to your tribal council.

NORMA

You're the boyfriend I've been hearing about.

DAN

Actually, I'm a consultant with the Hydro Company.

NORMA

A hired gun?

DAN

Yeah, right! Not quite, Miss Gray Wolf. (*Pause.*) What's that you're reading?

NORMA

Jack London. *Call of The Wild.* Have you read it? (*Short pause.*) You look surprised.

DAN

I just didn't expect an activist to be reading him.

NORMA

An activist? What did you expect? The *Communist Manifesto* or something?

DAN

Actually, yes. Well, in college the leftist activists read stuff like that.

NORMA

Really? This isn't college, Mr. O'Malley. (*Short pause.*) So why'd you expect I'd be a leftist? Or even an activist for that matter?

DAN

The file I was given says "possible subversive."

NORMA

What the hell are you doing with a file on me?

DAN

It's common practice. Companies keep tabs on the opposition all the time.

NORMA

So now we're the enemy? I thought it was a partnership. Who the hell changed that?

DAN

(*Tries changing the subject.*) This project will be a big benefit to everybody involved. Just think about it, Miss Gray Wolf.

NORMA

I have! (*Pause.*) Are you going to let me see that file?

Norma tries to grab the folder. The contents spill onto the ground.

NORMA

I'm so sorry. I didn't mean to do that.

DAN

That's okay.

Both bend down to pick up paper, but bump heads. They laugh as they rub their heads. Norma picks up a sheet of paper and begins to read it.

NORMA

> What is this? (*Pause.*) This is a note from Harvey Two Kill about me. That bastard! Is he working for the company?

Dan takes the paper from Norma and returns it to the folder.

DAN

> Look, Miss Gray Wolf, politics make strange bedfellows. (*Pause.*) Miss Gray Wolf, I've been authorized to do what-ever it takes to get the ball rolling. I'm prepared to pay substantial amounts of money to make that happen. I've been given a discretionary account from which I can draw money for people who are willing to get the thing . . .

NORMA

> (*Interrupts very angrily.*) You came to buy me off?

DAN

> I wouldn't put it exactly that way, Miss Gray Wolf.

NORMA

> Well, just how the hell would you put it, Mr. O'Malley? (*Short pause.*) I'm not for sale, Mr. O'Malley! Get that through your thick corporate skull. You can't buy me off!

DAN

> That's not what I said, and you know it!

NORMA

> That's how you people are.

DAN

> What? What did you say?

NORMA

> You heard!

DAN

> Yeah, I heard. (*Disgustedly.*) You know, Miss Gray Wolf, you don't know nothing about who I am or what I feel.

NORMA

> That's right! And I don't want to. So just get your ass away from me! (*Pause. Dan doesn't move.*) I said, get your company ass away from me. Now! (*Dan still doesn't move. He seems fascinated by her.*) I said get away from me or I'll scream, and you know what'll happen then. Go on—get out of here.

DAN

> (*Grinning sheepishly.*) Okay, Miss Norma. I mean, Miss Gray Wolf.

Dan exits.

Blackout.

Scene Six

SETTING: Company hotel suite.

As the curtain rises, Brenda and Dan argue.

BRENDA

(*Waves folder in Dan's face.*) You're protecting that God-damned Indian! Why didn't you tell me what was going on? (*Pauses and stares.*) I demand an explanation, Dan!

DAN

You demand? Who the hell are you to demand anything from me? For your information, I wasn't sure about him from the start. Anyway, you said you knew how to deal with people like him. I tried to warn you, but no—you knew it all. (*Pause.*) Now that the Indians know about him, what are you gonna do? We were the ones who actually compromised him.

BRENDA

Correction, Dan! You did it, not me. At any rate his information was all false. He's full of shit! He just outright ripped us off. (*Throws folder on the floor.*) I should have known better. (*Stamps her foot in anger.*) I'm really beginning to hate these damned Indians. We're trying to help them, for God's sake. Don't they understand?

DAN

Help them? Don't make me laugh! Do you have any idea what this project is doing to the land? To these people? Do you understand? I think that . . .

BRENDA

BORING! BORING! Dan, I told you before—that's nothing but rubbish. And another thing—I don't care what you think.

DAN

These people don't want another dam pushed down their throats, and frankly I don't blame them.

BRENDA

Daddy wants one . . . because the world needs electricity.

DAN

(*Laughs.*) This is all about money, and everyone knows it.

BRENDA

It's part of being civilized. Something these people hardly are. Look at how they live. Those cabins . . . God, they're so gloomy.

DAN

Have you ever gone inside one of them?

BRENDA

Of course not! I'm sure you have, though. Tell me, Dan, what were you doing inside one of them? Getting a little?

DAN

I was doing my job. (*Short pause.*) Aren't you even curious about how they live?

BRENDA

(*In Dan's face.*) READ MY LIPS! I don't care how they live! I just want them to pass Daddy's proposal. You're supposed to handle that, but no—you had to go sniffing around that Gray Wolf squaw. I feel so humiliated.

DAN

You're overreacting! As usual. I'm not sniffing around anybody. (*Pause.*) Why do you have to say "squaw"? It's derogatory and racist, and I don't like it.

BRENDA

I don't care what you like. And I definitely don't like the way that Harvey Two Kill ripped me off. What are you gonna do about it?

DAN

He took what was offered.

BRENDA

(*Laughs.*) You don't have a clue what was offered. (*Pause.*) I'm going to report him to our security and information branch.

DAN

Just what was offered? Huh, Brenda? (*No reply.*) Now you want to call in the goons? Come on, Brenda, you know what they're like.

BRENDA

They're highly professional. They get things done—which, incidentally, is more than I can say about you.

DAN

They're a bunch of burned-out mercenaries. They're dangerous.

BRENDA

You had your chance. I need results. (*Turns her back on Dan.*) They'll take care of this for me. They'll handle Harvey, Luke, and those trouble-making squaws too.

DAN

You have any idea what those guys are like? You have any idea what could happen?

BRENDA

Another thing, I want you to steer clear of those dissenters and their community center. Am I clear? Stay away!

DAN

>   How the hell do you expect me to do my job? I need to talk
>   to them, and that's where they hang out.

BRENDA

>   Dan! Listen to me! My orders to you are to stay away from
>   them. It's very simple. If you can't do as I say, then you give
>   me no choice but to call in Henry and his men.

DAN

>   That's like calling in the Seventh Cavalry. I have to talk to
>   them. I can convince them . . .

BRENDA

>   That's it! Henry will handle things. As of now, you, Dan
>   O'Malley, are off of this case. I can't trust you to do anything
>   right. And Dan, I mean it when I say stay away from those
>   stinking Indians! Do you understand? (*Dan puts on his coat
>   and exits.*) Where the hell do you think you're going? Get
>   back in here, Dan O'Malley!

Blackout.

Scene Seven

SETTING: Inside the Community Center.

*As the curtain rises, Norma, June, Monique, Teresa, and Jackson work
on protest posters. As they work, they talk.*

NORMA

>   At first I couldn't believe my eyes, but there it was in black
>   and white. When I first seen it my whole body went numb.
>   A note from Harvey to that Brenda woman. Of course I
>   didn't get to read all of it, but what I did read, it was plain
>   to see that he was working for them. He's spying on us, and
>   we need to do something about it.

JUNE

>   Do you believe Harvey would do us any real harm?

MONIQUE

>   He's a jokester! I bet he's stringing them along. You all know
>   how he likes to play tricks on people. But this could be
>   dangerous. I don't like it. I'm scared for him. I wish he'd
>   stop. Someone make him stop.

JACKSON

>   He likes money. Greed can do funny things to people.

Suddenly there is a loud knock at the door.

NORMA

I wonder who that is?

TERESA

Sure sounds like someone in a hurry.

Teresa goes to answer the door.

BRENDA

I'm looking for Dan O'Malley! Is he here?

JACKSON

(*Sashays to door.*) No, he's not.

BRENDA

And who are you? Tinker Bell?

JACKSON

(*Laughs and bows.*) Jackson Breyer at your service.

BRENDA

So you're Jackson Breyer, the militant faggot!

JACKSON

Touché! Touché! Touché all day, honey.

JUNE

What do you want?

BRENDA

I'm addressing that (*points to Jackson*), not you, you old hag.

JUNE

This is tribal property, and you're not welcome. (*Turns to Monique.*) Monique, you stay calm.

BRENDA

Please! I could buy and sell this place and everyone in it. (*Spins around to face Monique.*) So you're Monique Pepin—the community punchboard, as I hear tell.

Jackson steps forward to say something. Brenda points at him.

BRENDA

Stay out of this, faggot! This is between the drunk and me.

MONIQUE

Go get yourself laid.

JACKSON

(*Laughs too loudly.*) She can't! Danny Boy's missing.

BRENDA

Go cruise the gay bars or something. You're definitely getting on my nerves.

JUNE

He's not here. Just go home. You're embarrassing everybody—especially yourself.

BRENDA

Listen, you decrepit old squaw . . .

MONIQUE

Don't you talk to my elder like that, or I'll . . .

BRENDA

Or you'll what? Get drunk and get laid? (*Short pause.*) Your elder? That's a laugh! You're not even Indian—you're half-white. So what are you doing here?

NORMA

Did you pay Harvey for that information too?

BRENDA

She's nothing but half-breed white trash.

Monique goes after Brenda. Suddenly Luke charges through the door with Henry right behind him. Luke grabs Monique and Henry gets hold of Brenda. They separate the two women.

BRENDA

Dan is missing, and I think they may have kidnapped him. Do something, Henry! Arrest someone!

HENRY

By what authority? The Hydro Company has no such power, Miss Brenda. (*Pause.*) Anyway, Danny Boy stayed in the bunkhouse with my men. He couldn't stand being around you.

JUNE

Just get her out of here. She has no respect. Coming in here, calling us all down.

JACKSON

Ain't that about the truth.

BRENDA

You faggot! You're going to get yours too.

JACKSON

You're gonna get yours too! Go get laid, lady. Sex relieves tension, and honey, you're as tense as a spring. (*Looks suggestively over at Henry.*) If Danny Boy won't service you, this guy looks like he could unwind your spring.

HENRY

(*Laughing.*) Kid's got insight. You should listen to him.

There is an exchange of eye contact between Monique and Henry. They look at each other with interest. Brenda notices.

BRENDA

You'll all get yours, I promise you that. Just you wait. (*Pause.*) You interested in trash, Henry?

HENRY

None of your business what I'm interested in . . . unless, of course, it involves you.

JUNE

   Young lady, you need to learn . . .

BRENDA

   Shut up, you decrepit old squaw. Stinking Indians. I can't
   stand them.

HENRY

   Don't look like anybody here is too excited to see you either.
   (*Turns to June.*) I'm sorry, Grandma Beaver-Heart. I'll get
   her out of here right now. Come on, Miss Brenda, before
   you get yourself hurt.

Brenda and Henry exit.

LUKE

   This thing about Harvey being a spy is bugging the shit out
   of me.

NORMA

   When he comes over, I'll talk to him.

LUKE

   You let him know real clear-like that we don't appreciate
   what he's pulling. Tell him to stop or I'm gonna be dead on
   his Indian ass, aye.

Blackout.

Scene Eight

SETTING: Outside of the Community Center.

As the curtain rises, Brenda and Henry talk.

HENRY

   I'm just doing my job. There is nothing in my contract that
   says I gotta buy your ideology. It's NO MY YOB, LADY!

BRENDA

   Why do you say "yob"? You do it to irritate me.

HENRY

   (*Grins.*) That was a stupid thing for you to do.

BRENDA

   Don't you talk to me like that. Don't you dare!

HENRY

   Fire me, then! If you can. I got a contract, and I don't really
   give a shit what you like.

BRENDA

   You got a contract all right—you go to the highest bidder.
   I know your type.

HENRY

> I happen to agree with the Indians on this one, but they ain't paying me. Your daddy is. I'm here to do what he ain't got the balls to do himself. I'm a professional, Miss McGinnis. Don't you ever forget that. What I do, I do real good.

BRENDA

> Okay, Mr. Pro, I need you to do something for me.

HENRY

> I know what I'd like to do for you.

BRENDA

> Don't get cute, Henry.

HENRY

> It's like that gay boy told you—I could unwind your spring. And you'd like it. Guaranteed, Miss Brenda.

BRENDA

> You think so, do you? Well, Henry, I was raised a rich girl, and rich girls don't have anything to do with the hired help . . . even if they do have a contract.

HENRY

> But in your heart, you know . . .

BRENDA

> Not in this lifetime, Henry . . .

Henry grabs her and plants a kiss on her. She struggles at first, then relents. She starts to kiss back, but Henry pushes her away.

BRENDA

> What the hell are you doing?

HENRY

> Just showing you what you'll never get—unless you change your attitude, that is. Get over the idea that you're indispensable, Miss Brenda, because you aren't.

BRENDA

> You arrogant bastard! Don't you ever do that again!

HENRY

> You liked it, and you know it.

BRENDA

> Not likely. You're trash, Henry.

HENRY

> But women like you are trash collectors. I just want what Harvey Two Kill got. (*Pause.*) You know, I could have a little talk with Danny Boy for you. Let him know what kind of woman he's about to marry.

BRENDA

> Do you know Harvey Two Kill? And what do you THINK you know about me and him?

HENRY

I know everybody and what they do. Now as they say deep in the heart of Mexico, "THAT'S MY YOB."

BRENDA

Since it's your YOB—no, I mean job, with a J, it might interest you to know that the Indian son of a bitch is ripping us off.

HENRY

How's he doing that?

BRENDA

He sold us false information.

HENRY

So what do you want me to do? Be specific.

BRENDA

You're the specialist. Just clear up this mess.

HENRY

You know, this hinges on conspiracy. (*Pause.*) But then, I like the intimacy, to be perfectly honest with you.

BRENDA

I'm giving you a directive, Henry—nothing else.

HENRY

I'm very glad you clarified that for me. (*Pause.*) Aw, but Miss Brenda, the other thing. In time you'll be . . .

BRENDA

Let's get on with this business. I'm not interested in your little fantasy.

HENRY

I'll put out a memo to everyone involved. That'll stop his clock.

BRENDA

I want results, Henry, not paper work.

HENRY

What about the Ontario Provincial Police? Who's going to talk to them?

BRENDA

I will. It's time they started earning what we pay them. (*Pause.*) I'm flying out to Chicago for a few days. I want this done by the time I get back. Am I clear?

HENRY

You don't care how?

BRENDA

Do it right, Henry, and you'll make me a happy woman. (*Pause.*) There is one other thing.

HENRY

What's that?

Henry grins and steps closer to Brenda. She slaps him in the face.

BRENDA

Don't you dare ever put your hands on me again. You understand?

HENRY

We're gonna have us some fun. (*Rubs his face.*) I can see that.

BRENDA

Yeah, well don't count your chickens before they're hatched. (*Pause.*) There is one other thing.

Henry jumps back out of the way. Brenda smiles.

HENRY

And what's that?

BRENDA

You're real easy to train, Henry. (*Pause.*) Maybe too easy. (*Short pause.*) Now, about Dan. I want you to have someone watch him. I want to know who he spends time with.

HENRY

You'd do us all a favor by taking him back to Chicago with you.

BRENDA

You just make sure he's watched. I want a tail on him at all times. Starting now! Oh, by the way (*Pause. Puts hand on Henry's arm.*) . . .

HENRY

What?

BRENDA

Never mind, Henry.

Blackout.

Scene Nine

SETTING: In front of the Community Center

As the curtain rises, Norma and Harvey talk. He sits on a block of wood and she sits on a bale of hay.

HARVEY

Norma, Norma—I would never spy on our people. You should know that. Luke should know that too. You're my family.

NORMA

I told you, I read the note. Your goddamned name was signed to it.

HARVEY

What did the note say, huh?

NORMA

Something about a clandestine meeting.

HARVEY

(*Laughs.*) Oh, that! I was talking about those five old ladies that meet at Grandma Cabatie's house to play cards every Wednesday night. They play cards, drink tea, and gossip about the old men. That's all that was about. I took them a bag of those mint cookies. I give them to them for free because the old lady is a relation. Anyway, I got this crazy idea to say they were having secret meetings. That's what they wanted to hear anyway. That's not spying, Norma—hell, that ain't nothing but shucking!

NORMA

Yeah, well your shucking is making a lot of trouble. Harvey, do you realize how much danger you're putting yourself into?

HARVEY

Why? Those old ladies like them cookies. If they didn't, I'd give them something else. (*Pauses and laughs.*) You're a nice boy, they always say.

NORMA

Would you be serious?

HARVEY

If those white people are stupid enough to pay me $150 for something like that, then I'll come up with something every day.

NORMA

Why'd you do it, anyway?

HARVEY

To impress you.

NORMA

By spying?

HARVEY

I just told them what they wanted to hear.

NORMA

That could get you hurt. You know how the goon squad is.

HARVEY

But they ain't involved.

NORMA

They always are. (*Paces around, thinking.*) You never should have taken their money.

HARVEY

I didn't want to, but she kept on insisting.

NORMA

Who?

HARVEY

You know, that lady whose daddy owns the company.

NORMA

She asked you to spy? Did she give you money?

HARVEY

(*Laughs.*) She gave me more than money.

NORMA

I thought you had more brains than . . . that!

HARVEY

You're mad at me, aren't you? (*Pause. Norma shakes her head no.*) Norma, can I tell you something? Promise me you won't get mad.

NORMA

I promise.

HARVEY

When I was doing it with her, I was thinking about you. I pretended it was you. I just shut my eyes real tight and didn't see her white ass no more . . . and I thought about you. And damn, it was good too.

NORMA

Harvey! Would you get serious?

HARVEY

I am! (*Pause.*) Norma, I brought you five cans of that there Spam. Here, look—it's the good kind. (*Hands cans to Norma.*) I love you, Norma.

NORMA

(*Exasperated.*) Stop it, Harvey!

HARVEY

(*Looks dejected.*) Aw . . . you're mad.

NORMA

No I am not!

HARVEY

Yes you are.

NORMA

I said I wasn't angry with you, Harvey.

HARVEY

If you ain't mad, let me kiss you then.

NORMA

Are you crazy?

HARVEY

See—I knew you were mad.

NORMA

Harvey! I am not angry. (*Pauses.*) Okay then. Just a little one, though.

She shuts her eyes and pushes her face toward Harvey. He takes her face and kisses her full on the lips. Luke walks onstage just before he does so.

LUKE

Will surprises never cease? Be still my heart! (*Makes exaggerated motion of grabbing his heart.*) I thought you were going to talk to him—put him straight—you know what I mean? Not put him straight in a lip-lock.

NORMA

(*Startled.*) This isn't what it looks like.

HARVEY

Are you mad at me, Luke?

LUKE

Yeah, in a way, but I'm more concerned about your safety.

HARVEY

Sure you ain't mad?

NORMA

Watch out, Luke. (*Laughs.*) You know how he is. He might want to kiss you next.

LUKE

Bugger ain't gonna kiss me, aye, no matter what. I saw the whole thing. (*Turns to Harvey.*) That was pretty slick, Harvey.

HARVEY

I know. You sure you don't want a kiss too?

LUKE

Don't even think about it. (*Pause as he looks at the list of names on a clipboard he carries.*) You two are supposed to be going to Fort Francis for that workshop aren't you? You better hurry up before you miss the van.

NORMA

That's right. I totally forgot.

LUKE

You got Harvey on the mind.

NORMA

Come on—let's go, Harvey.

LUKE

Harvey, you better be careful. You hear me?

HARVEY

I ain't worried about it.

LUKE

Well, you should be. I don't know what's in your mind, but that was a really stupid thing to do. (*Pause.*) Now, get your arses in gear and get out of here.

Norma and Harvey exit. Luke sits on the bale of hay and begins carving on a stick. Dan enters. He doesn't see Luke as he goes to the Center's door and knocks.

LUKE

> Nobody's there, aye. They all went to Fort Francis for a workshop. Something about community-service work.

DAN

> (*Startled.*) You just scared the shit out of me. I was hoping to talk to someone. My name is Dan O'Malley. I'm here representing the Hydro Company. It's my job to try to get the proposal passed.

LUKE

> I see, and how are you doing that?

DAN

> First, I have to ascertain how the local community feels about it.

LUKE

> Ain't nobody too thrilled about it.

DAN

> It doesn't seem to be. Your name is?

Dan begins to consult a list of names. Luke watches him, quite amused.

LUKE

> Luke Frambeau, and I'm against the project.

DAN

> Oh yeah! Here you are. Umm. (*Shakes his head. Looks up at Luke.*) Huh. Huh. It looks like you're really opposed to this.

LUKE

> That's what I just said, aye. (*Pause.*) So, Mr. O'Malley, I hear tell you're some kind of Indian.

DAN

> (*Laughing.*) Yeah, I am. Some kind, anyway. (*Pause.*) I hear tell you're a radical Indian.

Dan writes something in his book. Luke is still amused. Both laugh.

LUKE

> That's a big folder. Lots of information in there, ennit? Can you let me look at it?

DAN

> You know better than that.

LUKE

> What if I just take it?

DAN

> Then we'll be boxing, and that would tend to screw up this whole day for both of us.

LUKE

Can we talk about it?

DAN

Now, that's a possibility.

LUKE

Can we talk about a Mr. Two Kill?

DAN

Two Kill? Oh—you mean Harvey. As a matter of fact, I think we should. I really do.

LUKE

(*Points at hillside.*) Who's that up there? Your bodyguards or something?

DAN

Up where?

LUKE

On the hill. Right there by that big old rock. One of them has binoculars. See that flash?

DAN

Yeah! Now I see them. What the hell? They're from the goons. What they doing up there?

LUKE

Goons? They must not trust you, Dan. What you want to do about them?

DAN

What can I do?

LUKE

We could do a Dukes of Hazard–type thing. I know these back roads like the back of my hand. We could have us some fun.

DAN

Sounds good to me. Let's do it.

LUKE

(*Picks up his stuff.*) We'll take my Jeep. This is gonna be a gas.

DAN

Wait a minute. I really do have to talk to people.

LUKE

There's a powwow tonight. Be lots of people you can talk to there. Wanna come?

DAN

I'd love to. You think it'd be cool?

LUKE

I know it would.

Blackout.

ACT TWO

Scene One

SETTING: Outside of the Community Center.

As the curtain rises, it's night. Inside, the sound of a powwow is heard. Luke and Dan come out to get fresh air. There are cricket sounds.

DAN

Nice powwow.

LUKE

Figured you'd dig it.

DAN

People having fun.

LUKE

Drum pulls our people together. Gives a sense of pride. You know what I mean? (*Dan nods yes. Luke continues.*) You know, for a long time the drum was banned as taboo.

DAN

No shit! Why?

LUKE

The Jesuits, aye. They recognized the power it holds.

DAN

What about freedom of religion?

LUKE

That's a joke! What about it? (*Pause.*) How's a guy like you end up with a name like O'Malley?

DAN

I was adopted by an Irish family when I was three. They were really into being Irish, so they tried to do what they could about me knowing who and what I am. They just weren't ever very lucky about doing it, but they sure did try. My mother used to get so mad at the churches and the government.

LUKE

That's a common story. Happens to a lot of Indian kids, aye. It's almost by design. Another form of genocide. They've never gotten over the fact that they want to wipe us out. Big business has never altered that. They still want what's ours.

DAN

Can I ask you something? (*Luke nods.*) How do you feel about guys like me? How's it feel when some sucker tells you he's Indian, but don't know what that means?

LUKE

That he's one lucky guy. (*Laughs.*) Really, we don't get much of that around here.

DAN

What's it really mean, Luke? You tell me.

LUKE

Up here it means second-class citizen, aye.

DAN

That's a crock of bullshit.

LUKE

You already instinctively know. I guess it's a matter of having this spirit about you. It's in the way you move, boy. (*Pause.*) You got what it takes. I can see that, believe me.

DAN

Not to change the subject, but there is something—a small favor—that I'd like to ask.

LUKE

What's that, Dan?

DAN

You don't mind? I mean, we just met and all.

LUKE

(*Steps away from Dan.*) Not blood brothers! No way!

DAN

No, no, no—it's none of that shit. (*Shuffles nervously.*) It's just that I want to ask this girl to dance with me.

LUKE

So ask her.

DAN

Show me how.

LUKE

Show you how to ask her? (*Short pause.*) Come on, Dan!

DAN

Show me how to dance.

LUKE

You can't be serious. You mean now? Here? (*Pause.*) You are serious. What if someone sees us?

DAN

No one will.

LUKE

Damn, I don't know about this. (*Pause.*) You sure you don't just want to be blood brothers or something? Hey, I got an idea. How about I adopt you? Hell—I'll even throw in an Indian name for you. Wolf Man or something! How's that? (*Pause. Waits for a response. Dan shakes his head no.*) You wanna dance? (*Dan nods yes.*)

DAN

I mean, take a good look. These are some fine women. I wanna dance with them. They're all looking real good to me.

LUKE

You're a goddamned Indian all right. Just got here and wanting to snag. Okay, then. (*Luke takes a careful look around.*) You take her like this. (*Dan starts jumping.*) No, no! What the hell are you supposed to be doing? Don't hop. You look like a goddamned rabbit. Be more relaxed. (*Dan still jumps about.*) No! There you go jumping again. Slow down. Move your feet like this. Just move your arms along with your feet. This is a two-step.

DAN

Like this?

LUKE

Yeah—like that. Now you got it.

DAN

Hey—this is fun.

LUKE

Just keep going like that. This is a social kind of . . .

GIRL'S VOICE

Luke Frambeau? What you doing with that there boy?

LUKE

(*Jumps away.*) Oh, shit! Now look what you've done.

SECOND FEMALE VOICE

I didn't know Luke was a two-spirit.

DAN

They're only teasing. What's a two-spirit?

THIRD FEMALE VOICE

Who's your good-looking friend, Luke? Does he swing both ways?

DAN

(*Asks Luke.*) So what's a two-spirit? (*Asks the girls.*) What's a two-spirit?

The girls all laugh.

FIRST FEMALE VOICE

He's a real virgin! Luke, what you got there? Are you sharing him?

LUKE

Don't say nothing to them.

DAN

They're just teasing. Let's go talk to them.

LUKE

Are you crazy? You don't know these goddamned Indians like I do. It'll take a year to live this down.

FOURTH GIRL

Does Teresa know about this? That's her chief, all right. Dancin' with a boy in the shadows. Good candidate. AYE!

All four girls laugh and say AYE!

Blackout.

Scene Two

SETTING: Inside the Community Center, in the hall.

As the curtain rises, Luke, Teresa, Norma, and Dan clean up after the powwow.

LUKE

Boy, it was nice of you to help us clean up.

DAN

Well, hell, I had a real nice time tonight. Thanks for inviting me.

NORMA

(*Laughing.*) I heard you even had a private dancing lesson.

LUKE

Don't start!

TERESA

I thought that was so cute.

LUKE

You would.

DAN

Well, I know how to dance now. When is the next powwow?

LUKE

Every last Friday of the month. Yo, Dan, give me a hand with this garbage can.

Dan helps Luke carry out a can.

NORMA

He makes me nervous.

TERESA

He's got cute buns. (*Short pause.*) Don't tell me you haven't looked.

NORMA

Would you get real?

TERESA

Come on, admit it. You've looked!

NORMA

Okay, I've looked. So what?

TERESA

You like? (*Smiles at Norma.*) Did you see the way those Spoon River girls practically mobbed him?

NORMA

Those girls! Especially that Wanda. I swear, she's a bitch. She makes me sick.

TERESA

You were jealous!

NORMA

Nah! (*Shakes her head no.*)

TERESA

AYE! Yes you were! I was watching you, and I know when you're jealous.

Luke and Dan come back into the room.

LUKE

(*To Dan.*) I meant to tell you that old man Beaver-Heart is making a talk on Saturday at sunrise. I thought you might find it interesting. He does them in English.

NORMA

When he gets started, he can talk a long time. Ennit, Luke? (*Luke nods.*)

DAN

Are you sure it's okay? He won't mind?

LUKE

No—in fact, he wants to meet you. He had a dream about you.

Norma and Teresa look at each other. Teresa goes and puts on a tape.

DAN

A dream about me? Must have been a nightmare.

NORMA

You should consider yourself honored. Among the men, he's a special teacher.

LUKE

The old guy wants to meet you. By the way, I have something I want to talk to you about.

Indian music comes on the tape player.

DAN

Well, I am honored. This whole evening has been so much fun. I don't know . . .

TERESA

Play your cards right, and it might even be more fun. Ennit, big sister.

Norma slaps playfully at Teresa.

DAN

(*Tries changing the subject.*) Who's that music by? I like that. Man, that's so pretty.

LUKE

Rewind it from the start, Teresa. (*Teresa rewinds the tape.*) That's Dennis Banks. Guy can sing, ennit. Listen to it. It's the AIM song. Their National Anthem. I think you'll really like it.

DAN

Wow! That's nice.

Luke sits and begins drumming on a chair and Dan begins to sing. As the song progresses, all four get into it and sing outloud. Dan is pounding a chair and moving his feet like he's dancing. Luke and the girls are singing hard and loud. Luke looks up and smiles. He indicates with his lips for the girls to look at Dan, who is totally involved at this point. Luke waves his hand, and Teresa shuts off the recorder. They all stop singing. Dan sings on for a second. He is way off-key and out of step, but totally engrossed. He realizes that they've stopped and looks around, embarrassed.

DAN

(*Grins sheepishly.*) What? Was I off-key or something?

Everyone laughs.

LUKE

No matter. You were into it.

TERESA

And you were steppin', aye. Oh brother, how you were steppin'.

They all laugh, and Norma hugs Dan until she realizes what she's doing. She jumps back, but Teresa already has a big grin.

DAN

You know what? I'm beginning to understand more about this community than I ever hoped to. This is great.

LUKE

Look, I just remembered—I have to get up real early to pull nets. I have to go. Would you see that Norma gets home okay? Come on, wife-type, let's head out. (*Turns to Dan.*) We'll work on your singing.

TERESA

Did he call me "wife-type"? Whatever! It was nice to meet you, finally. I've been hearing all about you from my sister. You know, she watched your buns all night long.

NORMA

Teresa! Would you stop? Sometimes, I swear, you're crazy.

DAN

You're gonna teach me to sing?

LUKE

Hell no! Carlos or Bobo will.

Luke and Teresa exit. There is an uneasy silence for a minute.

NORMA

(*Paces nervously.*) So, where's your girlfriend tonight?

DAN

She flew back to Chicago. She's due back here on Tuesday— probably get here by Wednesday.

NORMA

You're the first company person to ever show up at one of our events. The people liked that.

DAN

Aside from the company thing, I had my own agenda—and it had zilch to do with the project.

NORMA

And what was your agenda, if I may ask.

DAN

To meet people. Mostly to see you, though.

NORMA

(*Laughs.*) What a line! So—when the cat's away, the mouse will play. Well, anyway—I'm quite flattered, even though I believe it was PR work. The people sure ate it up, though.

DAN

I promise, it wasn't PR.

NORMA

All the attention from the ladies didn't seem to bother you either.

DAN

I'll admit that was flattering. Why didn't you ask me to dance? That's what I was really hoping for.

NORMA

Wanda had you all wrapped up. I can't stand her—never could and never will.

DAN

We can dance now. We have that music.

NORMA

(*Laughing.*) Are you sure this ain't some kind of PR trick? If it is, Dan O'Malley, I'll kill you.

DAN

Come here, Miss Gray Wolf.

NORMA

Oh—so formal all of a sudden.

DAN

Just come here. I won't bite.

NORMA

(*Laughs nervously.*) What if I like to be bit, Mr. O'Malley?

DAN

(*In a vampire voice.*) Then I'll bite you. Come on, shake hands.

They shake hands. Dan pulls Norma to him. He kisses her. At first she doesn't react, but then she kisses him back.

NORMA

I don't know about this.

DAN

Me neither, but it's been on my mind ever since I first saw you.

NORMA

Me too, but I never expected it to happen.

DAN

I don't regret it. Do you?

NORMA

Shut up, Dan O'Malley, and come here.

They kiss again. As the lights are lowered, "Because the Nights Were Made for Lovers" comes up. Once the lights are out, strobe light comes up, then someone is seen being killed in slow motion. Music stops.

Blackout.

Scene Three

SETTING: Inside the Community Center.

As the curtain rises, Teresa, Norma, and Monique sit around talking. Luke enters, crying.

TERESA

Luke—what's wrong? Is June all right?

LUKE

It's not June. Harvey's been murdered. They found him an hour ago. He was mutilated and scalped.

NORMA

Oh my God—no!

MONIQUE

I was afraid of something like this.

They embrace each other. Buffalo Springfield music comes up, then fades down, but continues.

LUKE

(*Enraged.*) I'll get them for this! What are we supposed to do? What choice do they leave us but violence?

Norma walks to a corner. Teresa stays close to Luke. Monique stands with her back against the wall. All of them are extremely angered.

LUKE

They're so violent toward us! What are we supposed to do? They've divided our council, aye. They've got us at each others' throats. Indian against Indian. Brother against brother. They've killed Harvey, and why? Because they want to flood our land—our goddamned land is what they want. They'll do anything to get it. Man, I wanna, I wanna . . . oh man!

Luke breaks down and sobs violently. Teresa cradles his head. Norma sits crying silently on the floor. Monique stands with her back against the wall, then crumbles to the floor.

LUKE

Oh man! (*Still sobbing.*) I have to fight! (*Still sobbing.*) No choice! (*Still sobs.*) My friend. He was my friend. I gotta fight. Oh man!

TERESA

(*Pulls Luke into her arms.*) Come here. (*Rocks him in her arms.*) Take it easy, Luke. We're going to do something.

Monique goes over and puts her arms around both of them. Norma also goes over to join them. They all sob. Buffalo Springfield music comes up a little.

TERESA

We have to do something. We've got to take care of his body . . . arrangements.

MONIQUE

> All my life—all my goddamned life, I get this. It's so hard. It's so damned hard. Who wants this land of ours, anyway? Some big company in the States? Why are they doing this to us—to people like me? I'm nineteen years old, and all my life I've had sadness. I wanna live . . . I wanna be happy. I . . . just . . . wanna enjoy. . . my life. What can we do? What? Someone tell me. PLEASE.

Monique breaks down and cries. Buffalo Springfield music comes up loudly for a minute, then lowers again. Enter June.

NORMA

> (*Sees June.*) Harvey's been killed! We don't know what to do.

JUNE

> I know. I heard.

TERESA

> Tell us, Grandmother, what should we do?

JUNE

> I don't know for sure, but right now we do nothing. We do nothing but take care of ourselves. That's the first thing we have to do.

MONIQUE

> I'm scared. I don't know what to think. Who's going to be next. Me? You? Luke? Who?

June hugs Monique, then goes to Luke.

JUNE

> Are you all right, Grandson? I came as soon as I heard.

Jackson enters, carrying a gun.

JACKSON

> I'm ready. How are we going to do this?

JUNE

> Oh Jackson!

JACKSON

> I'm not taking anymore, Grandmother. I'm ready. I've had it up to here. This is it for me. All my life I've had to take it from them for being an Indian . . . and gay. No more! Do you understand? NO MORE! Come on, Luke, we can do something—or die trying. I'm not ready to lay down or turn the other cheek. No more! I'm not taking no more!

Luke stands up, goes to Jackson, and hugs him. Both are crying.

LUKE

You're a brother warrior. (*Turns to June.*) I'm sorry, Grandmother, I shouldn't be crying, but I'm HURTING right now! And I want to fight. Maybe they'll kill us, but not before we do something to them. This is my brother. I've seen the pain he feels, not only because he's an Indian but because he's gay. And what does that got to do with his human worth? I'm proud to have him at my side in this fight.

JACKSON

And I'm proud to be there. I'll die for these people if I have to. They're my people, and that's why I'm crying—but I'm through crying now, and I'm ready.

JUNE

Oh, you boys! I love both of you so much. It's okay to cry. We're all humans. It's okay to be scared, Monique. It's okay to be angry, Jackson. I know what society has done to you because you're gay. We're all very angry and we react in our own way, but we are strong people. We'll do what we have to, but we'll do it right. Let me sit in this chair. (*Jackson helps, and June sits.*) Come here, all of you. Gather round me. Come closer, all of you. You don't know how much comfort you give to an old lady. (*They all gather round her on the floor.*) Remember how we used to do this? Oh, how my heart hurts right now. It feels like a piece of it has been torn away! (*She puts her face in her hands and sobs for a minute.*)

LUKE

(*Very angry.*) I'm going to get revenge. I'll blow them and their goddamned Hydro Project straight to hell. I'll get them for all the hurt. I swear to you people—they'll pay!

JACKSON

I'm with you too, bro. We're on their asses now. They'll pay—the bastards.

Music stops.

TERESA

(*Hugging Jackson.*) Jackson the militant faggot. Ain't that what that white girl said?

JUNE

Oh, you two! Our sweet, sweet boys. Always there to protect us. Our little warriors. You two were always our guardians, even when you were little boys. You remember when we used to pick blueberries along the railroad tracks? You'd both be carrying them little sticks, just in case a bear came along. You'd stand over us while we picked berries.

TERESA

(*Smiling.*) Because they didn't want to pick berries. "Girls work" is what they used to say. They just didn't like picking berries.

JUNE

Of course we all knew that, but it was good to have them standing guard, just in case. Remember how we used to stop, and they'd have this little fire going for us?

NORMA

So you could boil your tea. That was long before Jackson . . .

JACKSON

Came out of the closet. God, I remember those times like they were yesterday. And then when people started dating, I felt—aw, forget it!

JUNE

And Monique, you'd always bring along some bannock. We'd just sit there and enjoy the world around us. The trees, the birds singing, and the wind. Remember how we'd listen to the wind?

NORMA

And you'd tell us those stories.

MONIQUE

I remember that! I was so little. I used to make a big deal about our lunch—and Jackson would help me serve.

JACKSON

And Luke would tease me and call me "the waiter . . . ress." He always added the "ress."

JUNE

You'd cut up the bannock and make sure each of us got a fair share. And Norma, you'd lay on your back, at my feet, and look up at the clouds and tell us what you saw in them. Oh, you were the dreamer—our little Indian artist.

NORMA

Yes, I remember that. It was so much fun. Harvey would lay next to me, and . . . and . . . what will we do without him? He's always been a part of us. (*Norma cries.*)

JUNE

He'll always be with us in our memories. His spirit is still with us. Harvey Two Kill will never be forgotten. Oh, we're going to miss him every day for the rest of our lives, but we have to remember that life goes on. Teresa will bring us a baby. Maybe it'll be a boy, and we'll name him after Harvey. (*Pause. Looks around at the young people.*) We're going to do what we have to. We're Indians—don't any of you ever

forget that. Our history is part of this land. Our childhood
dreams and memories are here.

*June starts to hum an Indian chant. She reaches and pulls all of them
closer.*

JUNE

Every piece of ground that we walk on, we are walking on
the bones of our relatives and ancestors. Their spirits are
everywhere, and they'll protect us. We'll show them that
they can't come in here and scare us. (*Long pause.*) Come
here—all of you. Come hug me, Norma. We'll need your
compassion. (*Short pause.*) Monique, your fear will make us
cautious. (*Touches Luke's heart.*) Luke your anger will help us
be stronger. Come here, all of you, I want to give you
something. Come closer. Share our spirits. Come closer with
your bodies and your minds. Umbae Anishinaabe. (*Reaches
for Jackson.*) Come closer, Jackson—we need your strength.
Give us what you have always had to draw upon. Let's hug.

*They all embrace, and as a group they sway. Monique breaks away from
the group and begins to recite poem.*

MONIQUE

The Coyote spirit is silent,
trampled by the greedy feet of profit,
run, run to northern lights.

Rest of cast joins in.

The spirit journey has begun,
the soul has taken flight,
northern lights crackled on a silent night,
they buried him crying in Indian ground.
The weeping; an angered sound,
brown eyes flash in rage,
Native hearts churn,
the anguish strikes
like lightning storms.
A bond, an alliance formed,
spirits welded in common cause,
furious, like a panther's claws,
deception hidden in rich man's eyes,
for their brother a nation cries . . .

*Bass drum—boom, boom, boom. Rattle, fading out. A single female
Indian voice begins to sing, carrying into the next scene.*

Blackout.

Scene Four

SETTING: Inside the Community Center.

As the curtain rises, a group of people works at making protest signs. The phone rings. Norma answers it. Music stops.

NORMA

Hello, Joel—glad you called. (*Pause.*) They took him in to question him about the murder of Harvey? Wait a minute, Joel. She's right here. (*Turns to Teresa.*) Teresa—it's Joel. You should talk to him.

TERESA

(*Goes to the phone.*) Hey, Joel. What's going on? (*Pause.*) He would never kill anybody! What happened? (*Pause.*) Oh my God . . . no. This is a setup. (*Pause.*) What do you mean, stay away? Hell no! I'm coming down there right now to find out about this. (*Pause.*) Thank God! He was so angry about Harvey. (*Pause.*) Thanks, Joel. We will—you can bet your ass on that.

Teresa hangs up and turns to the others.

TERESA

Luke was arrested.

MONIQUE

For what?

NORMA

He wasn't really arrested. They just took him in for questioning.

TERESA

Joel said they took others besides Luke.

NORMA

Who?

TERESA

Billy John was the first.

MONIQUE

Billy John? He's just a kid. He's only seventeen.

TERESA

(*To Monique.*) They got your dad too.

MONIQUE

My dad? Arrested for murder? No way!

NORMA

We have to mobilize some people.

TERESA

Norma's right. Those guys need community support. I'm going over there.

MONIQUE

   I'm with you.

JACKSON

   Count me in. Man, I'm so sick of this. I wanna kick some
   ass. Some white official ass. This is one pissed-off faggot,
   aye! I'll show them the meaning of militant faggot!

MONIQUE

   Don't forget your purse.

JACKSON

   I got it, baby, and you know what? I'll use it too.

CAST

   Right on, Jackson!

NORMA

   They'd like nothing better than to arrest more of us. Be cool.

*Buffalo Springfield music comes up as the cast leaves stage. A protest
sign that says "Justice" is left in the middle of the stage. Light focuses
on the sign as the stage goes dark.*

Blackout.

Scene Five

SETTING: Police interrogation room.

*As the curtain rises, Luke sits handcuffed to a chair. Two police officers
question him—Officer Murray and Officer Ericson.*

ERICSON

   Now, let's go over this one more time. Where were you at
   two A.M.?

LUKE

   After the powwow me, my wife, and Norma Gray Wolf
   and Dan O'Malley cleaned up the Center, then I went home
   with my wife. That was about midnight. I stayed home.

MURRAY

   (*Slaps Luke.*) Dan O'Malley? He works for the Hydro Company. You're lying, Luke. You found out Harvey was
   working for the company, so you killed him. Isn't that right?

LUKE

   I didn't kill anybody.

MURRAY

   (*Grabs Luke by the hair.*) Bullshit! I know you killed Harvey,
   and I'm the one who's going to prove it. Now tell me the
   truth!

LUKE

> I didn't do nothing. I have nothing to tell, aye.

Murray slaps Luke and knocks him out of the chair. He starts to kick Luke. Officer Ericson pulls him off.

MURRAY

> You Goddammed blanket ass. You're going to confess.

ERICSON

> Back off, Murray! We're police officers, not SS troopers. I don't think he did it.

MURRAY

> The company wants it settled.

ERICSON

> I don't give a shit what they want. They ain't doing right up here.

MURRAY

> That's where we differ, you and me. (*Pause.*) Do you have any idea how many white men depend on that company to feed their white kids? Just think about it! (*Pause.*) Leave me alone with him for a minute—I'm not going to hurt him. I just want to talk to him. He needs to know some facts of life. Can you do that for a brother officer? Huh?

ERICSON

> Remember, no rough stuff.

Ericson exits. Murray bends down to talk to Luke, who still lies on the floor.

MURRAY

> (*Grabs Luke by the hair.*) Listen close to what I'm about to say. You have a nice looking little wife. You're not there to protect her, aye. You're putting her in danger by refusing to cooperate. (*Short pause.*) This Two Kill thing, I know you didn't do it, but your cards just fell wrong, Luke. If you don't give me a written confession, I can't promise that your pretty little wife is gonna be okay. Do you understand what I'm telling you, Luke? You're taking the fall on this thing. You have to do it to protect that pretty little lady of yours. Now what about it, Luke?

Luke starts singing an Indian chant. Murray kicks him and calls for a guard.

MURRAY

> Guard! Guard! Throw this blanket-ass Indian into a cell. I'll be back in the morning. Dream about your sweet little lady tonight, Luke.

Luke lies on the floor and calls Teresa's name. Spotlight on Luke dims slowly as instrumental portion of Cowboy Junkies comes up.)

Blackout.

Scene Six

SETTING: Inside the Community Center.

As the curtain rises, Norma and Teresa are deep in conversation. Music is still playing, but it is very low.

NORMA

It's important, Teresa. Right now we have to stay strong.

TERESA

I'm so tried of trying to be strong. My old man's been busted, and I'm afraid for him.

NORMA

That's natural. Don't worry—it'll go away.

TERESA

I'm worried about the baby too. All this stress! I tell you, it's not good. *(Pause.)* First Harvey! Then Luke! What else can go wrong?

NORMA

In a few days everything will settle down. Luke will be home, and we'll go on with our lives. You can practice at being a mom, and I'll think about how to be the best aunt in town. Won't it be nice to have a baby in the family? We'll spoil it rotten.

TERESA

(Sighs loudly.) I hope you're right. *(Short pause.)* Well we better get this place cleaned up.

Suddenly the door is kicked in. Three hooded terrorists rush in. One with a knife goes after Norma. The other two go after Teresa, who grabs a broom.

TERRORIST ONE

Get the bitch! That broom won't save you. You're mine.

Teresa swings at Terrorist Two. Terrorist One punches her and knocks her down. Terrorist Three in the meantime has managed to put the knife to Norma's throat. Teresa has fallen behind a scrim with back lighting. Terrorist Two has Teresa in a full nelson. Norma is quiet and breathes heavily. Her eyes are wide with fear.

TERRORIST ONE
> Hold her! Don't let her get away.

Terrorist One stands in front of Teresa and begins to undo his pants.

TERRORIST ONE
> These two bitches like demonstrations? I guarantee they're gonna see a demonstration tonight. Ever see your sister get laid, Norma? I'll demonstrate your rights, bitch. Make her look.

Behind the scrim, with back lighting, Teresa tries to kick Terrorist One in the groin area. He starts punching her. Teresa struggles silently. Norma is still breathing very hard, and her eyes bulge with fear.

TERRORIST TWO
> Stick it to the squaw. Give her the old John Wayne.

TERESA
> No, please! Get out! Please stop!

Teresa stops struggling and is quiet. The only sounds are the man's grunting and Norma's crying.

TERRORIST TWO
> (*In a loud whisper.*) Is it good? I get seconds.

TERRORIST THREE
> Then I get a turn with this hellcat.

As he talks, the knife moves away from Norma's throat. She bites his hand. He hollers and drops the knife. Norma dashes out the door.

TERRORIST ONE
> Oh shit! Why'd you let her get away?

TERRORIST THREE
> She bit me! Goddammed squaw bit me on the hand.

TERRORIST ONE
> We got to get our asses out of here.

TERRORIST TWO
> (*Whining voice.*) What are you talking about? I didn't get none! I want some too.

TERRORIST ONE
> No time! We have to get out of here.

TERRORIST TWO
> This ain't fair. You said we could do whatever we wanted to do with the squaws.

TERRORIST THREE
> He's right. We have to get out of here. Whole town'll be here in a few minutes.

TERRORIST TWO
> It's all your fault. Why didn't you hold on to that timber-nigger bitch?

TERRORIST THREE
> I done told you, she bit my goddamned hand.

TERRORIST ONE
> Let's head out of here. I mean right now!

Terrorists exit. Lights come down slowly as Teresa crawls center stage. She cries and calls for Luke. Indian music starts to play, continuing to next scene.

Blackout.

Scene Seven

SETTING: A hospital room. A small beeping sound suggests a hospital.

Indian music stops.

As the curtain rises, Teresa lies in bed. Norma enters slowly. Teresa sees her and reaches for her.

NORMA
> Oh Teresa, baby.

TERESA
> What will I tell Luke? (*The sisters hug.*)

NORMA
> The truth.

TERESA
> I don't want to hurt him—especially now. I'm afraid he might blame me. (*Pause.*) Norma, did you see them rape me?

NORMA
> They made me look.

TERESA
> I feel so guilty. (*Pause.*) I'm so ashamed.

NORMA
> None of this was your fault. Those animals attacked us.

They hug and cry again.

TERESA
> What's happening to Luke?

NORMA
> They charged him with murder. He's been officially charged.

TERESA

He didn't do it. There's no way. There's no way he could have. He was with me.

NORMA

Just relax if you can. Things will turn out all right.

TERESA

This whole thing's turned out to be a big nightmare. What's going to happen to us?

Norma has no answer for her question.

TERESA

Is this the end of us as we knew ourselves? I'm afraid, Norma. For you, me, Luke, and everyone else.

NORMA

You would be really proud of this town—the way things are coming together. The whole town—I mean Indians and whites. Everyone is mad at the company. The tribal council has suspended any and all talks.

TERESA

Time they got some spine about themselves. So I didn't catch this beating for nothing, aye.

NORMA

There's more, too. Dan's been helping out a lot lately. You know, he's a pretty sharp organizer. He's doing everything he can to get Luke out.

TERESA

Dan O'Malley? What about his old lady?

NORMA

They broke up. He's staying at the house. (*Short pause.*) It's not what you think, so get rid of that grin.

TERESA

Aye!

NORMA

Well, I can see you're getting better. Mind's still in the gutter.

TERESA

(*Yawns.*) I'm feeling sleepy, though. This medicine is kicking my Indian ass.

NORMA

(*Tucks blanket around her.*) Go to sleep, then. I'll be right here.

TERESA

Norma, I love you.

NORMA

I love you too.

TERESA

(*After a pause.*) They made me feel so dirty.

NORMA

Don't. You have to get past that. June said she'd come this evening.

TERESA

It's so unfair—to me, to Luke. I don't know if I'll ever be able to let him touch me like I used to.

NORMA

Luke loves you. He's not a stupid man. He'll understand.

TERESA

I hope you're right. (*Short pause.*) I just can't get it out of my mind. It keeps coming back.

Norma hugs Teresa and begins to hum a lullaby.

NORMA

Remember this?

TERESA

I sure do. (*Short pause.*) I miss Mom so much. Especially right now.

NORMA

I know you do. So do I.

Norma continues to hum the song as lights are lowered slowly.

Blackout.

Scene Eight

SETTING: Bare stage.

As the curtain rises, Brenda talks on the phone at the front of the stage. A male dancer dances slowly in background. Music is soft but gets louder as the pace of the dance picks up.

BRENDA

(*On phone.*) Daddy, it's me. Dan's left me! He's blaming the whole thing on me. (*Short pause.*) No Daddy, that's not the way it was. His name was Harvey Two Kill—ugh, he's some kind of Coyote spirit. (*Pause. Teresa enters the stage. She sits on the floor with a blanket wrapped around her.*) I know you've got a significant investment up here. (*Short pause.*) Naturally I'll do everything I can to protect that, Daddy. I'll do whatever is necessary. (*Pause.*) Yes Daddy, I did make threats, but I was mad. I lost my temper. The only one who could have heard me is Dan. He's become totally against us. It's like they've brainwashed him. (*Short pause.*) Norma Gray Wolf? She's a slut, Daddy. It was her sister that got herself raped.

The music begins to get faster and louder. The male dancer responds. He begins to move in Brenda's direction, then backs away. Teresa begins to sway with the music.

BRENDA

I'm feeling very isolated up here. I'm getting scared, Daddy. You know what I mean? I'm feeling like . . . ugh, I'm all jumpy. I keep smelling this smell. It's like they're burning sage or something. It's really weird. It wasn't my fault, but people are looking at me like it was. They don't say nothing—they just look. Even the whites are doing it. I want to get out of here, the sooner the better.

The music gets faster and louder. The dancer comes closer than before. He does lots of twirls and dips. Teresa covers her head with a blanket. Her body reacts to the music.

BRENDA

Daddy, things are getting out of control here. I need to get out of here. That guy, Harvey Two Kill. I'm scared, Daddy.

Suddenly the stage is lit up by the strobe light. The killing of Harvey Two Kill is repeated, at first in slow motion. Then it becomes faster and more violent looking. Teresa gets to her feet and dances too.

BRENDA

I will, Daddy. Stay away from everybody? I'll do like you say. I won't talk to anybody. Can I come back to Chicago? You'll send the plane? Oh thank you, Daddy. To Europe? Okay. Daddy, you're such a hero. Bye-Bye, Daddy.

Brenda stays seated, and the surrounding action is in a total frenzy. The male dancer is twirling. Teresa is fancy-dancing. Harvey Two Kill falls center stage. Blood comes from his throat, which has been slashed. Suddenly the music stops. Both dancers are in a crouched position. The lights are snapped off and a female voice trills. A newscaster's voice can be heard.

VOICE

And in tonight's news, we bring you a detailed report from the Canadian backwoods. A group of dissenting Native Americans went on the war path against the Hydro Electric Company owned by Chicago-area businessman George McGinnis. Reliable sources report that the rampaging Indians burned company headquarters, bombed a dam, and seized control of the local radio station. Company officials estimated the damage to be more than twenty million dollars.

In an unprecedented turn of events, Luke Frambeau, an activist with the group who had been arrested and charged with the murder of Harvey Two Kill, was released from jail and all charges were dropped. Henry Licorice, head of company security and information, reportedly cleared the young Indian militant in a statement to the Royal Canadian Mounted Police in which he named Ontario Provincial Police officer Reginald Murray as the assailant. Murray and two unnamed accomplices were also charged with the beating and raping of a local Indian woman. Licorice, a decorated war hero from the Vietnam era, reportedly has said he will join the resistance movement to block further construction of the project.

Businessman George McGinnis was not available for comment. His attorney, Gus Maxwell, stated that the company has abandoned all plans to further the construction project. Brenda McGinnis, daughter of George McGinnis, has taken an extended vacation in Europe.

Licorice went on to say that he has provided the Indian Tribal Council with documents and taped conversations which prove that company officials had doctored environmental-impact studies and altered contracts.

There is a happy ending to this whole episode. Dan O'Malley, formerly a consultant with the Hydro Company, announced that he will marry Norma Gray Wolf, a leader of the Indian resistance movement. And now—on to other news. Stocks on Wall Street . . .

Bass drum beats three times, then fades out with rattle.

Blackout.

Old Indian Trick, or
An Old Urban Indian Story
as Told by an Old Urban Indian
Who May Have Lied

A PLAY IN TWO ACTS

CHARACTERS

JOE RUNS FAST: Fifty-year-old Anishinaabe, dressed nicely. Relocated to Chicago as a teenager with the Relocation Act of 1952 from a small Indian reserve in northwestern Ontario. An old hustler/gangster, Joe owns a car lot and several hot-dog stands. Has a taste for younger women.

CARLOS HIGH FLYING: Anishinaabe, mid-twenties. A street operative for Joe. A very stylish dresser, who carries a gun, smokes fancy cigars, and likes women. Considers himself a ladies' man.

TINA SILVER-HAND: Navajo, early twenties. Attractive, wears lots of silver and turquoise jewelry. Graduated from high school. Has a child but no husband. Is having an affair with Joe. Aggressive, works hard at her job, and is loyal to Joe.

MANNY GARCIA: Joe's old pal, around fifty years old. A gangster with a bad reputation. Operates in Milwaukee, but wants Joe's operations. An old street soldier, he carries a big, big gun—a .357 Magnum. Is crude and rude to women.

LILLIAN SANCHEZ: A detective on Joe's tail. Is having an affair with Manny. Is into S&M and other sexual perversions. Wants Joe's operations and maybe even Tina Silver-Hand.

GAIL STEELE: Educated Lakota, with degrees in all kinds of things. Attractive and well endowed. Is the lover of Vernon, a Lakota medicine man whom Joe befriended as a younger man.

VERNON: A Lakota medicine man. Never seen, but his voice is heard in telephone conversations.

ACT ONE

Scene One

SETTING: A dimly lit alley, with several silver garbage cans sitting against the wall.

As the curtain rises, it is late night. William Tell Overture *plays softly, then, when house lights are lowered, comes up to an uncomfortable level. Lights are up halfway. Music stops. A man runs onstage, pleading with Joe and Carlos.*

CARLOS

I got the bastard. (*Grabs the man.*) Get up against the wall, asshole. (*Carlos throws him against the wall.*)

MAN

Please, Joe, I didn't mean to stiff you. I'll pay—I promise.

JOE

How many times you told me that before? I want my money. All of it, by five. Is that clear?

CARLOS

Answer the man, bitch.

MAN

Yes, it is.

CARLOS

No more chances. If you ain't got it, you're a dead man. You dig what I'm saying? (*Carlos punches the man.*)

MAN

Don't let him hurt me, Joe. I'll get the money.

JOE

All of it, by five, or Carlos comes after you. I hate to do this, but asshole deadbeats, like you, force me to.

CARLOS

Now, get your ass out of here. (*Kicks at the man and misses, pulls a leg muscle.*) Next time I won't miss.

The Man exits.

JOE

(*Sitting on garbage can and breathing hard.*) I swear, I'm getting too old for this shit. What's wrong with you?

CARLOS

(*Dances around holding his leg.*) I pulled something. (*Pause.*) From now on I'll work the streets. You kick back and relax. Hell, Joe, you earned it.

JOE

(*Looks at Carlos.*) Thanks, but I got other plans for you—besides, you're always hurting yourself. Even more than you hurt those other guys.

CARLOS

He was just lucky, that's all. (*Pause.*) What you got in mind?

JOE

I want you to go out west and work with Vito for a while.

CARLOS

Vito? Why him?

JOE

To learn how they run their numbers game. It'll only be for a year.

CARLOS

Shit, Joe, those west coast guys are a bunch of nuts. You can't trust them. Anyway, what's to learn? We don't need them.

JOE

(*Sternly.*) Listen, and I'll tell you.

CARLOS

Okay—I'm all ears, old man.

JOE

Don't call me old man. You're an Indian . . . though sometimes a piss-poor example of one. You're supposed to respect your elders, not call them "old man." (*Puts his arm around Carlos.*)

CARLOS

You're right! Okay? I listen.

JOE

Yeah, you gotta listen—and listen good, too.

CARLOS

You gonna preach at me?

JOE

You darned right I am. It's important. One screw-up and we both could be fish food. There is no room for mistakes. (*Short pause.*) No room—you got that?

CARLOS

Yeah, Joe, I dig what you're saying. I'll be careful. Count on it. Hey—that's why they call me the man out here, because I'm always careful. I'm a pro, Joe, don't ya know?

JOE

Okay! Okay! Cut with the riddles. Just remember when you go out west—be sure to watch your ass every minute. You don't, and we're screwed royal. (*Joe and Carlos exit.*)

Blackout.

Scene Two

SETTING: Joe's inner office, decorated with Indian accents. A couch and matching chair face Joe's desk.

As the curtain rises, Joe Runs Fast sits at his desk talking on the phone.

JOE

Vito, my man! It's Joe out of Chicago. (*Short pause. Joe grins broadly.*) Hey, pal, it's cold as a cat's ass. You know Chicago, it'll pass. You learn to live with it. It's the best you can git so you don't throw a fit. Anyway, ain't nobody gives a shit. (*Pause. Joe listens intently.*) I'm gonna be honest with you. The kid called out of the blue this morning, and I gave him the warning. (*Pause.*) Vito, the kid was flat broke. I promised him some bread and told him it was no joke. (*Pause.*) That's what don't make no sense, Vito. He didn't have bus fare on him. (*Pause.*) Hey, I want you to know that I appreciate you letting me do this my way. (*Pause.*) He knows that, Vito. He understands he gotta pay. (*Pause.*) That's right. You're right on the money. You look into it over there, and I'll do the same. I ain't making a move until I hear from you. Okay, my man. Chiao! I'll be in touch. Keep me posted.

Joe hangs up the phone and walks around nervously. Tina enters.

JOE

Good morning, Tina. Nice outfit. I like it. Is it new? It looks real good on you.

TINA

(*Poses for Joe.*) Glad you like it. It cost me an arm and a leg.

JOE

(*Looks appreciatively at her legs.*) Doesn't cover very much of them if you ask me.

TINA

You complaining?

JOE

No! No! (*Walks to his desk and sits down.*) I got a lot to do today. (*Picks up a folder.*) Would you mind typing out this form for me? When you're done, run over to city hall and get me those guidelines for minority status.

TINA

I'd be happy to.

JOE

Make sure you get the right forms this time. Okay? No screw-ups! You got that?

TINA

I understand. God—you worry so much sometimes. You're gonna give yourself a heart attack like that.

JOE

I gotta worry, Tina. Do you believe this city government? They don't recognize Indians as a minority. What the hell do they think we are, anyway?

TINA

I don't even try to understand their logic.

JOE

They say there ain't enough of us. (*Pause.*) That's a bunch of bullshit too. If we wanted to be technical, then all those Spanish people should be counted as Indians too. You know what I mean—every one of them is part Indian. They ought to be counted as Indians too. Hell do you realize that at least one in every six people in the whole world is some kinda Indian or other? There's a bunch of us. (*Pause, looks Tina over.*) Come here for a minute, would you? You're looking real good in that dress.

TINA

What you got in mind, huh? (*She poses provocatively and smiles.*) I can think of something. (*She walks behind his desk and begins to rub his shoulders.*)

JOE

That feels so good. Sometimes I don't know what I'd do without you.

TINA

(*Leans over and kisses him.*) How does that feel?

JOE

You know what you do to a man? (*Pulls her onto his lap and they kiss a long time.*)

TINA

Hmmm. Maybe I'll just stay in the office with you.

JOE

No can do, baby.

TINA

Then maybe we have time for a quickie before he gets here.

JOE

Who?

TINA

That guy. What's his name? (*Snaps her fingers.*) Oh yeah, Carlos Flying Feather.

JOE

High Flying, not Flying Feather.

TINA

Whatever! I knew it had something to do with flight. In more ways than one, too. You better be careful. (*Pause.*) What's he like?

Joe ignores her.

TINA

Well?

JOE

You ask too many questions, you know that. (*Joe gets up and walks.*) It's not always the healthiest thing to do. (*Pause.*) I guess he's a lot like me.

TINA

And just exactly what is that?

JOE

Never mind all the questions, okay? Get your sweet buns over to city hall and take care of some business. That's what I pay you to do. (*Pause.*) By the way, take the rest of the day off.

TINA

With pay? I can't afford no days without pay. I got a kid to support. She likes to eat.

JOE

Yes, with pay.

TINA

Thanks, Joe. You be careful . . . about this guy Carlos. Don't let him get you into trouble. I have this feeling, Joe.

JOE

Don't even go there, honey. Don't worry, I got everything under control. I don't want to hear anything about any of your goddamned hunches. (*Pause.*) And another thing— stay off of the phone when I'm talking. You understand?

Tina exits without answering. Joe walks to the window. There is a soft knock on the door. At first he doesn't hear it. On the second knock he turns to face the door.

JOE

It's open. (*Carlos enters, wearing a large coat and smoking a cigar.*) How are you, kid? Damn, it's good to see you. Come here, give me a hug.

The men embrace.

CARLOS

It's good to see you too, Joe.

JOE

> What's with the getup? Sure as hell isn't your style.

CARLOS

> You can say that again. Just being careful, Joe. You never know. (*Pause. He removes coat.*) Did you hear anything from the West Coast?

JOE

> I sure as hell did. What the heck went down out there, anyway? (*Pause. Carlos shakes his head.*) You know they put out a contract on you?

CARLOS

> What about the money? Can you let me get it? (*Joe reaches into his desk and pulls out a pile of bills.*) Joe, I want you to know that I appreciate this.

JOE

> I know you do. Now tell me what the heck happened. I told you to be careful.

CARLOS

> I was, Joe. I did everything like they told me. I didn't know they made me a counter so they could use me to rip themselves off.

JOE

> Is that what they did? (*Laughs.*) You expect anybody to believe that?

CARLOS

> I'm serious, Joe. Dead serious. I never took a dime from them. Not one thin dime.

JOE

> We'll get it straightened out, but it'll take time. You're gonna have to lay low. You never know who's gonna try to get famous. Vito's looking into it on his end, but that council insisted a contract be put out on you. It's pending.

CARLOS

> Those guys are animals. They rip each other off right and left.

JOE

> I know how they are. Honor among thieves? Don't make me laugh. (*Pause.*) There is one other thing, kid.

CARLOS

> Yeah, and what's that?

JOE

> The bastards offered me the contract.

CARLOS

> And?

JOE

> I had to accept it. You know that.

CARLOS

> Aw, don't be messing with me, Joe.

JOE

> I wish I was kid, but you know how it is.

CARLOS

> You know you don't accept a contract from them unless you plan to carry it out. Shit, Joe—those guys don't play. What the hell are you thinking about? You should have told them to go to hell.

JOE

> Yeah, right. Hey—I know they don't play. Neither did I. How do you think I got ahead of the game, anyway? I have a plan. (*Short pause.*) I have every intention of delivering.

CARLOS

> What?

JOE

> Like I said, I got a plan.

CARLOS

> You gonna kill me, Joe? No disrespect meant, but it's not all that simple. My gun's pointed at you right now.

JOE

> Like you're gonna shoot me! (*Pause and stare at each other. Carlos doesn't waver a bit.*) I'll be goddamned.

CARLOS

> I swear, Joe, I didn't take a dime.

JOE

> I believe you. (*Pause.*) Look—just give me a little time to work out the details. You lay low and give me some time. (*Pushes the money across the desk to Carlos. He picks it up and starts counting.*)

CARLOS

> Thanks, Joe.

JOE

> You got enough money there to take a short trip to the country. Go up north to a powwow or something. Go see that Menominee girlfriend of yours. Just let me know how to contact you, okay?

CARLOS

> Maybe. Maybe not. I'm tired of running.

JOE

> Look, Carlos, you have to trust me on this one. You're my guy . . . I'll do what I have to. You understand me, pal?

CARLOS

It's not that I don't trust you, Joe. It's just that I know how them guys are. (*Pause. He crosses the room to peek out the window.*) Okay, Joe—I'll do it your way but I ain't leaving the city. I'll go to a different neighborhood where no one knows me.

JOE

Just a few days, okay?

Carlos nods, and they hug. Carlos exits. Joe sits at his desk with a pistol that he begins to clean. There is a loud aggressive knock on the door.

JOE

Come on in. (*Manny enters.*) Manny! You son of a bitch! Where the hell you been?

The men embrace.

MANNY

Milwaukee. My businesses keep me humping. I practically live for them nowadays.

JOE

I know what you mean. Hey, but I know you—you love it. This is what we always talked about when we were young. Hell, Manny, we're living our dreams. Sit down, take a load off.

MANNY

You got a new girl or something? (*Manny sits in a chair next to Joe's desk.*) This place is so clean. How the hell do you get any work done?

JOE

What you doing in Chicago?

MANNY

Passing through. (*Short pause.*) You look good, Joe.

JOE

You don't look like you're missing any meals either. Now, what are you really doing here?

MANNY

Okay! Okay! Never could fool you. It's about business. (*Leans closer to Joe.*) Listen up. I ran up on a real good deal awhile ago. Got a truckload of those CB radios. You know, those kind truckers use. Some home-base radios too. Thought maybe you'd like some of them. I'll cut you a good deal.

JOE

That's why you stopped by? (*Laughs.*) To sell me some goddamned radios? Do they work?

MANNY

Hey, Joe! Come on, man, would I do you that way? I wanted to see you, too. You're my pal. We're a couple of old guys, me and you. What is it you used to call us? Oh yeah—old dog soldiers. You remember that, Joe? I sure do.

JOE

Sure I do.

MANNY

I'd be here more often if I wasn't so busy. I'm telling you. Those businesses are killing me. That's just the straight up stuff—my legitimate businesses. Hell, I don't even got time to go out and steal anymore.

JOE

You're too old to be out there stealing, anyway. (*Pause.*) You still drink Scotch on the rocks?

MANNY

Only the good stuff. No more of that rot-gut stuff. My system can't take it anymore.

JOE

For you, the best.

As Joe pours the drinks, Manny stands up and inspects the room. He looks in ashtrays, picks up a cigar butt, and puts it in his pocket as Joe turns around. Joe brings the drinks to his desk and sits down. He watches Manny pace around the room.

JOE

Manny—sit down and enjoy your drink, would you? You're making me nervous. What's wrong, anyway?

MANNY

I need a vacation.

JOE

That would be nice.

MANNY

Why don't we go camping like we used to do?

JOE

Last time you complained about everything.

MANNY

In the old days we would have.

JOE

We were much younger then.

MANNY

That's true, but we could always count on each other. Always!

JOE

You can still count on me, Manny.

MANNY

But things are so much different now. More complicated.

JOE

More complicated?

The conversation slows almost to a standstill. The mood is becoming intense.

MANNY

Like that thing about your boy Carlos. I hear things, Joe.

JOE

Like what?

MANNY

Rumor is that he stole lots of money. From Vito. Now why the hell would he do something like that?

JOE

I don't know. (*Picks up his drink.*) I haven't talked to him.

MANNY

Are you sure about that?

They stare at each other for a long time. Suddenly Joe jumps to his feet.

JOE

Jesus Christ, Manny, you're on fire.

Manny jumps up and starts slapping at his jacket pocket. He pulls out a half-burned cigar.

MANNY

The only guy I know who smokes these faggot cigars is Carlos. (*He throws the cigar into an ashtray and puts out the fire in his jacket by pouring his drink in it.*) This is a five-hundred-dollar jacket. He was here, Joe. Why you lying to me?

JOE

Me? Lying to you? Would you get serious? (*Laughing.*) I smoke them too now.

Joe reaches into his desk and pulls out a package of cigars. Throws them on the table.

MANNY

I gotta get out of here. I'll send you a bill for the jacket.

JOE

Why? I didn't put no lit cigar in your pocket. You did. Serves you right.

MANNY

Damn it, Joe. I gotta go. Bye!

Manny exits. Joe refreshes his drink and sits at his desk. He puts his head back as though he is very tired.

Blackout.

Scene Three

SETTING: Joe's office.

As the curtain rises, Joe and Carlos sit talking at Joe's desk.

JOE

Damn—didn't I tell you to lay low?

CARLOS

I know, but I need to know what the hell is going on. I can't stand being in the dark on this. You know what I mean?

JOE

You never listen to what the hell I tell you. What's wrong with you? What you got in that head? Shit for brains or something?

CARLOS

If it was the other way around, would you sit tight? (*Pause.*) Well, would you? I know you wouldn't.

JOE

But it ain't me who messed up.

CARLOS

Joe I done told you—I didn't take a dime. They're lying. The whole bunch of them.

A knock at door. Both men instinctively reach for their guns.

JOE

Who the hell is it?

TINA

(*Offstage.*) It's me, Tina. (*She enters.*)

JOE

What are you doing back here?

Tina and Carlos glance at each other with obvious interest.

TINA

You won't believe this, but I lost my keys.

JOE

Again? (*To Carlos.*) She loses them at least once a week. It's like some kind of Navajo ritual with her.

TINA

I'll ignore that remark. (*Looks at their guns, which are still in hand.*) You guys fixing to have a shootout or something? (*Pause.*) Did South Dakota call?

They both put away their guns, looking embarrassed.

JOE

No, not yet. (*Short pause.*) Tina, this is Carlos.

TINA

Hello, Carlos.

Carlos offers his hand and bows. Tina smiles.

CARLOS

May I ask you something?

TINA

Of course, long as it ain't too personal.

CARLOS

You take pretty pills or something?

TINA

(*Laughs.*) What a line! Joe, your friend is something else.

JOE

You don't know the half of it.

TINA

I can well imagine. (*To Carlos.*) I'm all natural.

CARLOS

Just the way I like a woman.

JOE

Okay, okay! Before it gets too deep in here, Tina, I want you to make sure no one disturbs us. We need to talk—and another thing—don't be listening through the keyhole.

TINA

Yeah, right, Joe. No problem.

As Tina walks toward the door, she stops and looks back at the two men.

TINA

Do you two realize you look alike?

CARLOS

Me, look like this ape? No way! I'm way too pretty.

JOE

We're from the same tribe.

TINA

Really! I swear you look like you could be relatives.

JOE

Tina, the front office, if you don't mind.

TINA

> What a grouch. Okay—I'm out of here. Don't have a cow, for Pete's sake.

Tina exits. Carlos picks up cards.

CARLOS

> You said you gots a plan.

JOE

> Gots? What the hell does that mean? (*Pause.*) Yeah, I'm working on a plan. Just give me a little time. Details soon.

CARLOS

> Well, when?

JOE

> When I get it all clear in my mind. It won't be long. Just relax. (*Joe walks to the window and looks out pensively.*)

CARLOS

> Easier said than done.

JOE

> I remember when I was a kid, my grandfather used to tell me to be proud of being Indian. Well, you know, I am. I can remember running around the reserve playing. You know, like kids do . . .

CARLOS

> Come on, Joe. This a bedtime story or something?

JOE

> Are you ever gonna learn to shut up and listen. Jesus H. Christ! Gee-tome-be-gis! Okay?

CARLOS

> Do you know how long it's been since anybody told me to shut up in our language? It sounds good to the ears. Shit, I must be getting old or something.

JOE

> Or something is right. How come you still remember it?

CARLOS

> Aunt Beverly. You remember her?

JOE

> Hell, yeah! She had a lot of heart. Took no shit from anybody. (*Pause.*) You know, Tina's like that too.

CARLOS

> Is she stubborn too?

JOE

> Like a mule with a big mouth. Just like your aunt.

CARLOS

> You ever try laying the law down to her?

JOE

>Laying the law down? Jesus Christ, Carlos, you know what would happen if a guy . . .

TINA

>(*Over intercom.*) Joe, its South Dakota on line two, and there's a guy here with a big box of toilet paper. He wants ten bucks for it. Do you want it?

JOE

>I'll take the call in here—and buy the toilet paper from the guy too.

TINA

>I don't know why you buy stuff from people. He probably stole it.

JOE

>Thank you, Tina. That'll do. (*Pushes button on phone.*) Vernon! Did you find out anything about that stuff we discussed? (*Pause.*) Oh, that's good. Can you do it? (*Pause.*) I need it ASAP, pal. (*Pause.*) It works that long? (*Pause.*) No, no. That's perfect, in fact. The longer the better. (*Pause.*) My secretary will make all your travel arrangements. She'll be at the airport to pick you up. (*Pause.*) Vernon, Vernon! I just told you it's okay. Cost doesn't matter to me—I need this done. Don't apologize. (*Pause.*) Okay, buddy, I'll see you in the morning.

Joe hangs up the phone and looks at Carlos with a happy grin.

JOE

>You're looking at a genius, young blood.

CARLOS

>You still fencing shit, huh?

JOE

>It keeps the economy moving. Everybody got to make a couple of bucks.

CARLOS

>South Dakota? Ain't nothing there but prairie dogs and cowboys.

JOE

>And some hellified Indians! Listen, I gotta run over to the Western Union office on LaSalle. Why don't you just make yourself comfortable. Kick back and relax.

CARLOS

>I'll do that pal.

JOE

>Visit with Tina. Hey, I know what. While I'm gone, why don't you lay down the law to her?

CARLOS

> I can handle her. You don't think I can, do you? Women like that are my specialty.

JOE

> Yeah, right! Do yourself a favor and watch the boob tube.

Joe exits laughing. Carlos gives him a finger, but also laughs.

CARLOS

> You think you're a comedian or something?

Blackout.

Scene Four

SETTING: Joe's office.

As the curtain rises, Tina and Carlos enter talking from outer office.

TINA

> So tell me about California.

CARLOS

> Wasn't no big thing.

TINA

> Did you get out to the beach?

CARLOS

> Yeah, I did.

TINA

> Did you surf?

CARLOS

> Did I surf? No, I didn't surf! I look like a beach boy to you or something?

TINA

> You don't want me to tell you what I think you look like.

CARLOS

> Really?

TINA

> Look—I know when someone's got problems. You got all the symptoms.

CARLOS

> (*Suspiciously.*) Did Joe say anything to you?

TINA

> He wouldn't do that. (*Pause.*) Frankly, I'm not even sure you deserve a friend like him.

CARLOS

> And who are you to judge? You know, Tina, him and me go back a long way.

TINA

Maybe so, but we're close too.

CARLOS

Just how close are you? What—are you sleeping with him or something?

TINA

That's none of your business.

CARLOS

You're sleeping with him! You should be ashamed of yourself.

TINA

It's none of your bee's wax, but if I was you I'd have nothing to say about it. We're both consenting adults, so what are you talking about?

CARLOS

He's a married man, and besides he's old enough to be your father—that's what I'm talking about. You know what that makes you, right?

TINA

Why don't you tell me.

CARLOS

What—I got to spell it out for you or something?

TINA

Yeah, why don't you?

CARLOS

Okay, lady, W-H-O-R-E!

TINA

I ain't no whore.

CARLOS

Yeah, okay!

TINA

You don't know nothing about our relationship.

CARLOS

(*Laughing.*) Oh, so now it's a relationship. (*Continues laughing.*) Do you actually call yourself a secretary?

TINA

And what do you call yourself?

CARLOS

We're discussing you and your dog morals, Miss Secretary . . . or . . . is it Sexitary?

TINA

(*Very angry.*) You're a punk! A pistol packing pen—I mean, punk!

CARLOS

(*Laughing even more.*) I see what you got on your mind.

TINA

You make me sick, punk.

CARLOS

I make you horny! That's what it is—I make you wet with desire. Don't I? (*Reaches for Tina.*) Come here—I'll give you what you want.

Tina reacts by punching Carlos. He falls back on the couch and holds his eye for a minute.

CARLOS

You hit me in the eye, you bitch. I'm gonna knock your ass out.

TINA

Come on, you little punk asshole. Don't you ever put your hands on me.

He jumps to his feet and they square off to box. He fakes a punch and she reacts by swinging and catching him a glancing blow to the head. Carlos begins limping. He's pulled his leg muscle again.

CARLOS

You did it again, you bitch.

As she circles, ready to swing, Carlos starts laughing.

TINA

What you laughing at?

Carlos can't stop laughing. He points at her and at his leg. They both laugh.

CARLOS

Hell, Tina, I'm sorry. I give up. My leg's been bad for years.

TINA

What an excuse.

CARLOS

I'm serious. It goes out on me at the damnedest times. (*Pause.*) I think I'm gonna have a black eye. Where the hell did you learn to fight like that, anyway?

TINA

I got a lot of brothers. I had to fight. (*Pause.*) I'm sorry too. You have a strange way of getting my goat.

CARLOS

(*Smiling.*) Your goat? (*Pause.*) If I can get your goat, I wonder what else I can get? Maybe I can get your . . .

Tina cuts him off.

TINA

> You don't quit, do you? (*She laughs and shakes her head.*)
> Okay, look—let's shake and start over, okay?

CARLOS

> Okay by me. (*He reaches out to shake her hand.*) I'm Carlos
> High Flying. And your name is?

TINA

> Tina Silver-Hand. I hold the Navajo female boxing champion-
> ship of Hog-Back, New Mexico. Hello, Carlos—I think you're
> very handsome.

CARLOS

> Handsome, you say?

TINA

> Don't let that go to your head. After all, I'm just a cheap
> whore with dog morals.

CARLOS

> I take it back. (*Looks in mirror at his black eye.*) I didn't mean
> it. Please accept my apology.

Tina walks overt to take a look at Carlos's eye.

TINA

> Grovel some first.

CARLOS

> I'm groveling already.

TINA

> Hmmm, this eye's gonna be black. I gave you a shiner.

CARLOS

> Am I forgiven or what?

TINA

> Okay. You're forgiven. (*Pause.*) So tell me all about it.

CARLOS

> (*Pretending to think real hard.*) Well let me think about this.
> (*Pause.*) Well, it's typical I guess. Once this woman, I met
> her in a bar, told me it was bigger than most, but I think she
> was just lying to make me feel . . .

TINA

> Not that, you nut. God you got a one track mind! Keep
> talking like that and I'll black your other eye.

CARLOS

> I thought that's what you were talking about. What, then?

Tina gets a towel and makes it wet.

TINA

> Whatever it is that you're afraid of.

CARLOS

Me, afraid? I keep a pistol in my pocket. People should be afraid of me. Very afraid.

TINA

I'm sure they are. (*Hands Carlos the towel.*) Put this on your eye. Helps keep the swelling down.

CARLOS

Thanks. What about you?

Tina goes by the window.

TINA

I'm attracted to you and that scares me.

CARLOS

I'm attracted to you too. I think you are one sexy woman.

TINA

(*Turns and smiles.*) Thanks. I'm really flattered.

CARLOS

You know, to me you look like you could really . . . (*Makes thrusting motion with pelvis.*)

TINA

(*Somewhat shocked.*) Don't even say it!

CARLOS

I was only gonna say what I feel.

TINA

Christ, Carlos—you don't say that to a woman.

CARLOS

Why not?

TINA

Well . . . it's kind of an insult.

CARLOS

An insult? I wouldn't be insulted if you said that to me. Come on, you can say it to me.

TINA

(*Laughs.*) I'm not gonna say that to you.

CARLOS

Why not? You're thinking it.

TINA

How do you know what I'm thinking?

CARLOS

It's all over your face and in your body language.

TINA

Maybe you're misreading my body language.

CARLOS

Maybe so, but I doubt it. At any rate, I was complimenting you.

TINA

You're serious, aren't you?

CARLOS

Damned straight I am. Woman, I ain't blind. The way you're built, I can plainly see that in bed you'd be dynamite. I mean, D-Y-N-O-M-I-T-E.

TINA

You better shut up while you're ahead.

CARLOS

I didn't mean to insult you. That's the last thing I want to do. (*Touches his eye.*) Or box with you, either.

TINA

You really are something.

Blackout.

Scene Five

SETTING: Joe's office.

As the curtain rises, Tina straightens out the room. Joe sits at his desk looking through paper work.

JOE

How'd you and Carlos get along?

TINA

He sure is arrogant.

JOE

Did he put you in your place?

TINA

I don't understand you men sometimes. My place? I blacked the guy's eye.

JOE

(*Laughs.*) No shit! Why?

TINA

His mouth. (*Pause.*) What's up with South Dakota? Who you talking to out there?

JOE

This Lakota guy I knew years back. He's a medicine man now.

TINA

You wired him some money.

JOE

How the hell do you know that?

Tina walks to desk and picks up a telegram form.

TINA

You should learn how to file this stuff.

JOE

I need it where I can find it. (*Pause.*) Air fare. I'm flying him in.

TINA

A medicine man? What the hell do you need with a medicine man? Does this involve Carlos?

JOE

You ask too many questions. You'll get your ass in trouble like that one day.

TINA

I'm just concerned about you, Joe.

JOE

Don't worry about me. I can take care of myself.

TINA

You'd be better off without him.

JOE

Hey, did I ask you what you think? Stay out of this, butt-in-ski!

TINA

Well, it's because I have this thing for you. We have this thing between us.

JOE

I'm so much older than you. You should look around some— find a younger guy.

TINA

I'm satisfied with the way things are. You aren't that old. Jesus, what's with the age hang-up anyway? We're both adults.

Tina begins to follow Joe around the room with her hands on her hips, demandingly.

TINA

Are you trying to blow me off?

JOE

(*Uncomfortable. He moves away but Tina follows him, hands still on hips.*) Of course not.

TINA

What then?

JOE

First quit following me around with your goddamned hands on your hips. You have any idea what the hell you look like?

TINA

Like I give a shit what I look like. I want an answer.

JOE

(*Resigned.*) Okay, okay! I can see you ain't gonna leave me alone. You and I need to come to an understanding. (*Pause. Tina continues to stand in front of him. He moves and she follows.*) Look, right now I have a lot on my mind. I need to focus.

TINA

Yeah? So what does that got to do with me? With us?

JOE

We have to stop the fooling around.

TINA

If that's what you want.

JOE

(*Sits on the sofa.*) That's what I want. Tina, it's what I need.

TINA

Just like that? You want to stop?

JOE

(*Nodding.*) I mean it's best all the way around, Tina.

TINA

Excuse me.

Tina exits from the room. Joe paces. He goes to desk and gets out a gun, studies it, puts it back in his desk. The phone rings.

JOE

Yes! (*Pause.*) Hey Manny—I thought you went back to Milwaukee? (*Pause.*) No, no—come right over. I'm just kicked back, relaxing some. Come on over—we'll have us a drink or something.

Hangs up and begins to pace. Suddenly he snaps his fingers like he has an idea.

JOE

Tina! Hey Tina!

TINA

(*Offstage.*) What do you want?

JOE

Come in here. I want you to go shopping for me. Buy some office supplies.

TINA

(*Offstage.*) With what?

Tina enters room. She's wiping tears from her eyes. Joe notices and reaches into his pocket to hand Tina a roll of bills. She counts it quickly.

TINA

> This is more than I make in a week.

JOE

> So buy lots of things. (*Pause.*) Get yourself something nice too, and get an outfit for the kid. Something nice and lacy. Take my car. (*Hands her the keys.*) Look, Tina—it's probably better this way.

TINA

> You're right, Joe. It was stupid of me to let myself get involved with a married man, anyway. I got what I deserved.

JOE

> Oh Tina, don't put it that way.

TINA

> Just exactly how would you have me put it, Joe?

JOE

> I don't know doll.

TINA

> Yeah—that's what I thought. Well, I better go.

JOE

> You make it sound dirty. It wasn't dirty, Tina. It was beautiful.

TINA

> You're right, Joe. (*Holds up the money.*) It was. It is beautiful.

Tina puts the money in her purse and exits. Joe gets a cup of coffee, sits at his desk. Tina reenters.

JOE

> I thought I said go.

TINA

> Someone's here to see you. It's a cop. A woman cop.

JOE

> Damn it. What does she want?

TINA

> She didn't say. She's not very friendly, Joe. Be careful.

JOE

> Well, show her in and then split.

Tina motions the officer to enter. Detective Sanchez enters.

SANCHEZ

> Detective Sanchez, Chicago Police Department.

JOE

> What can I do for you? (*Reaches to shake her hand, but she very purposely doesn't take it.*) Well, I can see this ain't a social visit. What do you want? (*Walks toward his desk, talking.*) I

already made my monthly donation to the Policeman's Ball
Fund. You know what I mean?

SANCHEZ

Just to clarify things. I've already pulled your jacket. I know
all about you, Mr. Runs Fast. (*Pause. She leans on desk close
to Joe's face.*) About this Carlos thing. We know what's going
down. We do have sources, you know.

JOE

Stool pigeons, you mean. Well, maybe they lied.

SANCHEZ

Not likely. You got the contract, and I know it.

JOE

You know what? I have rights, and you're starting to step
on them.

SANCHEZ

So does Carlos. I'm just trying to keep him alive. We can
offer him protection.

JOE

By harassing people. (*Pause.*) You know, I could have a
restraining order on you by closing time. You know that?

SANCHEZ

Huh! You're not up on the law, Joe. That's been changed.
You won't get one.

JOE

You keep on harassing me, bitch, and I'll . . .

SANCHEZ

(*Gets in Joe's face even more.*) Don't you threaten me. I'll have
you downtown so fast your balls will rattle.

JOE

I got connections. I'd be out within an hour. You're wasting
your time.

SANCHEZ

No, no, Joe—you're going down. Times have changed. I'm
gonna send you to the joint.

JOE

I'm calling my attorneys right now. I mean it.

Joe grabs phone and starts dialing. Sanchez consults a notebook.

SANCHEZ

Oh yeah. Here they are. Stigleone and Rossi! Both known to
be mob lawyers. Go ahead—call them. I'm sure the state
attorney's office would be happy about that. You're all going
down together anyway. You can play chess every day for
the next ten years or more.

JOE

(*Slams phone down.*) If you haven't got a warrant, or some kind of official business here, get the hell out of my place of business. I mean now!

As Sanchez starts to leave, Manny walks in. They stop and stare at each other for a brief moment. An evil smile crosses Manny's face. Sanchez looks a bit uncomfortable, but quickly regains her composure.

SANCHEZ

Manny the Beast!

MANNY

(*Grinning.*) Detective Nice Ass! Sanchez the "do-gooder." Out fighting crime and evil or looking for a spanking, huh?

JOE

Harassing citizens is more like it. Of course you two obviously know each other.

SANCHEZ

Nice company you keep, Mr. Runs Fast. This monster is . . .

MANNY

Just what you like on a rainy Milwaukee night. Cuss me, Sanchez. I just love the way you cuss. (*Joe and Manny have a good laugh.*) Remember our little motel thing? Oh, how you . . .

JOE

So you like the spanky, spanky, huh, detective?

MANNY

She sure does. She sticks that pretty hind end up in the air and begs for it. You ought to see her. And it's a nice ass too. OOOOEEE! I mean to tell you!

SANCHEZ

You're sick! A perverted slime ball, Manny! You should be locked up—you're a menace to society.

MANNY

You're really something, Sanchez—a real work of art. We're the same, you and me. It takes two to tango. Remember that, Sanchez.

JOE

(*Laughing.*) Goodbye, Detective! (*As she leaves he continues to taunt her.*) Spanky, spanky.

Sanchez slams door. Joe and Manny continue to laugh.

MANNY

Yeah, we had a short fling. Lilly that's her name—loves them S&M thang, and you know how freaky I can get?

JOE

> (*Disgustedly.*) Yeah, yeah, I know all about that. So what the hell you want to talk about?

MANNY

> (*Seriously.*) You, my friend, bullshitted me about Carlos. I don't appreciate that. He smokes those fancy little cigars, and your ashtray's . . .

JOE

> (*Slams his fist on the desk.*) Now look, Manny—I told you, I smoke them myself! (*Gets to his feet.*) What the hell is wrong with you?

MANNY

> (*Walks around desk and straightens Joe's collar.*) Don't get ruffled—I'm only trying to help out here. (*Pause.*) I got a call, Joe. They said, go see if Joe's okay. Help him out if he needs it. I'm asking you straight up, do you need me to handle things for you?

JOE

> Now you listen to me, pal. You're right—he's back. I'm gonna take care of this thing my way. The Indian way, okay? I don't need your help or interference. So quit worrying.

MANNY

> Okay, Joe, if that's the way it's gotta be. (*Pause.*) About those radios, though. I wanna drop them off with you.

JOE

> Don't do that, Manny. I don't want them sitting around my place.

MANNY

> (*Somewhat irritated.*) I thought you said you wanted some.

JOE

> I ain't said that. What's with you and the goddamned radios anyway? I'm too busy right now to deal with that.

MANNY

> Well, don't take all your life. They ain't gonna last forever.

JOE

> Don't bullshit me. You're scared you'll end up eating them.

Manny waves his hand in frustration. Joe grins.

MANNY

> Well, I gotta run.

JOE

> Later, Munchkins. Oh, by the way. There's a carton of ass wipe in my front office. Help yourself to a half-dozen rolls. You may need them.

MANNY
>   Screw you too.

Blackout.

Scene Six

SETTING: Joe's office.

As the curtain rises, Carlos sits at Joe's desk playing cards. He talks to Tina through the open door.

TINA
>   (*Offstage.*) It's going to snow. This rain's going to turn to snow. Everything will be a big mess.

CARLOS
>   Ain't nothing you can do about it, so stop worrying.

TINA
>   (*Offstage.*) I hate winters.

CARLOS
>   Do me a favor, Tina.

TINA
>   (*Offstage.*) What?

CARLOS
>   Come in here and rub my shoulders.

TINA
>   (*Offstage.*) I have work to do.

CARLOS
>   Come on—do me a favor, would you? I'll even say please.

TINA
>   (*Offstage.*) Okay, say it then.

CARLOS
>   You're gonna make me beg?

TINA
>   Say it.

CARLOS
>   Okay, Tina, would you please rub my back?

TINA
>   (*Offstage.*) Rub your own bony back. What do you think I am?

CARLOS
>   That was a low blow.

TINA
>   All right, but just for a few minutes.

Tina walks into the room and starts to rub Carlos's back.

CARLOS

> Oh man, that feels so good.

TINA

> How come a good-looking guy like you ain't married?

CARLOS

> For one thing, I never met the right woman. (*Pause as he enjoys the rubdown.*) But actually I been thinking about settling down. You know, maybe open a business of my own. Like Joe done.

TINA

> You could make some money.

CARLOS

> I wouldn't even have to make a lot of money to be happy. I'd just like to get out of this rat race. I don't know how the hell Joe put up with it for all these years.

TINA

> It would be a smart decision if you did.

CARLOS

> I wish I could say that about other decisions in my life. Like that shit on the West Side—I mean the West Coast.

TINA

> What is that about?

CARLOS

> I'm being accused of stealing a quarter of a million dollars.

TINA

> Is that why that lady cop was here?

CARLOS

> (*Surprised.*) There was a cop? Are you sure it was a cop?

TINA

> I think she was real. Joe sure wasn't very glad to see her. (*Pause.*) How did this happen?

CARLOS

> You mean how'd I get put into this trick bag? It started when they put me in charge of the gambling money. Sort of like a bookkeeper job. A couple of them asked me for some off of the top.

TINA

> Really?

CARLOS

> I should have said no, but what the hell—I figured it was their money. It wasn't much at first—a grand here, two there. It added up real fast. I was so stupid.

TINA

You can't blame yourself.

CARLOS

Not one of them told the truth when the matter did come up. Once I saw how those assholes were gonna act, I decided to split the scene. That was stupid.

Carlos puts his head between his knees and runs his fingers through his hair.

TINA

You poor guy.

CARLOS

You were right. I do have problems. Tina, I am scared shitless. (*Pause.*) I'm so tired of looking over my shoulder. I wasn't cut out for this. If you only knew.

Tina embraces Carlos to comfort him.

TINA

I wish I could make everything all right.

Tina kisses Carlos on the cheek. Carlos reacts by kissing her full on the mouth. She resists a little at first, but then returns the kiss. Joe appears in the doorway. He doesn't say anything. He smiles a mysterious smile, then backs away from the doorway.

Blackout.

ACT TWO

Scene One

SETTING: Joe's office.

As the curtain rises, Tina is on the phone talking to a friend.

TINA

Listen, girl friend, I have this feeling in my heart that he could be the one. (*Pause.*) It was mutual. (*Pause.*) I'll tell you, I'm getting tired of the shit they do. I said to Joe, I ain't your mother, you know. (*Pause.*) He laughed. All they want to do is sit around drinking coffee, talking, and smoking cigarettes. I don't know why I'm expected to clean up after them. I don't get paid for that. (*Pause.*) I was hired as a secretary, and that's all I should do. (*Pause.*) I know jobs are hard to find, but still. (*Pause.*) Damn snow—it's gonna get real nasty out there.

The door bell rings.

Somebody's here—I have to go. Call you later. (*Pushes intercom button.*) Door's open, come on in.

Detective Sanchez enters.

SANCHEZ

I'm Detective Sanchez, Chicago Police Department.

TINA

I remember you.

SANCHEZ

Good! Let's get right down to brass tacks. Do you know Carlos High Flying?

TINA

I know of him. I've heard about him. He used to work here as a car salesman. (*Sanchez laughs. Tina looks irritated.*) I can show you the files. He sold cars for Mr. Runs Fast.

SANCHEZ

A look at those files might prove interesting, but I'm afraid it'll have to wait for another day. Right now, I'd like to know the whereabouts of Carlos High Flying.

TINA

I can't help you—sorry.

SANCHEZ

Can't, or won't? (*Pause as she looks around the office.*) If you see him, give him this card, would you? (*Passes her a business card.*) Have him call me.

Sanchez starts to leave.

TINA

Look, Detective Sanchez, I only do the filing and typing.

SANCHEZ

Who does the books, I wonder.

TINA

An outside firm. Mr. Runs Fast likes to keep his records on the up and up.

SANCHEZ

(*Consults a big book.*) You're a funny girl. You're very beautiful. What you doing in a dead-end job like this?

TINA

(*Ignores her comment.*) That's a big notebook. (*Smiles.*) You must have lots of information. Anyway, it's Harrington and Harrington.

SANCHEZ

Ah yes! Here they are, currently under indictment for racketeering.

TINA

Innocent until proven guilty. This is still America, you know.

SANCHEZ

I don't need you to tell me that. (*Pause. Gives Tina a long hard look. Tina squirms uncomfortably.*) We want to talk to Carlos. He may have something to tell us.

TINA

I doubt that.

SANCHEZ

Oh—so you know him, then!

TINA

I didn't say that.

SANCHEZ

Oh yeah! The code of silence. (*Sanchez turns and walks back to the table, very deliberately. She looks at Tina's body suggestively.*) It breaks, girl. And when it does (*slams her hand on the table*)—they talk and heads roll.

TINA

I just told you I don't know anything.

SANCHEZ

You think these guys have some kind of honor or something? Don't kid yourself, honey. These are animals. Stealing, murderous, and raping lowlives.

TINA

(*Frightened.*) I don't know anything.

SANCHEZ

That's what they all say. We'll see you later. (*Looks suggestively at Tina again. Tina looks uncomfortable and Sanchez smiles.*) Yeah, we'll see more of you later. You might even like it.

Sanchez exits. Tina sits at Joe's desk thinking. Joe enters.

JOE

What's wrong with you?

TINA

That lady cop was here again.

JOE

What did she want?

TINA

She was grilling me, Joe—said all kinds of things. She has this big notebook full of information about you and Carlos. (*Pause.*) Are you a hit man or something?

JOE

(*Laughs.*) A hit man? She's just trying to scare you.

TINA

She is scaring me.

JOE

(*Agitated.*) You know what we do here. Once in a while I buy little things from the guys, but there ain't no real criminal activity going on. You know that. She's trying to make you afraid and doubtful.

TINA

And she is, Joe. (*Pause.*) She was also hitting on me.

JOE

(*Laughing.*) Now, that I don't doubt at all. I'll be goddamned— so she swings both ways.

TINA

Don't laugh, Joe. It's not funny. I don't like that shit.

JOE

(*Still laughing.*) I'll be dipped in shit. You know what we ought to do? If she tries that again, you should go along with it, and we can get some pictures. Use them to put her in her place.

TINA

You're absolutely crazy. What the hell do you think I am, anyway? I'm not some lesbo, Joe. (*Pause.*) I want to know what's going on here. Tell me, Joe.

JOE

The less you know, the better off you'll be.

TINA

> (*Reaches for phone.*) I'm telling you, I'll call her right now unless you tell me everything. I have a right to know.

Joe grabs Tina's hand.

JOE

> (*Quietly but forcefully.*) You ain't gonna call her, Tina. Not now. Not ever. (*Pause. Joe stares hard at Tina.*) I know that and you know that. Isn't that right, Tina?

TINA

> Right.

Joe smiles and puts his hand on the back of her neck, and walks her toward the door. It is a tense, threatening moment.

JOE

> That's my girl. Don't forget, you're going to the airport to pick up Vernon.

TINA

> I haven't forgotten.

JOE

> The expressways are a mess, so drive careful. (*Joe gives Tina the car keys and a roll of bills.*) If he's hungry, stop somewhere nice. I want everything first class. He's an important man, Tina, so treat him right.

TINA

> What about me? I get hungry too.

Joe grins at Tina.

JOE

> Get yourself a hot dog. (*Laughs.*) No—I'm just kidding. You get whatever you want. Whatever it takes to keep you happy.

TINA

> Just remember what you said.

Tina turns to exit.

JOE

> Within reason!

Tina smiles, exits, and Joe sits at his desk to relax. Carlos enters a few seconds later.

CARLOS

> Where did you disappear to last night? Where's Tina? You know, we waited for you until almost eight. We finally decided to go see a movie.

JOE

> I see you put her in her place. (*Looks closely at Carlos's eye.*) Did I tell you she used to be a female boxer?

CARLOS

> I mean, I could probably take her if I really had to. My leg acted up. (*Joe laughs.*) She got in a lucky punch.

JOE

> Maybe a couple of them. I see you got a good-sized lump upside your head too. Yeah, you put her in her place all right.

CARLOS

> So—did you give the plan any thought?

JOE

> Yeah—did you?

CARLOS

> Look, Joe, I got to ask you about something that you didn't mention.

JOE

> What's that?

CARLOS

> The guarantee?

JOE

> It's gonna be tough, but if we're careful it should be okay.

CARLOS

> Who do you figure they'll send?

JOE

> I'd guess it'll be Manny.

CARLOS

> I never did like him. He puts out some bad vibes. I don't trust him.

JOE

> He's a good soldier. Carlos—there's more. This woman detective, Lillian Sanchez, is on the scene too.

CARLOS

> I've heard of her. A real ball buster.

JOE

> She's looking for you. The bitch is ambitious. She came here this morning and caught Tina alone. Sort of scared her. What do you think?

CARLOS

> About Tina? You said she was solid.

Joe walks over to the window. Carlos sits on couch.

CARLOS

You know what I heard about her. She just busted a truck-load of radios, and—dig this, Joe—some of them come up missing. About a hundred of them.

JOE

A truckload of what?

CARLOS

Radios. CB radios.

JOE

That son of a bitch Manny.

CARLOS

What?

JOE

It might surprise you to know that Manny tried to sell me some radios just yesterday.

CARLOS

Nothing surprises me anymore Joe.

JOE

(*Sits on the sofa next to Carlos.*) You know what she wants. She'll offer you the Witness Protection Program. She'll tell you it's an option to consider.

CARLOS

It's for stool pigeons. I'm solid, Joe—you know that.

JOE

They'll threaten you with every crime on the books. You'd spend the next decade in the courts. And those West Coast guys are too jumpy.

CARLOS

If I did testify on them, I could tell a lot. I know plenty.

JOE

Then they'd put you onto me.

CARLOS

(*Stands up and faces Joe.*) Then it's no option. I'd never turn on you!

JOE

I know that, Carlos.

CARLOS

What are we gonna do, Joe?

JOE

Don't you worry. That medicine man and I had us a good talk. My plan's coming together.

CARLOS

I hope so. I swear, I hope so.

They sit and look at each other for a long time. The phone rings. Joe picks it up.

JOE

Hello. (*Pause.*) Tina, where the hell are you? (*Pause.*) That's a crock of shit too. He can't do this to me. (*Pause.*) Tina, I want you to tell her to get back on the plane. (*Pause.*) Tina, listen to me. We can't use her. (*Pause.*) Because she's a woman, what do you think? (*Pause.*) What the hell are you talking about. Don't you call me no chauvinistic pig. What are you supposed to be—a hippie or something? You're an Indian woman—you do like I tell you. (*Pause.*) Now you sound like a communist or something. Do you know who you're talking to? Nobody talks to me like that. You don't give a shit? (*Pause.*) Goddamn you Tina, you got a big mouth, you know that? (*Pause.*) Tina, Tina! (*Joe slams the phone down.*)

JOE

She hung up on me, that bitch. Called me all kinds of names.

CARLOS

Why get jacked out of shape?

JOE

She's at the airport with some woman the medicine man sent. He ain't coming.

CARLOS

What do you mean, he ain't coming? So what do we care if some medicine man ain't coming? (*Pause.*) Hey—wait a minute here! What are you up to, Joe?

JOE

I had a plan, and it involved a medicine man.

CARLOS

What the hell are you talking about? You ain't making no sense. (*Pause.*) Anyway, ain't no woman can be a medicine man, can they?

JOE

I don't know! (*Jumps to his feet and starts pacing.*) I don't see why not, Carlos. They've proven they could do most everything else. Even better than men in some cases. Then why not this? You know, in the old days Indian women had all kinds of political power.

CARLOS

This ain't the old days, Joe. And what's political power got to do with us? I don't know about this, Joe. What the hell do we need a medicine man for?

JOE

Holy shit! What are we gonna do now? I counted on him.

CARLOS

For what?

JOE

(*Sits down next to Carlos.*) It's time we have a heart-to-heart Carlos. Let me explain the whole deal. What I had in mind was . . .

Bring up William Tell music. Carlos can be seen reacting mostly negatively to Joe's plan, but it's not audible.)

Blackout.

Scene Two

SETTING: A dark alley, lit soft blue.

As the curtain rises, Manny sits on a garbage can. Neil Young music is playing very softly—"Harvest Moon," from a nearby apartment. He is joined by Sanchez. Blue lights come up.

SANCHEZ

I should've known you'd pick a place like this.

MANNY

Well, hello to you too.

SANCHEZ

What about the radios? Did he buy them?

MANNY

No, not yet—but he will. Relax—I got things under control.

SANCHEZ

(*Impatience in her voice.*) We can't keep them around too much longer. You told me you could move them real fast. So what's going on? (*Pause.*) You know I need some more information.

MANNY

(*Throw hands in the air.*) Sometimes I think that's all you want from me.

SANCHEZ

How can you say that? I'm taking a big risk with you.

MANNY

(*Gets up.*) Come here, closer to me. (*Sanchez moves a little closer. Manny looks longingly at her.*) You are one beautiful woman, Lillian.

SANCHEZ

Right now, I'm a frustrated woman. This job is really getting to me.

MANNY

It won't be long. Once we get rid of him and Carlos, I'll be running the whole show.

SANCHEZ

That's why it's so important that he buys them radios. Don't you understand? I tip off the Feds and he's gone. Hijacking is a bad offense. Even if he tries some kind of Indian defense, it'll fall under the Major Crimes Act. He's a goner. You take over his turf, and we'll be sitting pretty.

MANNY

We can move to Florida just like we planned. No one will know any better. You are one brilliant lady, Lillian. You've got it all here. (*Points to her head.*) I never met anybody like you.

SANCHEZ

(*Seductively.*) It's all for you, Manuel.

MANNY

Girl, come over here and give me a kiss.

Sanchez gives Manny a kiss.

MANNY

Would you like to dance?

Up music as they dance for a minute or two.

SANCHEZ

Oh Manny, what I'd really like to do is slip into something cozy and have some fun.

MANNY

Did you bring the handcuffs? (*Pause. Sanchez shows Manny the cuffs. He smiles.*) We'll need them tonight.

They both laugh as they exit arm in arm.

Blackout.

Scene Three

SETTING: Joe's office.

As the curtain rises, Joe and Carlos play cards. Offstage a car door can be heard as it slams. Carlos rushes to the window.

CARLOS

It's them! Would you look at this!

JOE

Hubba-hubba, ding ding! Take a look at that thing.

CARLOS

> She looks like a college lady, Joe. How are we gonna get rid of her?

JOE

> I'm not so sure we want to.

CARLOS

> Joe! Would you stop with the ogling. This is dead serious!

The women enter carrying a suitcase and a shopping bag.

TINA

> Hi, guys! Joe, Carlos, this is Gail Steele.

JOE

> Miss Steele? So old Vernon hasn't hog-tied you yet, huh? (*Bows.*) It's nice to meet you.

GAIL

> Call me Gail—and no, I'm not hog tied. We live together. Have for several years. (*Gail reaches for Joe's hand. Joe kisses her hand.*) Why, I'm very honored to meet you. Vernon speaks very highly of you.

JOE

> Really? How is that old horse thief?

GAIL

> Fine, except that you'd never guess what happened to him just last night. His horse kicked him and broke his knee. He couldn't travel, so he sent me.

CARLOS

> (*Throws his hands in the air.*) A Lakota with a WOUNDED KNEE! It figures.

GAIL

> (*To Carlos.*) And you must be Carlos! I can tell by the enthusiasm.

Gail reaches for Carlos's hand, but he makes a sign of the cross and cringes in mock fear.

CARLOS

> Stay away, witchy woman!

JOE

> Carlos! Be nice. (*Turns to Gail.*) Miss Steele . . . I mean, Gail— I'm not so sure that we want to go ahead with this. I mean, after all, my deal was with Vernon.

GAIL

> I understand, but . . .

JOE

> I don't mean to offend you, but I don't know shit from shinola about you. I'm gonna have to call Vernon.

GAIL

I would do the same. In the meantime I'll tell you all about my credentials.

CARLOS

I don't care about your credit. I pay cash for everything. Good old American dollars, by golly.

TINA

(*Slaps Carlos playfully and laughs.*) She doesn't mean that, stupid. She means her college degrees.

CARLOS

(*Surprised.*) I knew that. I was just messing with her head.

TINA

Yeah, right you were!

CARLOS

I got a GED, you know. I ain't stupid.

TINA

So shut up and listen.

Joe dials the phone and makes a sign for them to be quiet.

JOE

Both of you shut up.

CARLOS

Well, tell her I ain't stupid.

JOE

Well, don't act like it then! Shhh. It's ringing.

JOE

Vernon. Ya-ta-hey, Cola. This is Joe. What's the deal here? What's with this woman? (*Pause.*) No, no! I don't give a shit if the person doing the job wears B.V.D. briefs or a pair of frilly bloomers from Victoria's Secret—I just need it done. It's just that none of us knows anything about her. We don't know what to think. No, no. You're misunderstanding my point. I just want it done right. I want to hear you say she knows what's she's doing. (*Pause.*) That's what I wanted to hear. (*Pause.*) Okay, Vernon, you say she's okay, then she's okay. (*Turning to Carlos and Tina.*) He says she knows what she's doing. What do you guys think? (*Tina nods yes emphatically, and Carlos shrugs.*) That's good enough for me. Okay, Vernon, we'll do it. (*Pause.*) I know she's your lady. Hey— don't you worry none about that. She'll be well provided for. Nothing but the best. (*Pause.*) Okay, pal, we'll see you later. Hey—keep that Wounded Knee in bed. I swear, you Lakota guys and your Wounded Knees. Hey—just joking— don't be calling me no rabbit choker! (*Pause . . . laughs.*) That's a good one. I'll see you later, buddy.

Joe hangs up the phone and turns to Gail.

JOE

> Well, tell us about yourself. Joe says you're on top of this thing.

Carlos throws his hands up in resignation.

GAIL

> I'm a psychiatrist. In college I minored in psychology and did graduate work in the study of psychopathic personalities.

TINA

> Boy—did you land in the right place!

CARLOS

> And what the hell is that supposed to mean?

GAIL

> I specialized in dealing with people whose sense of reality is impaired by impulses such as fear. (*Pause. She looks at Carlos.*) Vernon said this would be right up my alley. I think he was right.

CARLOS

> Here's some reality for you, Miss College Degrees. You ain't messing with me.

JOE

> Carlos—what the hell do you think you're doing?

CARLOS

> No way, Joe! (*Begins to put on his jacket.*) I don't know nothing about this voodoo stuff, but ain't no woman doing anything like that to me.

JOE

> Where do you think you're going?

CARLOS

> I'll take my chances with those thugs on the street.

JOE

> I got a lot of money invested in this deal. I can't let you walk out.

Joe steps forward to stop Carlos. Carlos punches Joe and knocks him to the floor.

TINA

> Carlos—what the hell? (*She runs to Joe.*) Look what you've done.

CARLOS

> Joe, I'm sorry. (*He exits.*)

GAIL

> (*Checks Joe quickly.*) He's okay—just shook up.

JOE

Tina—go after him and try to talk some sense into him.

Joe gets up and feel his jaw.

GAIL

Good idea. He needs to talk to someone.

TINA

(*Puts on her coat.*) I'll call as soon as I find something out. Joe, you better give me some money. Just in case.

Joe pulls out a roll and begins to count out some bills. Tina grabs the whole roll and runs out the door.

JOE

Hey! What the hell are you doing? (*He see's Carlos's gun on the desk.*) Oh no! He left out of here without his pistol.

GAIL

We know he can handle himself.

JOE

Do you have any kind of idea what it's like out there? Miss Steele, it's a dog-eat-dog world. (*Pause.*) Well, there's nothing we can do now. Boy, I sure made a mess of this.

GAIL

All is not lost yet. His reaction is typical. He'll come back once he thinks about it.

JOE

I hope you're right. He's a good kid. (*Pause.*) Miss Steele, are you hungry or anything?

GAIL

As a matter of fact, I'm starved. That bag of peanuts and the beverage of my choice on the plane didn't help much.

JOE

I know a real nice steak joint. Come on, we'll go there and eat. Maybe Tina will call with some news. I got a feeling this is going to be a long night.

Blackout.

Scene Four

SETTING: A nice restaurant.

As the curtain rises, Joe and Gail have finished eating and sit at table sipping coffee.

GAIL

What do you do for a living, if I may ask?

JOE

I buy and sell things.

GAIL

A broker? Obviously you've done okay at it.

JOE

Yeah, I survive.

GAIL

Can I ask you something? Why are you and Carlos carrying guns?

JOE

It's a long story. (*Pause.*) Maybe we're overreacting, I don't know, but it's better to be safe than sorry.

GAIL

In some cases—but with loaded guns?

JOE

He got into some trouble with some West Coast associates of mine. They ain't the most ethical business people.

GAIL

Vernon did mention that you run in some unusual circles.

JOE

They put out a contract on his life, then gave it to me. I have no choice, but you know I'm not going to kill anybody.

GAIL

I would hope not.

JOE

Especially Carlos. Hell—he's like a son to me.

GAIL

How'd you get involved with organized crime?

JOE

It's a long story. I always made a living in the street. The nine-to-five thing just never seemed to work for me.

GAIL

How does this involve Vernon and the solution he sent? I'm not exactly clear on that.

JOE

Well, Miss Steele, I recalled a conversation that he and I had many years ago about this old guy who was a holy man or something. He said this guy could make people appear like they were dead for several days.

GAIL

I see. You figured that Vernon might know how to do this too.

JOE

> Exactly! I mean, I'm desperate here. I think to myself, if this
> stuff can work, maybe it's worth a shot.

GAIL

> So to sum this up, you figured you could fool your West
> Coast associates—the unethical business people—and can
> I assume they are gangsters of some kind?

JOE

> You'd be fairly accurate if you assumed that.

GAIL

> I see now. You figured to trick them into thinking Carlos
> was dead. Am I correct?

JOE

> That was my thinking. You think it was a good idea, or
> what?

GAIL

> I think it was an ingenious idea. A little on the diabolical
> side, but very clever . . . extremely original, I must say . . .
> and remarkably resourceful on your part, may I add.

JOE

> Now the only problem is Carlos. If we can convince him to
> do it, do you think it might work?

GAIL

> I do. But what if they demand an autopsy?

JOE

> They wouldn't do that. I know these guys—they aren't
> rocket scientists.

GAIL

> What if he's guilty?

JOE

> I wouldn't have accepted the contract, and some street thug
> would have tried to kill him. I accepted it to keep him alive.
> The only thing he's guilty of is being young and gullible.

Manny walks into the restaurant. Joe sees him and grimaces.

JOE

> Don't say anything in front of this guy. (*Joe points toward
> Manny.*) He's trouble, real trouble.

GAIL

> I understand.

JOE

> Yo, Manny! Over here. What the hell are you doing here?

Manny comes over to their table.

MANNY

Who's this angel, Joe? Nice of you to offer an introduction. He never wants me to meet his squeezes.

GAIL

Is that what you think I am? One of his squeezes?

MANNY

My name is Manny Garcia. What's yours?

GAIL

Dr. Gail Steele.

MANNY

Doctor? Sounds professional. You sick or something Joe? (*Pause and grins.*) Hey—sell me your business before you get too sick.

JOE

Too sick for what? You're always after my businesses, ain't you? Well, forget it. It all goes to Carlos.

MANNY

If he's around, that is. (*Shows concern.*) Really, Joe, are you sick?

JOE

Well actually she's . . .

GAIL

(*Laughing.*) I'm a psychiatrist, not a medical doctor.

MANNY

A shrink? What the hell you doing with a shrink?

JOE

Having dinner. See the dirty plates, the cups, the silverware? We had a social dinner.

GAIL

In reality it was a private session, Mr. Garcia.

Both Joe and Gail laugh.

MANNY

A private session? Oh, I get it. (*Slaps himself on the forehead.*) Two's company, three's a crowd. (*Manny looks over Gail.*) You sure can pick 'em, Joe. I'll give you that.

JOE

(*Winks at Gail.*) I try, my friend, I try.

MANNY

(*To Gail.*) You're some kind of Indian, right?

GAIL

SOME KIND OF INDIAN? (*Pause.*) Yes, I am. I'm a full-blood Lakota. From the Pine Ridge area.

MANNY

That's nice. Listen here, Doc, if he don't treat you right, you just give old Manny a call. I'll be right over there at the bar.

GAIL

I'm sure he'll do just fine. Well, Mr. Garcia, it's nice to have met you. (*Turns back to Joe.*) Now, as I was saying, by all indications treaty law would cover that kind of infraction.

JOE

(*Looks at Manny and grins smugly.*) But I would think the idea is to create a situation where the people see that it's in their best interest to cooperate.

MANNY

Excuse me, I see you guys are making heap big Indian talk (*laughs at his own joke*), but if I may, I must interrupt. Joe— did you hear from our young friend again?

JOE

Why do you ask?

MANNY

The natives are getting restless out west, Joe, and besides I like to stay on top of these things. (*Mimics Joe's voice.*) I just want to create a situation where everyone sees that its best to cooperate. (*Speaks more intensely—almost threateningly.*) You get my drift?

JOE

(*Nods and answers very slowly.*) I think I do.

MANNY

(*Becomes much lighter now that he's made his point.*) What about those radios? I could have my man drop off fifty or so. I need to move them. You want me to drop them off?

JOE

I'm not sure. I gotta talk to some friends of mine.

MANNY

No big thang. You just let me know when you're ready, and I'll scoot them over to you. (*Bows to Gail.*) The pleasure was all mine, Dr. Steele.

He takes Gail's hand and kisses it, then turns to leave. She shakes her hand as though to get rid of the kiss, as Manny goes to the bar. Joe watches him and is silent.

GAIL

I see what Vernon meant about unusual circles. God—the evil drips off of him. How do you do it?

JOE

Well, we'd best get going.

Joe and Gail exit. Manny watches them. He signals for the bartender for a phone, takes it, and goes to Joe's table. He sits, looks around for the waitress, then picks up the twenty-dollar tip Joe has left.

MANNY
Who the hell is he trying to impress?

He reaches in his pocket, pulls out two singles, throws them on the table, pockets the tip Joe has left, then dials a number.

MANNY
This is Manny Garcia. (*He has a diabolical grin on face.*) Hello, Vito . . .

Up music, Peter Gunn. Music throughout set transition, opening of following scene.

Blackout.

Scene Five

SETTING: Joe's office. Music still plays, but very low.

As the curtain rises, Gail sits on the couch reading. Joe paces around, goes to look out the window several times. He appears very impatient.

JOE
Where the hell can he be? I never should have let him leave.

GAIL
Any idea where he might go?

JOE
No telling with him. I hope Tina caught up with him. You think she did?

Gail shrugs and continues to read the magazine.

GAIL
Is there anybody you can call? Other relatives maybe?

JOE
Maybe his mother, but I doubt it. I'll try, anyway. I have to do something. How can you just sit there and read?

Gail looks up at Joe but doesn't answer. There is a loud noise at the front door. Joe grabs his gun and indicates to Gail to take cover. Tina and Carlos enter. She is helping him. Blood can be seen on Carlos's shirt. He's been stabbed.

GAIL

Let me look at that. Sit him down here. (*Gail indicates the couch. Tina helps Carlos sit, and then Gail peels away his blood-soaked shirt. She looks it over carefully.*) Joe—give me that bag there, please. Tina—would you mind getting some towels? Soak them first with hot water.

CARLOS

It ain't nothing. Just a scratch.

JOE

Who the fuck did this to you?

CARLOS

That deadbeat gambler—what's his name? Oh yeah, the guy they call Cicero Mike and his silent partner. You know, that dumb guy—Kenny the Junkie.

JOE

How'd they do it?

CARLOS

I didn't see them until it was too late. They came right up on me.

GAIL

You're very lucky these weren't more serious.

JOE

Goddamn, Carlos—I told you to be careful. Didn't I tell you that?

TINA

Back off, Joe. It wasn't all his fault. His leg went out on him.

CARLOS

Yes it was. I let my guard down—I got mad. That's dangerous. (*Pause. Gail finishes applying bandage to his wound.*) I'm sorry, Joe. About everything. I know you're right. You always are. I was such a schmo. I didn't listen to you!

JOE

Don't worry about it. The point is, live and learn. It might be a good idea to go see a doctor about that leg, too.

Everyone laughs.

CARLOS

About punching you—I'm really sorry about that.

JOE

Not as sorry as you will be once you get on your feet.

CARLOS

Whatever! I know I got it coming. I'll take it like a man. Those assholes thought they had me—and they did too, but they forgot about Tina. She saved my ass.

JOE

(*Interested.*) What she do?

TINA

It was nothing. Anybody would have done the same thing.

CARLOS

She was great, Joe. Man, this woman got some heart.

JOE

(*Puts his arms around Tina and holds her close to him.*) I know that to be true. This is a good Indian woman. The kind you don't mess with. I owe you, Tina.

TINA

(*Laughing.*) I was scared shitless.

CARLOS

(*Gets to his feet.*) You should have seen her. She slammed a garbage can over Silent Kenny's whole body. His arms were pinned like this. (*Shows how Kenny was stabbing about in the air.*) God—was it funny. Then she kicked the other guy's nuts up to his Adam's apple.

TINA

He called me a bitch, that dickless asshole.

GAIL

Right on, sister!

JOE

That was a major mistake on his part.

Everyone has a good laugh. Then they all get quiet.

GAIL

Just to clarify things, I need to know if we're going to proceed as originally planned?

JOE

(*Points to Carlos.*) It's his call.

TINA

So what's up with that? What you gonna do?

CARLOS

(*Hesitates. Everyone leans forward to hear his decision.*) After tonight? Let's proceed, Doctor Steele.

Both Tina and Joe cheer.

JOE

My man!

TINA

No Joe, my man. I SAVED HIS ASS. He owes me his life. He belongs to me.

JOE

Oh really?

TINA

Just joking.

CARLOS

Maybe I can change that.

TINA

Not likely, so don't hold your breath.

GAIL

I'll have to do some preliminary procedures first, but I see no major complications.

Joe and Gail get busy with the medical equipment that Gail has in the shopping bag.

GAIL

You'll have to remove your pants.

CARLOS

Why?

GAIL

It's procedures. Nothing to worry about.

TINA

(*Looks up from work.*) You scared or something?

CARLOS

(*Arrogantly.*) I know what you're interested in. Well, ladies, feast your eyes.

Carlos drops his pants. He has on bikini briefs with a leopard-skin design on them. Tina reacts first.

TINA

Holy cow! Would you look at those! He's a cross-dresser!

CARLOS

What's that?

JOE

A man who wears women's bloomers.

CARLOS

What the hell you talking about? Hey, these ain't women's bloomers. Man, these are the cutting edge of today's men's fashion.

TINA

Yeah—cutting into your ass! Just look at them.

JOE

They look like something Tarzan would wear.

TINA

You mean Jane.

They all laugh. Carlos gives them a finger, but laughs with them.

JOE

Where the hell did you buy these?

CARLOS

Saw them advertised in *Playboy*. I'll tell you something—
they cost, pal.

JOE

How much?

CARLOS

It's what the men of the seventies wear. Come on, get with
it. Cost doesn't mean shit.

JOE

If they cost a dollar, that's ninety-nine cents too much.

TINA

I can't believe any man would actually wear those things.

CARLOS

Excuse me! You may have saved my ass, but please don't
talk about what covers it. (*Laughs, then turn to Joe.*) Three
pairs, twenty-nine ninety-nine. Hey—it's worth it. See how
these women reacted? Tina's just acting like that to cover
up her lust. Ask Doctor Steele.

TINA

They look like panties for women. Weird women!

CARLOS

Yeah, right, Tina. Your eyes lit up like a Christmas tree.
These shorts were made to please women like you, and . . .
so was I, for that matter.

TINA

Don't flatter yourself!

JOE

All right, already! That's enough. It's getting deep in here.
Come on, Tina, the front office. Leave Tarzan alone with
Doctor Steele.

*Tina and Joe exit laughing. Gail puts a thermometer in Carlos's mouth
and begins to take his blood pressure.*

GAIL

Your temperature is fine. Your blood pressure is just a little
higher than I'd like it to be.

CARLOS

(*Seriously.*) What's gonna happen to me?

GAIL

You'll be heavily sedated. All body functions will be, in a
sense, arrested.

CARLOS

Will I be able to hear? (*Pause.*) Smell?

GAIL

I would think all your senses will be affected in much the same matter.

CARLOS

Could I ask you something?

GAIL

You can ask me anything.

CARLOS

There is one thing that I sort of worry about. (*Pause.*) It's just a little on the embarrassing side. I find it hard to talk about in mixed company.

GAIL

Like what?

CARLOS

Some things—like politics, sex, and religion—ain't no problem.

GAIL

(*Becoming perplexed.*) What exactly are you talking about then?

CARLOS

(*In a conspiratorial tone.*) This is strictly confidential?

GAIL

Yes it is, Carlos. Now what is it?

CARLOS

Wait a minute here—what exactly do you mean by confidential?

GAIL

That I won't tell anybody.

CARLOS

Okay. That sounds cool. (*Pause.*) Say, "Spit to die, make an Indian cry."

GAIL

I'm not going to say that. It's ridiculous and childish.

CARLOS

Say it if you're serious, because I am.

GAIL

Okay, then! Spit to die, make an Indian cry. Are you happy now?

CARLOS

(*In total sincerity.*) Okay! It's the problem of bodily functions that you mention. Will I still do, you know, like number one and number two?

GAIL

(*Laughing.*) Oh, Carlos! You are so funny. Don't even worry about—

Joe and Tina enter, arguing. Tina follows Joe around with her hands on her hips.

TINA

You can't be serious.

JOE

I'm as serious as a heart attack.

TINA

I put up with enough shit here already. I ain't putting up with no more. You give me a raise, or my ass is out of here.

JOE

Yeah, well, don't let the door hit it on the way out. Now come over here and give me a hand with this.

They pull a rollaway bed into the room, go get blankets.

CARLOS

See why I was concerned?

GAIL

I sure do. In bed! I'll worry about it.

Carlos climbs onto the bed. Gail prepares to administer a needle.

CARLOS

That's absolutely necessary?

GAIL

It makes things easier and quicker. You lay back and make yourself comfortable.

CARLOS

And miss the show?

GAIL

What do you mean, show?

CARLOS

You know! The voodoo thing.

GAIL

I won't do a voodoo thing. (*Pause.*) What you need to do now is relax.

CARLOS

I'm totally kicked back.

GAIL

Now picture yourself in utopia.

CARLOS

What's that? Sounds like a fancy drink or something.

TINA

Kinda like the perfect place.

CARLOS

The perfect place? What's that supposed to mean?

GAIL

> (*Becoming concerned.*) Joe—it's real important that he relaxes if the solution is going to work. Otherwise there's the danger of shock.

JOE

> Come on, Carlos—relax. Concentrate on relaxing. On that there utopia place.

CARLOS

> On utopia? I don't even know what that is.

JOE

> You heard the lady, son.

CARLOS

> I can't think! My mind is a blank.

TINA

> That's not unusual. Hey—I have an idea that might work. Carlos—just think of you and I someplace.

CARLOS

> You and me. (*Pause.*) And you're letting me do whatever I please?

TINA

> Well, not quite, but close. You're doing what I want you to.

CARLOS

> Now that I can picture. You mean it, Tina?

TINA

> Yes, Carlos, I mean it.

CARLOS

> Oh yeah! Hold my hand, Tina.

GAIL

> He's got to relax. He's going to encounter difficulty if he doesn't.

JOE

> Just hold his hand. It won't hurt nothing.

TINA

> So why don't you hold his hand?

JOE

> I would, but he wants you to.

Tina takes his hand. Carlos smiles.

JOE

> Get closer so he can smell your perfume.

Carlos smiles again and pulls her hand to his heart. Tina doesn't resist.

CARLOS

> I picture us at a lake. We're skinny-dipping. The sun on our nude bodies feels so great. So relaxed. I hear a drum. We're

at a powwow. The drum is like magic. Now we're making love to the beat of the drum. Hmmm . . . Tina . . .

TINA

I feel like a dirty movie or something.

GAIL

(*Laughing.*) I just heard a new and interesting definition of utopia.

JOE

A good one, though. Ain't nobody happier than an Indian when he's . . . (*Joe thrusts his hips like he's copulating.*) You ladies know what I mean?

TINA

Would you cut it out, Joe? You're as bad as him. (*Pause.*) Hey—he's out now. Sleeping like a baby.

GAIL

(*Checks Carlos's heartbeat.*) He's under.

TINA

(*To Joe.*) See what I do for you?

JOE

(*With total sincerity.*) Don't you think for minute that I don't appreciate it, Tina.

TINA

That's why you're going to give me a raise, right?

JOE

Books come out right, doll, and you got it.

TINA

Fair enough.

GAIL

(*Holds up syringe.*) Well—this is it folks. Modern medicine doesn't even know about this stuff. Time for the solution. (*She injects Carlos. He moans softly.*) Here you go, Carlos.

JOE

That's it? Somehow I expected more. A ceremony of some kind. You know, this is the start of a whole new life for this young man. Somehow it feels like there should be more. Like some singing or something.

GAIL

The voodoo thing?

TINA

Somehow I get this feeling like there will be more—a lot more!

Blackout.

Scene Six

SETTING: Joe's office.

As the curtain rises, Carlos lies on the rollaway bed. Joe and Tina enter stage talking.

TINA

That Miss Steele is a nice lady.

JOE

A lot of class there, I mean to tell you.

TINA

Joe? (*Pause.*) Do you think I got class?

JOE

Hell, yeah. You got a style that's all your own.

TINA

You really mean it? Are you just saying that to be nice to me?

Tina gets up, walks to the window, and looks out pensively.

JOE

Yeah, I mean it. You got a bug up your ass about something. What is it?

TINA

(*Becomes alarmed.*) Oh no, Joe! It's that lady cop again. What are we going to do?

JOE

Quick—help me get him into the storeroom. (*They move Carlos. Sanchez knocks loudly on the door.*) Who is it?

SANCHEZ

Police! Open up!

JOE

Come in.

SANCHEZ

(*Enters.*) Okay where is he?

JOE

Where's who?

SANCHEZ

Don't play stupid with me. (*Looks hard at Tina.*) Where is he?

TINA

In Hinsdale. I gave him your card. He tore it up and said you could stick it in your . . . well, never mind where he said.

SANCHEZ

Hinsdale? Illinois?

TINA

    What can I say?

JOE

    You don't have to say anything.

SANCHEZ

    If anything happens to him, you've had it. (*Turns to Tina.*)
    Both of you! Is that clear?

JOE

    This is police harassment! And another thing—why you
    hitting on my secretary?

SANCHEZ

    She was giving me a big come-on. All I could do was keep
    her off of me. (*Laughs.*) Oh yeah, you got a hot one there,
    Joe, but I'm sure you, above all, know that.

TINA

    That's a bare-faced lie and you know it.

SANCHEZ

    It is? The way you stand, with your hands on your hips and
    your pelvis stuck out! That's a come-on-and-get-it sign.
    Whores stand like that.

JOE

    (*To Tina.*) See—I told you, didn't I? (*Turns to Sanchez.*) You
    stay away from my secretary, too. You understand?

SANCHEZ

    Private stock, Joe? I don't think so. Give me five minutes
    with her, and I'll have her.

TINA

    I don't think so!

SANCHEZ

    I'll be back. Just remember what I said. If any harm comes
    to Carlos, I'll be on you like stink on shit. Got that, slime ball?
    You too, Miss Hot Pants.

Sanchez exits. Joe plops down on the couch. Tina sits at his desk.

JOE

    God, I hate that woman. (*Pause.*) Hinsdale?

TINA

    It's so pretty. Almost like a movie scene. I'd love to live there,
    except there isn't enough Indians. Maybe a dozen or so. You
    see them in the supermarket buying flour for their fry bread.

JOE

    Fry bread? In Hinsdale?

Suddenly there is a loud knock on the door.

TINA

Don't tell me she's back already.

JOE

Who the hell is it?

MANNY

It's me—Manny.

JOE

(*Through the door.*) What do you want?

MANNY

You know why I'm here. (*Pause.*) Open up Joe.

Joe opens the door. Manny enters.

JOE

I took the contract, I do the job. What the hell is this shit?

TINA

What does he want?

MANNY

Who the hell is this?

TINA

Who are you, asshole?

MANNY

Just let me do it, Joe, and I'm out of here.

JOE

My gun, Manny. They're trying to weasel out of paying me.

MANNY

You're just being paranoid. I don't give a shit what gun. I just gotta see it happen. You know how it is.

JOE

(*Extremely excited and mad.*) Okay then! Watch this!

Joe grabs his gun from the desk, runs over to the storeroom door and shoots Carlos. Manny starts pulling out his gun. Joe points his gun at Manny.

JOE

Hold it right there. (*Manny puts his hands out in front of him.*) You gonna shoot me too and collect double or something?

MANNY

It ain't nothing like that, Joe. Would I do that to you? It's the broad. Let me shoot her. Come on—we don't need no witness.

TINA

Give me that gun. (*Tries to grab Joe's gun.*) I'll shoot this miserable bastard myself.

MANNY

Who is this bitch?

JOE

> I told you, she's okay.

Tina lets loose a barrage of curses at Manny.

MANNY

> What's she gonna do? Hit me with a wet noodle? (*Laughs and makes kissing gesture in Tina's direction*) Shut her up, then. I'm falling in love. I like a woman to call me names. Such passion—listen to her. You know what I like.

JOE

> (*Disgustedly.*) Yeah—I know what you like. Did you know it makes me sick—your perversions? (*To Tina.*) Shut up. You're only making matters worse. (*Turns to Manny.*) You saw—so split!

MANNY

> Hey—take it easy, big guy. Okay? Ain't no need to get rude. I saw what I had to see. I'm out of here.

JOE

> You're right, Manny. I'm sorry.

MANNY

> Let's get together soon for steaks. I'll call in a couple of weeks. Maybe you can bring the dame with you. (*Throws a kiss at Tina.*) What do you say, baby?

TINA

> Get out of here, asshole. YOU FREAK!

MANNY

> Oh—I love it!

As Manny exits, he emits a low groan and licks his lips vulgarly at Tina. She gives him a finger. The door closes and Tina collapses on the couch. She sits for a few seconds, then remembers Carlos.

TINA

> Oh my God. What are we going to do? (*She jumps up and runs to the storeroom, pulls the bed onto the stage. Starts to pull back the blanket, then stops.*) He's dead!

JOE

> Would you calm down?

TINA

> We have to call the police. We'll say Manny did it.

JOE

> You don't know what you're talking about.

TINA

> We're going to the electric chair! I know we're gonna fry. Do something, Joe!

JOE

>(*Laughs.*) What's to be done? I suppose I could shoot you so there will be no witness. Maybe Manny was right.

TINA

>Don't talk like that, Joe. Oh God—how did I get into this? (*She sits down next to Carlos and then screams and jumps.*)

JOE

>What now?

TINA

>I just stuck myself with that needle, and it still has some of that stuff in it! What are we going to do, Joe?

JOE

>Are you sure?

TINA

>Yes I am.

JOE

>Well, don't panic. I'll call Gail. (*Pauses as he reaches for phone and dials.*) Why the hell couldn't you be more careful?

TINA

>Call Gail! (*She starts to wail.*) Oh my God! Why?

JOE

>(*On phone.*) Miss Steele's room, please. (*Pause.*) Gail? I'm sorry to bother you, but we've had an accident. Tina sat on that needle with the root solution in it. (*Pause.*) You better hurry, then! (*Pause. Turns to Tina.*) How do you feel?

TINA

>Like I took too many quaaludes or something.

JOE

>She feels groggy. (*Pause.*) Okay, I will. Yes ma'am, I will.

Joe hangs up, gets a towel. He hands it to Tina, who has moved to the couch.

JOE

>Put this on your head.

TINA

>Shouldn't it be wet?

JOE

>Oh yeah, you're right. (*Joe gets towel wet.*) Everything will be okay.

TINA

>What did she say? What if I die, Joe?

JOE

>(*Returns to Tina.*) You ain't gonna die.

TINA

> What about Carlos? (*Tina is becoming incoherent.*) I'm starting to go under.

JOE

> (*Very concerned now.*) Don't do that Tina! Stay awake.

TINA

> There's going to be hell to pay for this, you son of a bitch.

JOE

> (*Gets another towel.*) Oh, don't I know that to be true. (*From outer office.*) Keep talking. Stay awake.

TINA

> (*In a very slurred voice.*) Joe, do you care about me? I mean ... umm ... not as lovers, but as friends.

JOE

> Of course. You don't have to ask that. I love you, Tina. Always will. (*Joe notices that Tina is beginning to fall asleep.*) Don't fall asleep, Tina. Just keep talking.

TINA

> (*Very groggy.*) Okay. I'll try. (*Pause.*) Joe, are you going to give me a raise for real?

JOE

> (*Strokes her hair tenderly.*) You know I will. How much do you want, baby-doll?

TINA

> I think I deserve 25 percent at least.

JOE

> (*Shocked.*) You want a 25 percent increase in pay?

TINA

> I deserve it, Joe.

JOE

> (*Throws her head onto the couch and stands up.*) Shut up and go to sleep, Tina.

TINA

> (*Very groggy.*) See how you are? You treat me so bad ... so bad ... so ba ...

Joe paces floor. Tina lets out a moan and is asleep. Gail enters. Joe points to the couch. Gail rushes to her.

JOE

> Is she going to die?

GAIL

> No, she'll be just fine after the solution wears off.

JOE

So she's going to be okay? (*Gail nods.*) She ain't getting no raise then, either. I have to contact her family. I don't know how I'm gonna explain this.

GAIL

Maybe I should talk to them. What are they like?

JOE

They're Navajos. They stay close to each other. If they suspect foul play, they'll have the cops all over the joint. Hell—they'll even have the BIA in here.

Suddenly the door is kicked in. Sanchez enters with gun drawn. Gail freezes. Joe slaps his forehead.

JOE

Not you! That's all I need.

SANCHEZ

Up against the desk, scumbag! Both of you. Put your hands on the desk and don't move. Don't even blink.

JOE

Come on, what do you think this is? Starski and Hutch or something. (*To Gail.*) This bitch better have paper.

SANCHEZ

Don't need it, jag-off. We have reports of gunfire coming from this office.

Sanchez pats Joe down. Gail turns to speak.

GAIL

I just walked in the door—I didn't have anything to do with this. Joe will confirm that.

SANCHEZ

Shut up and turn around.

JOE

This woman is a respected doctor.

SANCHEZ

Right now, she's a murder suspect. Respected or otherwise.

JOE

A murder suspect? You're jumping the gun aren't you?

GAIL

This is ludicrous! Absolutely absurd!

SANCHEZ

I said shut up. (*Sanchez looks around the room. She sees Joe's gun on the desk, picks it up and smells the barrel.*) This gun was just fired.

JOE

> I can explain that.

SANCHEZ

> I bet you can—and you will. (*Sanchez goes over to shake Tina.*)
> Wake up, hot crotch!

JOE

> She won't wake up.

SANCHEZ

> Double murder. You're gonna fry, Joe. (*Goes over to look at
> Carlos.*) Where'd you shoot him? I thought you shot him in
> the head.

JOE

> (*Laughs.*) What did I tell you about stool pigeons? They lie.

SANCHEZ

> I want to know what the hell is going on around here. Is this
> some kind of trick?

GAIL

> I can assure you that neither of these people has been shot.
> We administered a solution—I mean, I gave it to him and
> she accidentally injected it. They are not dead—just sleeping
> very deeply.

JOE

> It's an old Indian trick.

SANCHEZ

> I'll bet it is.

Gail walks over to Tina who has just stirred.

SANCHEZ

> Where do you think you're going?

GAIL

> This woman needs my attention. I am a doctor, believe it or
> not.

SANCHEZ

> But I thought you were a shrink.

JOE

> Who told you that?

SANCHEZ

> Never mind. Just get back up against that desk.

GAIL

> Are you going to shoot me if I don't?

SANCHEZ

> Well—do what you have to, then.

GAIL

> (*As she leaves for the outer office with a towel in her hand.*) That,
> Detective, is what I intend to do.

SANCHEZ

Okay, Joe—what's happening here? I want the goddamned truth.

JOE

Okay, Sanchez—listen closely. This whole idea . . .

Phone rings. Sanchez indicates to Joe that he should answer it.

SANCHEZ

Switch to conference.

JOE

(*Does as he is told.*) Yeah?

MANNY

Listen up, Joe. This is Manny. They called off the hit.

JOE

They what?

MANNY

They found out it was one of their own guys ripping them off. Carlos is in the clear. What should I tell them?

JOE

You know what happened here. Tell them that. And another thing, I know you been stool pigeoning on me, too.

MANNY

Not really, Joe. Look—it's complicated, and I'll explain it to you another time, but here's a tip. Get rid of the body, because I just got wind that the "spank-me-daddy" freak is on her way over there to bust you. She's plotting to take over your operation and mine, by busting both of us. I was going along with her—you know for the sex-sational evenings. She's a real bitch. Dump the body and do it now.

Manny hangs up the phone.

SANCHEZ

That son of a bitch. Did you hear what he just called me? That lying bastard!

JOE

(*Laughs.*) What did you expect? Loyalty?

SANCHEZ

I guess not, but the facts are—the reality is—that I got you, Joe. I'll get him later. He ain't worth a plugged nickel now. Not to me, anyway.

JOE

I have some reality for you to think about, woman.

SANCHEZ

Shut up. I have reports of gunfire. Someone's going to jail. It might as well be you—and Miss Fancy Bloomers.

JOE

I'll walk out of court. These walls are sound proof. I had them built that way.

SANCHEZ

That doesn't matter. It's just a matter of time. I know all about you, Joe.

JOE

And I about you.

SANCHEZ

Yeah, right!

JOE

You should see my collection of photos. (*Pulls folder from desk drawer.*) Just for openers, this one even shows the mole on your left thigh. You see what else it shows?

SANCHEZ

So what? That's my right thigh. Don't you know a left thigh from a right one?

JOE

(*Looks closely at photo.*) So it is. Here's something else. I know about that truckload of radios too, and you and Manny's little scheme to call in the FBI.

SANCHEZ

Sure you do.

JOE

I got it in your own words. Taped your little meeting with Manny in the alley.

SANCHEZ

You're bluffing.

JOE

Let's see what this adds up to. One, stealing evidence, number two, obstruction of justice, and number three, conspiracy. Not to mention consorting with a known criminal. Holy shit, Sanchez, you could be the one heading for the big house. You know what's waiting for you there?

SANCHEZ

(*Resigned.*) You bastard! What do you want?

JOE

To retire and go back to my reservation. I want you to get rid of my police record.

SANCHEZ

Everything is computerized.

JOE

So delete it. You're smart—you'll figure out a way.

Gail enters.

SANCHEZ

(*To Joe*.) You got a diabolical mind. (*Pause*.) Okay, we deal.

JOE

Put the gun away first. It makes me nervous.

SANCHEZ

(*Laughs*.) We still have the problem of Fancy Bloomers.

JOE

You mean Carlos?

SANCHEZ

No, I mean her. (*Points at Gail*.) The Society Lady. She's broken an Illinois law, and I'm compelled to arrest her.

Phone rings again.

SANCHEZ

Leave it on conference again.

JOE

Hello.

VERNON

Joe? Vernon here. Is Gail available?

Joe looks at Sanchez. She nods.

JOE

Yeah, she is. Go ahead.

VERNON

Listen, Gail—we have a slight problem. You took the wrong solution. You haven't administered yet, have you?

GAIL

Actually, I have. About six hours ago . . .

VERNON

Oh no!

GAIL

And there's more. Due to an accident, we have two people under right now. Both were injected with the solution labeled "A."

VERNON

That's the solution I usually give people who've lost their sex drive. It's an aphrodisiac. Did you water it down?

GAIL

No, I didn't.

VERNON

Well—what will happen is, they'll sleep for about ten hours and wake up with a greatly increased sexual drive. They'll be in overdrive.

Eye contact between Gail and Joe.

JOE

> An aphrodisiac? Wow, man—I don't believe this. (*Laughing.*)
> Boy—Carlos and Tina are in for a surprise.

GAIL

> Is there anything I should do to counteract that?

SANCHEZ

> (*Interrupts.*) Hello! My name is Detective Sanchez, Chicago
> Police Department. Are there any negative side effects?

VERNON

> Detective? Gail—are you all right?

GAIL

> Not to worry. Just answer her as best you can. Please be
> brief, too.

VERNON

> Well, Detective, unless they don't want to have sex—and
> a lot of it, I might add, the only side effect is that they'll
> wake up with a heightened sex drive that will last prob-
> ably about thirty-six hours, especially since the solution
> wasn't watered down. A one-to-one mixture will certainly
> be enough.

JOE

> They wake up horny!

SANCHEZ

> For thirty-six hours? OY!

VERNON

> That's it in a nutshell. Joe? Has that mess been cleaned up
> for you?

JOE

> Actually it has, Vernon. The good detective was about to
> leave.

SANCHEZ

> Not so fast, Joe. As a law office, I have to confiscate what's
> left of that solution.

JOE

> Oh, sure you do.

SANCHEZ

> (*Picks up the vial.*) I assume this is it? Is there more?

GAIL

> Yes—I have another full bottle in my bag.

SANCHEZ

> Give it to me. Give it all to me right now.

JOE

> (*Laughing.*) Ain't this something?

GAIL

> (*As she digs in her purse.*) You have to be very careful with that. You can cnly take a very small amount. It's much stronger than stuff like Spanish fly.

JOE

> She doesn't care about that. She likes to orgy.

SANCHEZ

> Shut up Joe. (*To Gail.*) I'll be the judge of that, Miss Society Lady. I guess you Indians didn't share everything with us, right?

GAIL

> Are you still going to arrest me?

JOE

> She ain't going to arrest nobody.

SANCHEZ

> You got it, Joe. Ain't no crime been committed here. Now you can go ahead and retire. (*Turns to Gail.*) Go back to the prairie that you came in from.

VERNON

> Gail—are you sure you're okay? Joe—what's going on?

JOE

> Everything's fine. Just hold on a minute, Vernon.

Gail hands over the other larger bottle of the solution to Sanchez. She grins at Joe and Gail and backs toward the door.

SANCHEZ

> Adios, amigos.

VERNON

> What's happening? Did I hear the detective say she was confiscating the solution?

GAIL

> She took it, Vernon. She also took the bottle that you had labeled as "B."

VERNON

> She's in for a nasty surprise. "B" has the exact opposite effect. If taken by a man, his penis won't experience an erection for several weeks. Actually, if too much is taken, it'll shrivel up to the size of a baby's.

JOE

> What if a female takes it?

VERNON

> She'll experience frigidity for weeks. Is that detective still there?

JOE
>She left, Vernon. She ripped us off.

VERNON
>She should be warned.

JOE
>It wouldn't do any good. I know that woman.

VERNON
>Is she sexually active?

JOE
>(*Laughing.*) And how! Oh—this is great! It couldn't be better.

Phone clicks off—sound of disconnection.

JOE
>Well I'll be dipped in shit! So there is some justice in this world after all. Another day! Another old Indian trick! THIS IS GREAT!

Up music—William Tell Overture

Blackout.